PAULIN

Broken Alpha

Book 2 of the Broken Trilogy

CHAPTER 1 – LEAVING

"Raven, hurry up your guests are starting to arrive." My mother mind linked me.

"Be right there mom." I linked back.

My cousin Clair and I are getting ready for my graduation party. I had graduated from high school as valedictorian and my parents were very proud. My father had promised that if I graduated first in the class, I could attend any university I wanted. I couldn't wait to leave. The further away the better.

"You think he'll bring her with him?" Clair asked.

"Of course, he will. She's his mate." I replied, dreading seeing them together.

Clair was talking about Zach, our future Gamma at Crescent Moon. He was tall, tan, and handsome, and I've had a crush on him for as long as I could remember. Zach stole my first kiss last year and I was sure he would be my mate. He was even present when I shifted for the first time two months ago, hoping that my wolf would recognize him as my mate.

I was heartbroken when he wasn't my mate. A week later, Dr. Ross's daughter Sydney, turned eighteen and discovered Zach was her mate. The last two months have been agonizing for me, pretending to be happy on the surface is much harder than it seems.

We made our way downstairs and out to the backyard where the party was.

"There's my girl." Aunt Payton said and engulfed me in a hug followed by my Uncle Max.

My Aunt Payton is the best, everyone always says I'm a younger version of her. I was on the short side for a she-wolf, standing at five feet, six inches tall, and had the same light skin and big blue eyes. Aunt Payton wore her raven colored hair short, while mine was waist length.

"Give your favorite uncle a hug." I heard a deep voice call from behind me.

"Favorite uncle? That would be me!" Max said with a big grin on his face.

I turned to find my Uncle Ranger and gave him a hug. Uncle Ranger is the Alpha of the Dark Moon pack, he never had any children, so he spoiled us. My oldest brother Knox is the future Alpha of Crescent Moon and his twin, Peter, is the heir to Dark Moon.

"How are my two favorite nieces?" He said to Clair and me.

"We're your only nieces!" Clair giggled and hugged him.

Clair had two younger brothers, which isn't as bad as having five brothers! I'm the only girl out of six children. Knox and Peter are my older twin brothers, after I was born my parents had three more boys. I was drowning in overprotective Alpha testosterone and couldn't wait to go away to school.

"Praying my father doesn't change his mind about letting me leave for school." I told Uncle Ranger.

"Well, you are his princess and you're going halfway around the world. I'm surprised your mother was able to convince him to let you go." He chuckled.

"If I'm going to take over LaRue Enterprises someday, I should get my business degree." I smiled.

"You don't have to go that far." Max chimed in. "We could always enroll you in an online university instead." He joked. At least, I think he was joking; I'm sure my dad had already considered that too.

"Oh, hush now. Raven needs to spread her wings and is perfectly capable of handling anything that comes her way. There's nothing wrong with a little independence and adventure." Aunt Payton told them both and winked at me.

My father's voice rang out, "Friends and family, thank you for joining us to celebrate our beloved daughter today and to wish her well on her new adventure to study abroad. Raven has selected to attend the University of Athens, where she will be studying in a city that has produced geniuses like Plato and Socrates. If she fails to video call her father every week, I will not hesitate to drag her back home." My father smiled sheepishly, and I suspected he wouldn't hesitate to find a reason to drag me back home.

"In honor of her departure to Greece tomorrow, dinner will be Greek-themed tonight and is ready to be served." My mother announced.

Clair and I walked over to the table to find our seats. "I

can't believe you're leaving me tomorrow." She pouted.

"You're going to have a little more to pack," said Aunt Megan who was standing with our Delta Elliot. She handed me a gift bag from Shari's Designs. "I had Ms. Hall make a few Greek Goddess worthy dresses for you." She smiled with tears in her eyes.

I hugged them. "I love you both."

I took my seat next to Clair to eat and looked around at my family and friends. Zach was seated at the other end of the table next to his parents Gamma Zeke and Vannica, his sister Zoe and his mate Sydney. Sydney was a very nice girl and I had nothing against her, but she had Zach, and my heart panged with jealousy at the moment. I managed to push my feelings down and keep it together while we ate.

After dinner, I walked around to speak with our guests and say goodbye. When I had made my rounds, I came face to face with Zach who gave me that heart-melting smile.

"Hey, Rave." He always called me Rave.

"Hey Z." I replied, trying to look casual.

"So, Greece it is?"

"Yeah."

He stood silent for a moment. "We're going to miss you around here."

"Thanks. I'm sorry I'm going to miss your mating ceremony. I'm happy for you and Sydney." I lied. This wasn't fair, the Moon Goddess had clearly made a mistake. Zach was perfect for me and had been my best friend since we were pups. I felt a lump in my throat as he pulled me into a hug.

"Take care." He whispered and then walked back to his mate.

I made my way to my bedroom. This was the last night I would spend in the castle for a while. Tomorrow night I would be sleeping in my new dorm. My bags were packed and sitting by the door ready for the morning. I took a shower, put on my pajamas, and brushed my teeth and hair.

I was ready for bed when I decided to go up to the astronomy observatory one last time. This was my father's favorite part of the castle and I knew he would be there sulking about my leaving.

I opened the door and saw the back of his large frame. He sensed me entering and took a deep breath before he turned to me. His blue eyes looked like they glistened for a moment and he pulled me into a long hug before he finally let me go. I knew this was very hard on him, but I was of age already and could have easily found my mate and left the pack. He had been hoping that my mate would have been someone in our pack, and I was hoping it would have been Zach. After two months, I still had not sensed my mate at Crescent Moon.

"I can't believe my baby girl is leaving me." He said.

"Dad, I'll call every week, visit during the holidays and I'm sure business will bring you to Europe a few times a year. It won't be that bad and it won't be forever." I assured him.

"Raven, promise you'll call me if you need anything."

"I will dad. Don't worry."

"And be very careful with your gifts, you're going to be in the human world." He warned.

"I know dad."

We stood for a while looking out at the view when my mother came in.

"There you are!" She said and walked over to hug my dad who pulled her in a kiss.

"Eww, child present." I said and covered my hand over my eyes. Twenty years later and my parents still acted like lovesick new mates.

They both burst out laughing. "You know, your father and I had one of our first dinner dates right here in this room and we spent the night watching the Northern lights." My mother beamed.

"Someday I hope to be as lucky as both of you." I said.

"Not too soon." My dad said and my mother laughed.

"Come on, you have an early morning flight and should get some sleep." My mother said and wrapped her arm around me.

I made my way to my room and plopped down face first on my pillow. I tried not to think about Zach and focused on the adventure ahead. My eyes were heavy, and I drifted off to sleep, next stop, Greece!

CHAPTER 2 – DORM

After a twelve hour flight, I finally set foot in Athens. My father had hired a private escort to take all my luggage and me to the university dorm. I exited the terminal and was greeted by a smiling man who instantly recognized me. I assume my father had sent a photo.

"Ms. LaRue, how nice it is to see you again." He said.

"I'm sorry, do I know you?" I asked.

"I'm Kosta, I was your family's escort when you vacationed here two years ago and took you to Santorini." He told me.

"Of course, now I remember. You stopped to get us the Souvlakia when I was hungry." I remembered him. He was more than an escort; he was a wolf and built like a house.

"I have all your luggage on the cart, shall we?" He led the way.

"Thank you."

"Are you hungry, we can stop and get you some Souvlakia?" He asked. I was starving and grilled meat is exactly what any werewolf would like.

"That would be wonderful, thank you." I smiled.

A short while later, we pulled over and Kosta got out to get the food. I sat in the car people watching and he returned. He handed me a bottle of water and a food bag. I pulled out the pita sandwich stuffed with Souvlaki, potato, and veggies; it was delicious.

"Mmmmm," my wolf Rae purred inside of me happy with the meaty sandwich.

Kosta continued to drive and pointed out the sights. I was excited to venture through the Plaka District and other points of interest. I could also see the ancient Acropolis in the distance. There was so much history here and so many places to explore.

"Take my business card and put my number in your phone. If there's anything you need or places you want to go, you call me. Athens is neutral territory for the five main packs in Greece, but you are no ordinary wolf." He said.

"What do you mean?" I asked, did he know about my gifts I wondered.

"Raven you are a LaRue, you're from the largest pack in the world and powerful family. You are practically royalty in the shifter world. You need to be careful." He said.

"And our mother is the golden wolf of the century." Rae snickered in my head.

"Did you know that Greece is the birthplace of werewolves, legends, and the home of Gods? Maybe we'll learn something new." I told Rae.

While both of my twin brothers inherited the water element from our father, I received both the gift of water and the fire element. No one outside of the family knows this. I had promised my parents not to use my elements, unless absolutely necessary.

"Here we are. Go ahead and check-in with the dorm advisor and I will bring your luggage up." Kosta told me.

It was Friday afternoon in Greece, and we were ten hours ahead of home. I sent my dad a text to let him know we had arrived, and I was at the dorm. Then I knocked on the door of the dorm advisor who answered right away.

"Hi, I'm Raven, I've just arrived." I said.

"Yes, we've been excepting you, I'm Karla, come in." She said with a thick Greek accent. She was short, warm, and in her late forties. She reached for a manilla envelope and handed it to me.

"Looks like you're on the penthouse floor." She teased.

"Excuse me?" I asked, wondering if there was a penthouse level.

"The top floor is the single occupancy floor, and all the dorms have their own private bathroom. The other floors are double occupancy with shared bathroom facilities and common rooms."

I waved to Kosta who managed to bring all my luggage to the elevator. Karla walked with me towards him and pressed the elevator button to call it to the lobby.

"You're on the sixth floor and the laundry facility is in the basement. The most important thing to remember in Greece, you don't flush anything in the toilet. Not even toilet paper, our pipes can't handle it."

Amazing, here we are in Greece, the cradle of western

civilization and yet the plumbing is still flawed. We pulled my luggage into the elevator and Karla pressed the sixth floor number.

"The stairs are next to the elevator and can take you to the rooftop for fresh air. We have a lovely rooftop patio and tables up there." Karla said and we piled out of the elevator with my luggage in tow.

"Ah, here we are, six A, as in Alpha. Your keys are in the envelope and the box you shipped is already in the room. If you need anything, you know where to find me." She smiled and left.

"Do you think she knows? She said A is for Alpha?" I whispered to Kosta.

He chuckled. "No, Alpha is the first letter of the Greek alphabet."

"Oh, that's right." I laughed back.

I opened the door and stepped inside; it was like a small studio apartment. A queen sized bed, closet, tiny bathroom with shower, a study desk, and chair. There was a small kitchen space that had a little refrigerator, microwave, hot plate, and sink. It had a few shelves and cupboards stocked with plates and cups; with room to store food.

"This is pretty nice, once you decorate it. Do you want to go shopping?" Kosta asked me.

"We already shipped some things from home in the box, I think I'm okay." I told him.

"There's a market on the corner down the street if you want to buy any groceries." He said.

"That's convenient. I'll settle in and maybe take a walk this afternoon to the market." I said.

"I'll leave you then. Don't forget to call me if you need anything. I live nearby, okay?"

"Thank you, Kosta." I smiled and closed the door when he left.

Classes start on Monday and I have two and a half days to get settled in. I opened my first large suitcase and hung up all my clothes in the closet. I was surprised by how much I was able to fit in it. The second suitcase contained shoes, jackets, a coat for the winter, pajamas, T-shirts, and sweats. The smaller suitcase had underwear, socks, toiletries, and accessories.

There was a smaller dresser with three drawers, I stuffed my underwear and other clothes in. I also had a backpack with my laptop, iPad, and other belongings. Once I was done with the suitcases, I tucked them into each other like nesting dolls and slid them under the bed for storage.

We were required to bring our own bedding and towels, so my mom had shipped over a big box. I opened the box and found bath towels, hand towels, and washcloths. I took some to the bathroom and put the rest away in the closet on the top shelf.

Then I took out two sets of sheets, my favorite blanket, and a comforter. I found two pillows at the very bottom of the box and a note from my mother with a framed family photo. I set the photo down on the desk with the note and made the bed. I stored the extra set of sheets in the closet.

I removed the tape from the box and folded it down to store under the bed in case I needed it later. Then I set up my laptop and other desk supplies on the desk. I placed the family photo on my desk.

I tried not to cry when I opened the note from my mom, it said, "We miss you already, Love Mom and Dad."

I sat on the bed and debated if I should take a shower and try to nap, but I wasn't really tired yet, I had slept on the plane.

"Let's go have a look around and maybe go do some grocery shopping." Rae suggested.

We went upstairs to the rooftop and I was pleasantly surprised. There were three propane gas grills to cook on, tables, outdoor furniture, and beautiful potted plants up here. The city view was also beautiful. I could see the market from here.

I took the elevator down to the Lobby but somehow ended up in the basement at the laundry facility. I looked around and noticed a dozen washers and a dozen dryers. There was a young man with blonde hair and brown eyes who smiled at me.

"You must be new, I'm Leo." He said.

"Yes, I'm Raven." I extended my hand.

If I didn't know any better, I could swear this was a male wolf, but he had no scent. I stood confused for a moment as he smiled at me. I could feel an aura around him, like a ranked wolf. Maybe it was just strong male testosterone?

"So, this is the laundry facility." I said looking around.

"Yes, everyone has a locker on that wall to store their laundry supplies, the key to your locker should be with your room key." He continued to smile.

I looked at the keys in my hand and noted the small key. "So that's what this little key is for." I walked over to the lockers and tested the key on six A. It was empty and I needed to remember to buy some detergent when I was at the market.

"You're in six A?" He questioned.

"Yes."

"We're neighbors! I'm in six D, as in Delta." He grinned.

I couldn't help but feel he knew and there was a double meaning here. No, I'm probably just paranoid, Delta is the fourth letter of the Greek alphabet after all.

"Well, then I'm sure we'll be seeing each other again." I smiled and turned to leave.

"If you need anything, don't hesitate to knock." He said.

"Thank you, I'm heading to the market." I said.

"Well take one of the folding carts with you so you don't have to carry back all your items. We have several in the closet; right there for anyone to borrow. Just remember to bring it back or Karla will hunt it down." He laughed.

"Great, I will. Thanks again, Leo." I said and took a folding cart from the closet. I noticed my shoe was untied and bent down to tie the lace when the elevator door opened again.

"Leo, did you catch the scent of the new she-wolf on our floor?" An excited female voice asked, and I froze in place.

CHAPTER 3 – NEW FRIENDS

"Something strange is going on here." Rae said to me.

Someone scented me as a wolf, but I couldn't pick up on any wolf scents. I lifted my head up and slowly stood up to look at the female. She had that uh-oh look on her face while Leo had an uncomfortable grin.

I looked at Leo with my eyebrow arched and gave him a questioning head tilt. "Why can't I scent you?" I asked.

"Hi, I'm Rocky." Said the female who looked to be about the same age with long brown hair and big hazel colored eyes.

"I'm Raven." I said.

"You have a strong Alpha aura radiating!" Rocky said as she stepped closer with a curious look on her face.

"Why can't I scent you? Are you using magic?" I asked.

"Leonidas and I are from the same pack in the Northeastern region of Greece. There are only five packs in Greece: northeast, north, central, Sparta, and Crete. Athens is neutral but it doesn't mean that someone won't notice you. The islands are also neutral but there is a large roaming rogue population on the islands. Humans can't scent you, but other wolves can. We use herbs to hide our scent so other wolves can't scent us." Rocky told me.

"Are you in some danger if another wolf scents you?" I

wondered.

"No, not on neutral territory. Our Alpha would just prefer us to be left alone and unnoticed when we are away from the pack. He makes everyone take the herb when they leave pack territory." She said.

"The herb is native to the Mediterranean and we like to keep it a secret." Leo told me.

"How many more wolves are in the dorm?" I asked.

"Just us. Rocky is in six B, for Beta." He smiled.

"Are you heading to the market?" Rocky asked pointing to the utility cart in my hand.

I nodded. "Yes. I just arrived today and to get stocked up."

"I need to go shopping too, is it okay if I join you?" She asked and grabbed a folding cart.

"I'd like that." I said and we made our way to the market.

I learned that Rocky is the daughter of the Beta and Leo is the son of the Delta. What a strange coincidence that I was in six A, she was in six B and Leo was in six D. "What about the other dorms on our floor, C, E, and F?"

"Humans." She said.

We walked into the market and I grabbed laundry supplies, paper products, food, snacks, and drinks. My utility cart was fully stocked with no room left; I was glad I brought it to carry everything back in. At the checkout, I found a tourist guide to Greece and purchased it as well. The metro line was by the market which was convenient transportation to get around Athens and check out some of the sights I wanted to see.

We walked back to the dorm building, and took the elevator upstairs to unload our carts. Rocky was just across the hall from me. I stood in the kitchen and unloaded the groceries. The kitchenette had basic cooking utensils and necessities. I had purchased dish soap and a sponge to do the dishes.

"Are we having the steak tonight?" Rae asked practically drooling at the fresh piece of meat I had bought for dinner.

"You are such a carnivore." I told my wolf.

I left the room with the utility cart; my laundry supplies were still in it. I made my way to the elevator to return the borrowed cart to the basement and store my laundry supplies in the locked cabinet I was assigned.

Rocky also stepped out of her room with the empty cart and stepped into the elevator with me. "Are you staying in tonight?" She asked me.

"I don't have any plans, just settling in." I said and the elevator doors opened up to the basement.

"Leo and I are going to the club tonight; you're welcome to come with us." She smiled.

"Is there an age restriction?"

"Oh honey this is Greece, they don't even check, but it's eighteen." She smiled.

I walked over to the cabinet and put my laundry supplies away, then I set the utility cart back in the closet. We took the elevator back up to our floor and the doors dinged open. "Just think about it. It will give you a chance to let your hair down before classes start on Monday. We're leaving at ten, you know where to find us."

"Thanks. I'm a little jet lagged but I'll take a shower and think about it." I told her.

An hour later I had taken a shower in my little bathroom in what must have been the world's smallest shower. I stood at the hot plate cooking my dinner and it smelled delicious. I had sliced the steak in strips and cooked it with onion, mushroom, and zucchini. I dumped the contents in a bowl and sat at my desk to eat.

I checked my phone and saw a missed call from Clair and a text message from my Dad. I texted my dad back and called Clair. I reached her voicemail and left a message. Thoughts of home and Zach flooded through my head as I sat silently chewing my food.

"We should get out and see the nightlife, no sense in sitting around thinking about Zach." Rae said to me.

She was right. This was my new life and Greece was going to be my adventure. I was surrounded by Greek Gods without the overprotective eyes of my brothers. I was going to get past Zach one way or another and dancing sure sounding like it would be a good start.

I went into the bathroom and blow dried my long hair before adding some loose ringlets in it with my curling iron. My hair was indeed raven black, and it stood out with my pale complexion. I finished my makeup with black mascara on my blue eyes to make them pop and a dark merlot lip stain. I stood in front of the closet, what does one wear when partying in Athens?

"The little black dress." Rae purred back.

I slipped on my silver heels with a black form fitting dress. It was mid-thigh with three quarter length sleeves and off the shoulder, exposing one shoulder. I slipped on my silver earrings and bracelet and grabbed my silver purse.

"Eeeek!" Rocky squealed as she ripped the door open and hugged me. "I'm so glad you're coming with us. YOU LOOK HOT!"

She was wearing black heels and a red dress. Her brown hair was semi clipped back and curled. "Let's go. Leo's got a taxi coming in five minutes."

"Hey, look who it is!" Leo smiled at us when we stepped out of the elevator. He was wearing black slacks and a blue button up shirt, his biceps nearly straining the shirt. "Come, the taxi is here."

We stepped into the night club and the music was pulsing in the air. It was sleek, dark, and had strobe lights buzzing. I scented humans and at least a dozen different wolves. We made our way to the bar and Leo ordered shots of Ouzo. "When in Greece, do as the Greeks. Yamas!"

We downed the shots and my throat burned with the taste of black licorice. Leo then ordered a round of beer. Alcohol had very little effect on a werewolf because our system burned it quickly.

A human redhead made her way to Leo and Rocky rolled her eyes. "Come on, let's go hit the dance floor." I followed her and noticed a few wolves shamelessly eyeing me like candy. The place was so crowded, and we squeezed out a spot on the dance floor.

I had that awkward feeling of eyes boring holes into me, I was so exposed on the dance floor that I couldn't tell whose eyes they were. Before I knew it, I felt a heated body pressing against my back and grinding against me. I turned to find strong arms and a dazzling smile on a handsome wolf.

"You're new." He said with a Greek accent.

"What makes you say that?" I asked.

"It's not every day a beautiful little wolf steps into Athens smelling like honeysuckle and vanilla." He smiled.

"I'm not new to Athens." Technically it wasn't a lie, I had vacationed here before with my family.

"I'm Eros from the northern pack in Greece." He said and slipped his hand on my hip. I could feel his aura, he wasn't just an ordinary pack wolf, he was an Alpha. Rae also sensed him. I noticed his eyes trail down to my exposed shoulder and then to my chest.

"Eros? Named after the God of lust, it's nice to meet you, Eros." I lied. I had no intention of getting to know him better or giving him my name. He was devouring me with his eyes.

"She knows her Greek mythology." He smiled, "What

a coy little wolf, she will not give me her name." He stared intrigued. His wandering hand and gaze were making me very uncomfortable. He leaned into my ear and inhaled deeply before he whispered a warning. "You're not safe, the beast is here tonight and he's watching you."

I heard a low growl coming from the upstairs balcony area and a chill ran through me. Rae was uncomfortable and something felt off. Eros walked away and I turned to find Rocky and Leo waving me over. I quickly made my way to them and Rocky spoke first, "I need some air, will you both step outside with me."

I thought we were going to get some air, but Leo quickly hailed a taxi. "Quick get in." He said looking anxious and pulled the door open for us.

"What happened? Why are we leaving so soon?" Not that I minded.

"The beast of Greece was in the club tonight and he can sense all werewolves. It's not safe for anyone." Rocky said.

"The beast of Greece? Sounds like a demon or boogeyman." I let out a nervous giggle.

"He may as well be." Leo said.

"We are never going back there." Rae whispered to me.

Wait a minute, a dreadful thought hit me. Didn't Eros say the beast was watching me tonight?

CHAPTER 4 – HOWL

I'm not sure what I was expecting but all of a sudden, I felt like the boogeyman might bust into my room at any moment.

I got up again and checked to make sure the door was locked and then padded over to the window. I was on the sixth floor, it's not like someone was going to climb up. I laid down and hugged my pillow close. I had wolf hearing, why was I being paranoid.

I replayed what Eros had told me and thought about the chill that ran through my spine when the growl ripped through the club. Did he notice me or sense my power? Was he upset because I was an Alpha born wolf in his territory? But wait, Athens was neutral, and he didn't get close enough to fully sense me. Maybe I'm just overthinking things.

Perhaps Eros was just trying to scare me, it's not like we had been at the club that long for anyone to really notice me. I turned and tossed a bit more. This entire dorm room was tiny compared to my bedroom at home.

I woke in the morning and looked at my phone to check the time, it was almost noon. I had slept in; this time change adjustment was hitting me hard. I decided to take a shower and explore a little today, maybe I would walk to campus and look around.

"Ah, there she is." Karla called out to me as I stepped

out of the elevator.

"Good morning Karla." I waved.

"What good morning? It's almost one o'clock" she said with her arms moving. Karla reminded me of the quintessential Greek lady who was opinionated, in charge, and in everyone's business.

"Time change." I simply stated and stood smiling.

"A nice man dropped this off early this morning, he said you dropped it yesterday." She handed me the silver bracelet I was wearing last night.

I took the bracelet and stared at it for a moment. I hadn't even realized I had dropped it. Maybe it was the taxi driver?

"Thank you." I shoved it in my purse.

"Off to see the great city?" She asked.

"I'm thinking about starting at the campus and the surrounding areas." I told her.

"Watch out for the pickpockets, especially in the metro." She called out.

The campus was two blocks east and I could see the Acropolis in the distance. I walked around looking at the old buildings and found my way to the big library. I took note of the buildings so I could easily find my way next week. My stomach growled at me and I decided to get something to eat.

There were several eateries and shops in the vicinity of the campus. They had indoor and outdoor patio dining areas. I walked by a big window and saw a rotating chunk of meat on a spit.

"Mmmm Gyros." Rae purred and my stomach grumbled again.

Ten minutes later, I was seated on a patio chair and taking a big chomp into the fresh and flavorful Gyro with delicious tzatziki sauce. I had decided to spend the rest of the afternoon walking along the shops and taking in my new environment.

I walked by an ice cream shop and heard a knock from the inside window. Rocky was waving at me, so I stepped inside Richy's Temple of Sweets.

"Hey Raven, how's it going?" Rocky asked.

"There's so much to take in."

"The only thing you need to take in right now is the new sweet seduction chocolate ice cream Richard just got in. He's now offering twenty-one flavors." She said.

"Ladies, would you like a sample of my sweet seduction?" He asked with his eyebrows dancing up and down. We burst out laughing at his cheesy catchline.

Rocky and I strolled out of the ice cream shop with our large sweet seduction ice creams. I had some nagging thoughts in the back of my mind about last night, so I decided I would ask her.

"This beast of Greece, what can you tell me about him?"

"Well, I've never actually seen him myself. He's the Alpha of one of the strongest and deadliest packs in

Europe. He killed his father for the title when he was sixteen." Rocky said.

"How could he do that at sixteen? We don't get our wolf until we are eighteen?" Shock in my voice.

"He's not an ordinary wolf. He got his wolf early and they say he's a descendant of King Lycaon, who was turned into a wolf by Zeus, after trying to trick him. He's monstrous and his aura radiates death, they say his family is cursed. We try to avoid him."

"Cursed? In what way? What's the name of his pack?" I made a mental note to ask my father since he knew most of the major packs in the world.

"I'm not sure what kind of curse, but it's said to be very unnatural. The name of the pack is Olympus Blood Moon, their territory is in the central part of Greece and a few of the islands belong to them." She informed me.

"The man I was dancing with at the club said that the beast was watching me." I told her anxiously.

She nearly dropped her ice cream and gave me a shocked look. "I saw a man dancing with you, but I didn't get a look at his face."

"He said his name was Eros, he was a wolf." I added.

"Eros? As in the Greek underboss?" She asked.

"I have no idea. Wait, underboss? As in mafia? There's a Greek Mafia?" I asked in complete shock.

"Whom better to run human mafias? Arms, drugs, trafficking, sex, all of it. The black market is run by the lowest unethical wolves, the corruption runs deep."

Goddess what kind of world have I been living in? I thought to myself. No wonder my father wanted to keep me close to home.

"The beast may have noticed you, you have a strong aura" she said.

"Does he have a name?"

"Yes, but most are afraid to even say it." She looked over her shoulders and then whispered, "Dimitri Theodorus."

I felt a sensational chill run through my spine at the mere mention of his name. "Dimitri," I heard his name roll off my lips. Rae tensed up and I thought maybe she could use a run.

"Rocky, is there a safe place to let my wolf out for a run?"

"Yes, Athens has some neutral forest lands. Leo and I will usually run once a week near the Kaisariani Monastery. We're going tonight."

"Would it be okay if I joined you?"

"Sure, we run in human form to the forest, it's about a thirty minute run east of here. Then we let the wolves out." She said.

We headed back to the dorms and I spent some time looking through my university schedule and class syllabus. I was sitting at my desk when I noticed a small binder in the top drawer that contained take-out menus for local restaurants that delivered.

"Sweet, let's order something." Rae yipped.

I might be small, but Rae is an Alpha born wolf and she's bigger than most wolves. We burn a lot more calories quicker. My fingers dialed a local Greek restaurant, and I placed the order. I plopped down on my bed and flipped through the tourist guide I had picked up. I was reading up on the Temple of Apollo at Delphi and felt an instinctive pull to visit since mom was a descendant of Apollo.

I was lost in thought looking through the guide when I heard the elevator door open and a knock at my door. A handsome young delivery guy was holding my bag of food. "Kalispera." He smiled.

"Umm, hello." I smiled back. He had said good evening, but my Greek was terrible and I wasn't about to make a fool out of myself.

"I have a leg of lamb specialty plate and fresh baklava for Ms. Raven." He held out the bag.

"Thank you." I smiled. I had already paid over the phone but tipped him five euros.

Three hours later, I was dressed in yoga pants, a shirt, and running shoes, running with Leo and Rocky. We looked like normal college students out for a run. The cool night air felt wonderful on my skin as we jogged east towards the forest.

We finally reached the forest and went in a little deeper before we found a spot to shift. I removed my clothes and hid them in a bush next to the tree before stepping out in my black Alpha wolf. Rocky and Leo both turned to me and bowed their heads in submission at Rae who emanated a strong power. Rocky was a dark brown wolf with hazel eyes and Leo had light brown fur with brown eyes.

Leo let out a bark and we took off running. Rocky and I followed behind and I had no idea where we were going. The night was clear, the air was crisp, and the forest felt still. I wondered if other predators lived in the forest. It certainly did not feel like we were alone.

Rae kept trying to pick up scents, but we couldn't even pick up Leo and Rocky who were running along with us. The Mediterranean climate was so much different than the Canadian Rockies I was used to. We stopped at a small stream to lap some water up, the moving water was the only sound that could be heard.

We started to run back in the same direction and a loud howl pierced through the air. Leo, Rocky, and I started running with great urgency to our starting point. Leo and Rocky were from the same pack so they could still mind link, but I was completely in the dark. I thought this was neutral territory.

We reached our starting point and I shifted back. I reached into the bush for my clothes and found they had been scattered around. I picked them up, put them on, and quickly ran out of the forest tree line to meet Leo and Rocky.

"What the hell was that?" I asked.

"Obviously we weren't alone. Leo and I have been running here for the last year and we've never come across any other shifter's." Rocky told me.

"Raven, you smell different." Leo sniffed in my direction.

I pulled my shirt to my nose and inhaled, he was right, caramel and spice. I looked at the forest behind us and saw a pair of glowing eyes staring from the darkness. I blinked and they were gone

CHAPTER 5 – SIGHTS

This was yet again another night I spent turning and tossing in my dorm room. Leo had explained that the forest is usually pretty quiet on a Saturday night. Athens has so many other diversions to offer, that even the other wolves are usually too distracted to be out running.

I rolled out of bed and made my way to the tiny kitchenette to start breakfast. The hot plate was now warmed up and I dropped a few slices of bacon in it, when it was done, I scrambled two eggs and sliced a pear.

The sun was peeking through my curtains and I sat on my bed eating my breakfast. Today was a good day to venture out to the new Acropolis museum and take in some sights. After I washed my dishes, I took a shower and got ready for the day. I slipped on a long maxi dress that Aunt Megan had picked up from Shari's Designs for me. It was dark blue with brown and cream flora designs and made my eyes stand out.

I put on my brown sandals, then slipped my purse around my head and shoulder. I went down in the elevator and when I stepped out on the first floor, Karla was standing there watering the plants.

"Oh, look at you! Are you off on a date with a lovely Greek Boy?" She smiled.

"Good morning." I smiled. "I'm going to the Acropolis

museum today."

"Lots of wonderful Greek history to see there. If you want some company, I have a very nice nephew." She suggested.

"Thank you, Karla, but I'm okay." I laughed and waved.

I walked towards the corner store and stepped inside to buy a bottle of water and ask if there was a metro schedule or bus route. The young lady suggested I take a bus which would be stopping in front of the store in five minutes. I paid for my water, thanked her, and stepped outside just as the bus pulled up.

Forty-five minutes later, I was walking towards the museum which was situated just below the Acropolis. The sun was shining, the breeze was fresh, and the streets of Athens were buzzing. In the distance, I could hear church bells ringing.

I stepped up to the museum ticket office and a young man greeted me good morning in Greek. "Kalimera."

"Good morning." I smiled back. "One ticket please."

"That will be five euros." He said and handed me a booklet, map, and entrance ticket as I passed him the money.

"Thank you." I said,

"Efharisto!" He called out you're welcome as I waved.

What a cutie, something about him reminded me of Zach. Oh Zach, I needed to stop thinking about Zach. His mating ceremony was coming up and he was off limits. "Come on Raven, you're in the land of Gods for crying out loud, you can get over him." I told myself.

"Maybe we'll find our mate in the land of Gods." Rae gushed.

I entered the beautiful museum; I walked through the lobby and passed the turn styles. I stood on the glass floor gallery looking down at archaeological excavation finds, then I made my way through the museum taking in the ancient Athenian culture and studying the statues. The marble and glass usage in the museum's design gives it a light and airy feeling.

The Parthenon Gallery at the top level was stunning with a perfect view of the actual Parthenon that stood about three hundred yards away. I stood for a while taking it in, it was almost twenty-five hundred years old. Before I left the museum, I stopped at the base to look down at an archaeological excavation that uncovered an ancient Athenian city in the open pit below.

I looked up and scanned the crowd, I had a feeling someone was watching me, but nothing stood out. After seeing those glowing eyes yesterday, I was left feeling uneasy. I tucked the brochure in my purse, checked the time, and decided to venture into the neighboring areas.

The Plaka District was nearby, and I started walking towards it. Plaka was also called the neighborhood of the Gods because of its close proximity to the Acropolis. It's one of the oldest neighborhoods in Athens, built on top of ancient Athens. The narrow streets are cobblestoned, and the neoclassical architecture gives it a small island village vibe.

The cafes, eateries, and boutiques lined the narrow streets. The tables outside made it impossible to drive a car through. I made my way to a small restaurant and was seated outside. It was midafternoon and I was starving. I ordered a dolmades appetizer, the Greek chicken, and a salad dish.

I ate my lunch and watched the mixture of tourists and locals walk by. I had even scented several wolves and was amazed at how easily they blended right in. I was looking at a flyer on the table about the Cina Paris, an outdoor rooftop movie theater. I had heard about its breathtaking views of the Acropolis under the night sky while watching a movie. I would have to visit once my Greek was better, I'm sure the movies are in Greek.

"Are you planning on visiting the cinema tonight?" I heard a deep voice ask.

I looked up to find Eros in a two-piece suit smiling at me. "Be nice Raven." I told myself. If this guy was a mafia criminal, I certainly didn't want to make an enemy of this wolf in nice clothing.

"Hello again." I forced a smile on my face.

"Hello, little wolf." He smiled back.

He may have been dangerous and possibly corrupt, but he sure was Greek handsome. Dark thick hair, brown eyes, olive skin, pearly white smile, and the carved muscles. He had to have been about fifteen years older than me, luckily, I didn't have any daddy issues, or I would have been attracted to him.

"Are you going tonight?" He motioned to the flyer.

"Oh, um no. My Greek isn't very good yet and I'm sure the movies are all in Greek." I said.

"I can always translate for you." He grinned.

"Thank you, but it's also a school night for me." I said. Then I mentally head slapped myself, why am I telling him personal information?

"Perhaps another night then. I think you will be with us for a while if you are attending the university. I can also have the cinema play an English speaking movie for you."

He can have them show an English speaking movie just for me? What kind of power or influence did he have, I wondered?

"That's very nice thank you." I replied.

The waiter came out with my bill and bowed his head to Eros. "It's on me." Eros said and waved him off.

"Yes Sir." The waiter turned and left with my bill.

"Oh, you didn't have to do that." I said.

"In my country, you just say thank you." He smiled.

"Thank you, Eros." Slipped out of my mouth and he smiled at the mention of his name.

"You're welcome. Raven." He said and nodded his head as he walked away. It sent a chill down my spine hearing him say my name. I had never told him my name.

I left the restaurant and soon found a charming clothing boutique. Sometimes when you go out on a mission to shop for clothes, you never find anything you really like. Other times, when you're not even looking for clothes, you find a lot of things that you absolutely must have. This was one of those unexpected times where I knew I was going to buy several things!

This boutique had the cutest and trendiest of things. Soon enough I was in a dressing room with several items on the keep rack. I made my way through the streets of the Plaka carrying four full bags. I turned down a narrow street and noticed graffiti on the walls. Some was artwork and some would be considered borderline vandalism. There are lots of stone stairways and zigzagging narrow streets through here. I'm not exactly sure which direction will get me out.

I walked faster and could hear someone behind me. I turned around and found no one. I caught a glimpse of a shadow on the rooftops of the buildings in this narrow back street and looked up for a moment. I couldn't see anyone, but it sure felt like someone was there.

I finally made my way back out to the main street. I walked back towards the Acropolis to see if I could find a taxi to take me back home. I noticed a few missing posters of young females and wondered if they were runaways or actual abduction victims. Rocky has mentioned something about the black market and human trafficking.

"Raven? Is that you?" I heard a man's voice ask.

"Kosta! Thank the Goddess." I said relieved.

"Here, let me take those for you." He reached out and took my bags.

"Thank you. What are you doing here?" I asked.

"I live nearby in the Monastiraki area." He said. "Are you leaving?"

"Yes, I was just going to find a taxi." I told him.

"I will take you, come." He said.

We walked to his car and he opened the door for me and placed my bags in the back of the car.

"You should have called me, I'm happy to take you anywhere. I work for your father, so my services are at your disposal." He told me. "You need to be very careful, the Plaka has many dangerous people lurking around. Between the criminal activity and our shifter unrest, you don't want to be caught in the line of fire." He said.

"I have your number saved Kosta, I promise to call the next time I venture far from the university." I said, in case he was reporting back to my father. Speaking of my father, I have to remember to video call him to-night.

Kosta got out of that car and I moved to the back to grab my bags. Karla was walking towards us holding a takeout bag of food.

"Ah, I see you've been shopping." She said to me. Then she turned to Kosta, "Kalispera Kosta." She greeted him with a good evening.

He responded with, "Kalispera Karla."

I stepped into the elevator with my bags, I wondered about the shifter unrest that Kosta mentioned. Then I wondered when Kosta and Karla had been introduced; they seemed to be familiar with each other.

CHAPTER 6 – ODD

It's been two weeks since the start of class and the professors have been moving at a fast and unrelenting pace. Leo and Rocky are second year students, so I don't have any classes with them.

Angela sat across the table from me in the library, she's my assigned partner for a project we're working on. It was getting late, and I wanted to have some dinner before I went to bed. Angela was a great partner and is actually in the same dorm on the second floor. We left the library and started walking back towards the dorms.

"I'm going to stop and pick up some food at the corner restaurant, do you want anything?" I asked her.

"I'm good thanks. My roommate picked up a pizza, so I'm going to head back." She said.

"Sounds good, I'll see you on Monday." I said to her and stepped inside the restaurant.

Ten minutes later, I had a takeout box with some meat filled moussaka and walked the remaining block alone to the dorms. It was Friday night, and the dorms were pretty quiet. Most were out enjoying the nightlife of Athens. I entered my dorm room and opened the window to let the night breeze in.

My phone is connected to the bluetooth speaker in my

room, so I played some music. I opened the takeout box and found a generous helping of moussaka, bread, and Greek salad. I sat at the desk eating and feeling the fresh breeze blowing. Halfway through I started feeling stuffed and decided to take a shower before I slipped into bed.

I washed my hair, soaped myself up with my favorite French vanilla wash, and shaved my legs. I stood under the hot water thinking about tomorrow. Tomorrow was Zach and Sydney's mating ceremony. Here I was, halfway around the world, and yet I still felt painfully close.

I dried off and put on my pajamas. Then I ran a large-tooth comb through my towel dried hair. I stepped over to the window and looked out for a moment. My view faced east, over the top of a tree. I could see other buildings and the forest in the distance. I closed and locked the window before I pulled the curtains shut.

I turned off the music and reached for the takeout carton to place in the refrigerator for tomorrow. The rest of the moussaka was gone, I had only eaten half. Someone had finished the rest of it while I was in the shower.

I checked my front door to make sure it was locked. Maybe Leo had stepped in and helped himself? I sniffed around and there was no scent of anyone in my room. Of course, Leo and Rocky can't be scented while they're taking those masking herbs.

I laid in bed staring at the ceiling. The stolen food was forgotten as I frowned thinking about Zach's ceremony tomorrow. I suppose it's a good thing I didn't have to suffer through it tomorrow in person. Maybe I should do something fun and distracting tomorrow. I drifted away to sleep after sulking for a few moments longer.

I woke up in the morning to the sound of my phone ringing. My father was on video chat. He had been so worried the last few times I had spoken to him, that I hadn't asked him about the Olympus Blood Moon pack that belonged to some fabled beast. The last thing I wanted was for him to send a babysitter over to watch me.

"Good morning dad." I answered.

"Hello, Princess. Did I wake you?"

"No, I was just getting ready to start my day with some breakfast and maybe go out to Delphi to see the temple."

"That's over two hours north of you. Is Kosta taking you?" He asked.

"I was thinking about taking a bus." I told him.

"Nonsense Raven, Kosta is available to take you anywhere. I'll call him for you." He insisted.

"Dad, I'm perfectly capable of making my way there." I said.

"I know you are, but a private car with an experienced tour guide will be much more comfortable for you than a crowded tour bus."

He had a point; I'd be stuck with the tour bus all day. "Fine, call Kosta." I conceded.

"Do you need anything?" He asked.

"No dad, I'm good. What's mom doing?"

"She's been busy with Vannica getting things ready for the ceremony."

"Of course, she is. Listen, I should get going, I need to get ready."

"I love you, Princess."

"I love you too dad, give mom a kiss for me." I hung up before I had to listen to any more mating ceremony news.

I walked over to the bathroom to brush my teeth, hair and get ready. There was going to be a lot of walking on the sacred path at Delphi, so I put on my sneakers with denim shorts, tank top, and a light jacket. My phone dinged, I looked down to find a message from Kosta. "Be there in five minutes, don't eat breakfast."

I grabbed my sunglasses and headed out the door. There was some commotion in the lobby downstairs when I exited the elevator. Sara was Angela's roommate and was talking to Karla and a university security guard.

"Here comes Raven, maybe she knows something." Karla said.

"Good morning." I said.

"I'm Gus, university security. We found Angela's backpack just outside and she did not come back to her dorm last night. Do you know anything? When did you last see her?" He asked me.

"I was with her last night at the school library. We left just after 8:00 pm and walked back together. I stopped down the street at Cristopalous Taverna to pick up dinner. Angela walked back alone because Sara had ordered pizza." I told them.

"She never came back to the dorm." Sara said.

"It was Friday night, maybe she had other plans?" Karla suggested.

"Does she have a boyfriend?" Gus asked.

"I don't know." Sara said.

"Okay, we'll keep an eye out. Karla, please call me when she gets back. Hopefully, she's just been out having a good time, this isn't the first time this has happened, certainly won't be the last." He said.

"Should we call the police?" I asked.

"You have to wait two days before an inspector will look, but I'm sure she will be back soon." He bowed out the front door.

That's odd, Angela seemed like a quiet and reserved person, not the party type at all. I saw Kosta's car pull up, "I have to go, I'll see you later." I said.

"Where are you off to?" Karla asked.

"Kosta is taking me to Delphi." I told her.

"Ahh, good. Enjoy the trip and take some pictures." She called out behind me as I walked out waving goodbye.

"Kalimera, Raven." Kosta smiled as he held the door to

the back seat open.

"Kalimera." I wished him a good morning and stepped up into the black Mercedes G-Class.

We pulled out into traffic and a motorcycle pulled up alongside of us. I couldn't see the driver because he had a full-face covering helmet on, but he had a very muscular body and his biceps were as big as my head. He could have easily passed us but was maintaining the pace next to us.

"There's a small taverna that has excellent breakfast just ahead, we can stop in and get something." Kosta said.

"Sounds great, thank you." I said. Kosta had to be well into his forties, but sometimes it's hard to tell with a werewolf. I wondered why he was living in the city and if he belonged to a pack or had a mate. I wasn't at that level to ask him just yet, so my curiosity had to wait.

Kosta parked the car on the busy street and opened the door for me. We stepped into the restaurant and the delicious smell of food and Greek coffee hit me.

"What is that?" I pointed to something coming out of the oven that looked like pizza.

"That's Ladenia, a flatbread with tomato, onion, and olive oil. It's very good with a side of sausage." Kosta told me.

"Sounds great!" I smiled and Rae yipped in my head.

Kosta ordered the same for both of us, the Ladenia with sausages. He carried the food to the car, and I carried a coffee for him and a tea for myself. Soon enough we were driving outside of Athens, eating and talking.

"This is fantastic." I said and continued to enjoy my breakfast.

"This Greek sausage is so delicious and juicy." Rae purred at me.

We continued to drive north, Kosta was pointing out landmarks and sights during the drive. He was a wealth of information on Greek history. The first werewolves descended from Greeks thanks to the Greek Gods. He told me the story of the first werewolf, King Lycaon of Arcadia was turned into a werewolf by Zeus.

"Is the beast of Greece really a descendant of King Lycaon?" I asked.

Kosta nearly spits his coffee out at the mention of the beast. "You know about the beast?" He asked nervously.

"Leo and Rocky are the other two wolves in my dorm. They told me about him." I answered, not wanting to give him the full details at the nightclub in case he was reporting back to my father.

"The beast in an old children's tale to get naughty pups to behave." He told me. I could sense a nervous undertone.

"Look, we're almost there." He said changing the topic. We were climbing the beautiful hillsides on a two lane road. The scenic view was spectacular! It made me wonder how the ancients made the journey to the higher elevation.

We slowed down and Kosta turned into the second parking lot. A motorcycle passed us by, and I tried to get a better look at the driver. He looked like the same rider from this morning, surely this wasn't the same motorcycle from Athens. Was it

CHAPTER 7 – DELPHI

"Know Thyself." Kosta read the Greek inscription at the front of the temple entrance as I stared up at it.

"It's one of the many Delphic commandments inscribed around here. There are one hundred and forty-seven of them, like words of wisdom; nothing in excess, obey the laws, respect your parents, worship the Gods." He added.

"Do you have a favorite one?" I asked him.

"Be on your guard." He replied.

"Really? Is that really one of the commandments?"

"Of course it is. Ancient Greeks were always at war or preparing for war." He said.

This ancient site was not only where the temple of Apollo was; but also had numerous treasuries from different Greek tribes dedicated to several Gods in which tithings and tributes were offered to the Gods. Every time a Greek tribe won a war, they paid homage to the Gods by erecting treasuries filled with offerings. We walked the sacred path and looked at statues, sanctuaries, and alters. The area had lots of olive trees growing and even some almond trees, I reached out and grabbed a few almonds off a tree to crack open.

"Did you know that Delphi is the belly button of the earth?" Kosta said. "Legend says that Zeus released two eagles from opposite ends of the world, and they crossed paths right over here, he declared it the center of the word. There's a stone just over there called the omphalos, which is the navel, marking the spot."

We visited the Tholos at the Sanctuary of Athena, the site of the oracle, the stadium which was home to the Pythian games, and the theater with stunning views from Mount Parnassus. I looked out at the mountains and Kosta pointed out the fault line where tectonic plates clashed causing earthquakes that were often attributed to the Gods in Ancient Greece.

Kosta stepped away to find a restroom and I stood in front of the slope at the Apollo temple taking pictures with my phone. There was such a mystical feel in the air and a connection that pulsed through me. This place would have been mesmerizing to see in its prime all those centuries ago.

I lifted the camera and aimed it towards the temple, a man caught my eye who appeared to be watching me. I snapped the picture and acted like I hadn't noticed him. Turning around slowly, I zoomed in on the photo to get a better look at him.

"Should we take a selfie together?" His voice startled me; he was looking over my shoulder smiling.

"Who are you?" I turned to face him; I could feel his wolf but couldn't scent him.

"I think the more important question here is, who are you?" He asked.

This was definitely the motorcycle rider from Athens, he was wearing the same black riding boots, jeans, and jacket. His light brown hair was wavy and ear length, his eyes a beautiful shade of green.

"Are you following me?" I asked.

"Maybe you're following me. You are the one snapping pictures of me after all." He grinned at me.

"You seem a little full of yourself." I laughed.

"I like your kefi, you've got spunk." He smiled. I understood the Greek word kefi to mean spirit or passion and wondered if he was patronizing me.

"Niko?" Kosta called out. "What are you doing here?" He seemed to know the young man.

"Same as everyone else. I'm taking in the sights; it's been a while since I've been here." He smiled.

"Imagine that, a true Greek, born and raised here and he's out sightseeing like a tourist." Kosta said laced in sarcasm.

"The same could be said about you." Niko replied.

"I've got a visiting client."

"I see that. Are you not going to introduce us, Uncle?"

"No, I'm not." Kosta folded his arms across his chest with his biceps bulging.

Wait, did he just say Uncle? Niko had to be a wolf too. Damn these Greeks and their scent masking herbs.

"Princess must be pretty special to have you at her service." Niko said.

"She's no one that would interest you." Kosta told him.

"Her aura would suggest otherwise." Niko replied and eyed me.

"You are mistaken, and we are leaving." Kosta said and held my elbow leading me away.

"Keep walking." Kosta whispered to me. He was looking around, scanning our surroundings, and went into high alert. We walked quickly to the car and Kosta opened the door. "Quick, quick." He said.

Moments later we were back on the road heading down the slopes of the mountain. I looked behind us to see if the motorcycle was following but saw nothing.

"Kosta, was that your nephew?" I asked.

"Yes, my late brother's son."

"He's a wolf." It was more of a statement than a question.

"Yes, he is."

"Why did we have to leave so quickly?"

"My job is to protect you and Niko runs with some very dangerous people. It's best to avoid them altogether." Kosta said sounding nervous and looking at his rear-view mirrors.

"What is this herb that masks scents? Should I try to find some?"

"It's a Greek weed called Evvie, it grows in the northern mountains. Difficult to find, but not impossible.

You steep it in water and drink it. It will mask your scent for three to five days depending on how strong it is." He told me.

"Where can I find some? I'm getting tired of everyone scenting me when I can't scent them." I asked.

"It's mostly found on the black market for wolves, it might hide your scent, but another wolf will still be able to sense your aura. You're an Alpha wolf and you radiate strength; you won't be able to hide that Raven."

"I was able to sense Niko, is he a higher ranked wolf?"

"He's Beta Born, just as I am." Kosta told me.

"What happened to your brother?" It slipped out before I could control myself, but I was glad when he answered.

"He was killed trying to do the right thing. Our pack fell apart and some of us now live amongst the humans. Not necessarily rogues, more like lone wolves." He said.

His phone rang and he answered it speaking in Greek. I looked down at my phone and zoomed in on the picture of Niko. He didn't look dangerous or scary to me. His Beta aura was strong, much stronger than Rocky's. I could sense his immediately.

"Should we stop for some food?" Kosta asked me.

"That would be great."

We stopped at the Hermes Souvlaki and Gyro stand near Delphi. I ordered the chicken souvlaki pita and Kosta had the Gyro. We grabbed our drinks and headed back to the car. Kosta seemed anxious to get back on the road and further away from here. I wondered if we were near pack territory.

The ride back was uneventful, and I replayed the conversation Niko and Kosta had. I wondered why Niko had been interested in me and why he had followed us to Delphi. It was late afternoon when we arrived back at the dormitory.

Kosta opened the car door for me and then walked me to the front lobby doors. "Raven, it's best if you avoid any unknown wolves. If Niko is interested in you, it can't be good."

"Thank you, Kosta, I promise to stay away from anyone I don't already know." I smiled at him.

I walked into my dorm and stripped off my clothes, then I stepped into the shower. After my shower, I realized that my laundry hamper was piled up and I had just used the last clean bath towel. I slipped on a shirt and shorts, then I carried my laundry hamper into the elevator.

I stepped off the elevator and into the laundry room. Then I loaded my laundry in two machines and opened my locker to get my detergents out. I dropped a token into each machine and started it. We had to purchase tokens from Karla to run the washers and dryers.

The elevator doors opened up and I heard Rocky call out my name. "Raven."

"Hi, Rocky. How's it going?" I asked.

"Well, Leo and I just finished a big project and my brain is a little fried." She laughed.

"I feel you on that, Angela and I have been working on a project as well. Has she come back yet?"

"No, Karla has been pacing the floor waiting for her. If she's not back by tomorrow, they will have to notify her family. She may have just gone out on a party cruise to one of the islands. Last year Leo and I got stuck for two days when we missed the return time and the boat left without us." Rocky laughed.

"Hope she doesn't leave me hanging for the rest of the project we're working on." I said.

"This is Greece! The Dionysus festival starts next weekend. People will go missing for days and will eventually turn up."

Rocky collected her laundry from the dryer, and we went back up the elevator to the sixth floor. We stepped out and Leo was just coming out of his dorm.

"Hey girls." He smiled.

"Hey, Leo." I smiled back.

"I was thinking about grilling steaks on the rooftop tonight for dinner." He said.

"Now he's speaking my language." Rae pepped up.

"Sounds great." Rocky said.

"I'm going to run over to the market and grab the steaks." Leo told us.

"Hey Leo, did you eat the rest of my moussaka last night?" I asked.

"Oh, you had moussaka last night. And didn't invite me?" He grinned.

"I'm being serious. Yesterday I got home late, picked up my dinner from Cristopalous Taverna, sat down at my desk, and ate half the moussaka. Then I took a shower and when I got out of the shower, it was gone." I said.

"It wasn't me." Rocky said holding her hands up in surrender.

"It wasn't me either and I love moussaka." Leo said confused.

I wonder if Karla had an extra key. I would have scented a human in my room. It's not like someone could climb up to a sixth floor window.

"Get to the store Leo, we'll meet you on the roof, I've got vegetables to grill with the steaks." Rocky said.

"Be right back." He smiled.

Rocky and I took the stairs to the rooftop. We sat in the patio club chairs waiting for Leo to grill dinner. "We're going to the beach tomorrow, to an island about forty-five minutes away from here. The water is crystal clear like the Caribbean, and the sand is beautiful. Would you like to come with us?"

"YES! That sounds wonderful." I said.

"Great, we'll be leaving about 8:00 a.m. to catch the ferry."

"I went to Delphi today, met a man, well actually a

wolf, who I believe is from Athens."

"Ohhhh, do tell!" She leaned in smiling wide.

"Handsome, tall, early to mid-twenties, beautiful green eyes, his name was Niko." I told her.

"Niko is a very common Greek name; did he say which pack he was from?"

Ugh, why didn't I ask him? Why didn't I ask Kosta? Now that I think about it, Kosta may have deliberately not wanted to tell me his pack name. In fact, he wanted to make sure I stayed away from him. He even warned me about some of the dangerous people that Niko associates with.

"No, I didn't get a chance to ask, but I have a feeling I'll be seeing him again soon." I smiled.

CHAPTER 8 - AGISTRI

I was running late. I jumped out of bed and dashed to the bathroom to brush my hair and teeth. I really wanted to tie my hair up in a ponytail but clipped the top half back instead. I rarely ever wore a ponytail because I didn't want anyone to see the crescent moon mark on the nape of my neck. I might be able to pass it off as a pack tattoo since I was from Crescent Moon Pack, but I wasn't sure if someone might recognize it as the mark of a gifted wolf.

I slipped on my two-piece turquoise bikini, then a yellow sundress and sandals. I grabbed my backpack and stuffed my towel, sunscreen, magazine, lip balm, cell phone, sunglasses, lighter, and money in it. I knocked on Rocky's door and she opened it ready to go. Leo also stepped out of his dorm and we took the elevator to the Lobby.

It's Sunday morning and Karla was probably still at mass, so we didn't see her on the way out. We took a taxi to the Port of Piraeus on the Athens coast; it was a thirty minute ride. We made our way to the high-speed ferry ticket booth and purchased three round trip tickets on the flying dolphin ferry. The high-speed ferry was nearly twice as fast as the regular ferry and a little more expensive.

We zipped across the beautiful crystal blue waters of the Aegean Sea, the smell of the sea breeze and the mist of the water excited my senses and elemental gift.

In the distance I could see our destination come into view, Agistri Island seemed to be covered in pine trees.

"A forest! Think maybe I could stretch my legs out?" Rae asked.

"Leo, what's the island population like? Do you think we might be able to go out for a run in the forest?"

"This is one of our favorite islands to run at." He smiled back. "The island has less than twelve hundred inhabitants in three main areas. The forest has a steep trek, so the tourists tend to stay away and prefer the beaches."

"I could use a run too." Rocky said.

"We'll take the last ferry back at 5:00 p.m. so that we could run later in the afternoon when most tourists are either eating or going back to the mainland." Leo explained the plan and we nodded our head in agreement.

The ferry reached the port of Myloi and we disembarked. We walked through the village of Megalochori, it looked like something from a postcard with its beautiful scenery and architecture. "I need something to eat." I said as my stomach growled at me.

"There's a place up ahead, we can grab something there. We usually have a late lunch at Raina's Taverna, they have the freshest seafood on the island." Rocky told me.

"Sounds great." I said. Ten minutes later, we walked out of the small cafe and I was enjoying delicious spanakopita with a coke. We strolled through the village, towards the beach.

The village has a quaint little charm to it, and everyone seems so happy. The roads and walkways are paved with brick, some are more artistically designed than others. The buildings are mostly whitewashed in that typical Greek island fashion and everything seems so clean.

This island had a nice laid back contrast to the hustle and bustle of the city. The beach was beautiful, and the water was a gorgeous clear blue. We walked to the far end of the beach for more privacy to claim our spot. Leo set up a pop-up shade canopy in case the sun got too hot. We set our bags down, stripped off our top layer of clothing, and made a run for the water.

"This feels amazing." I called out.

The water was at the perfect temperature and I couldn't get over how clean and clear it was. I could see my own shadow beneath me as I swam around. Leo and Rocky had grown up together and were very competitive, they had a swim race out to a floating navigation buoy and back. I was the referee and watched as Rocky, who is smaller and more agile than Leo, swam back faster, beating him to the finish line. Once we cooled down, we headed back to the shore.

"Leo, could we bury you in the sand?" Rocky asked.

"Oh wow, I haven't done that to anyone since my brothers and I buried my dad when we vacationed in Jamaica." I said excitedly.

"No way! I'm here to work on my tan, have to get ready for next weekend." He smiled.

"What's next weekend?" I asked.

"The Dionysus festival! Lots of parades, floats, costumes, wine, plays, festivities, and debauchery for three days!" Leo's face glowed with excitement.

"Sounds like the Greek version of Mardi Gras." I said.

"We celebrate carnival here in Greece too, we call it Apokries. It's one of the largest celebrations of the year in this country." Rocky told me.

"I can hardly wait." I smiled.

We pulled our towels out of our backpacks and dried off, then we rolled the towels up to serve as pillows. We laid on the sand soaking up the sun and flipping through magazines. Rocky and Leo argued over several celebrities featured in the magazine trying to determine who was a werewolf and who wasn't.

A few hours later, we were seated at Raina's Taverna in the outdoor dining area overlooking the beautiful sea. Our table was under the shade of a tall tree and the location was picturesque. A pitcher of ice water was placed in the middle of the table, it was beautiful and made from Greek blown glass. We sat quietly and studied the menu for a few minutes.

"Kalispera." The waitress greeted us.

"Hello." I responded.

"Ah! English, no problem." She seemed to recognize that I didn't speak Greek, even though Rocky and Leo could've easily translated for me she switched to English.

"Good afternoon, welcome to Raina's, I'm Nathalie and I'll be taking your order today. Do you have any menu questions I can assist you with?"

"Hello, Nathalie." Leo gave a flirty smile.

"What are the specials today?" Rocky asked.

"Today's special is a whole grilled seabass with a shrimp skewer, lemon rice, and spinach." She said.

"That sounds great, I'll have that." I said.

"Me too." Rocky nodded her head.

"Make that three specials and also bring us two orders of the Greek mussels and a large order of the fried squid." Leo smiled handing Nathalie back his menu.

"Excellent! I'll be back with that soon. Would you like anything else besides water to drink?" She asked.

"I think we're okay with just the ice water thank you." Rocky told her.

"Excuse me, where's the restroom?" I asked.

"You can go through the restaurant and down the stairs, or you can go down the patio stairs over there and enter the first floor on the side door to the restrooms." She said.

"Thank you," I told her and excused myself from the table.

I took the scenic route down the stone steps of the outside patio to the first level. The restroom was just inside the side door to the restaurant. A few minutes later, I exited the restroom and stepped outside. A meowing black cat caught my attention, cats usually run off when they sense a predator, or in this case a wolf. I was looking down at the cat when I walked right into a brick wall.

I realized the wall had moved and took a step back. It wasn't a wall; it was a hard-muscled chest. I looked up and my breath hitched in my throat. The side of my face and hand that touch him was tingling. My knees even felt weak.

Rae was anxiously stirring inside of me. I could sense a strong Alpha aura pulsing from him even though he had no scent. He was wearing relaxed jeans and a white linen shirt. His thick hair is dark brown, cut short, and modern. His beard is also short and well-groomed, I fought the urge to reach out and touch his face.

He wore dark tinted aviator sunglasses and something inside of me desperately wanted to look into his eyes. I had to tilt my head back to look up at him, he must have been at least six feet, six inches tall, and built huge. I felt small standing so close to him and my heart was racing. I couldn't understand what was happening to me.

"Excuse me." I apologized, hoping he would say something nice to me. Maybe even take off those sunglasses so I could look into his eyes. He didn't make a sound, he didn't speak to me, he just side-stepped me and kept walking.

I felt Rae whimper inside, I assume it's because we were just snubbed by another Alpha. Surely he had to have scented me and felt my Alpha aura. I wondered why he didn't speak to me and why it bothered me so much. He seemed annoyed that I had walked into him, it was a genuine accident, besides it's not like I hurt him. Maybe he was a rogue or lone wolf since he was masking his scent? No, he was too well dressed and groomed to be a rogue.

I turned to look at him, maybe call for him, but he was gone. I felt flush and my palms were sweaty. I wanted to run after him but instead, I went back up the stairs to the patio and my eyes wouldn't stop searching for him.

"Ahh just in time." Leo said as the fried squid and Greek mussels were delivered to our table. We devoured them and our sea bass was served next.

"Earth to Raven, Hello? Come in Raven?" Rocky's voice broke me from my deep thought.

"I'm sorry, I was just thinking about someone." I smiled.

"I had just asked if you were still up for taking a run and you were in a trance." Rocky said.

"Heck yes, we're still up for taking a run." Rae practically jumped for joy.

"It's been a while since Rae has been out, a run would be great." I told them.

CHAPTER 9 – STALKER

After lunch, we strolled towards the northern side of the island where the pine trees were thick. It was a bit of an uphill trek and most island beachgoers came here for the sand and water, not the forest.

We walked into a thick area of the forest and sniffed all around. No human or wolf scent was detected by any of us. We found large enough bushes to strip off our clothes and hide them. Our wolves took off running like children at a play park. Rocky kept nipping at Leo's wolf teasing him.

Rae loved the feel of fresh dirt under her paws and the smell of pine in the air mixed with a light sea breeze. It reminded me of the time we vacationed at the northern California coast, where the giant redwood pine trees grow along the Pacific Ocean coastline. It's such a relaxing and distinctive smell.

We ran a while before we found ourselves at a cliff-top overlooking a beach below us. I laid down on the ground and admired the breathtaking views. This truly was spectacular. Rocky and Leo were about a hundred yards away from me, trying to corner a family of squirrels.

I sat watching another family from the cliff, a human family with five small boys on the beach. It reminded me of my five brothers when we were pups. The youngest who was about five years old waded into the water and was being pulled out with the undertow. No one seemed to notice he was in the water and his little arms flapped around in panic.

Before I knew it, I had willed the water to lift him and glide him back towards the beach. My dad used to glide us as children around the water top for fun and we loved it. I wasn't sure if I could reach him with my power from this distance and was surprised that I could. He stumbled back on the shore and ran for his mother.

I heard a low bark come from behind me and Rocky motioned her head back to the direction we came from. I understood it was probably getting close to our time to head back if we wanted to catch the last ferry for the day. We ran back together and made our way to our bushes.

My clothes had been scattered again. I shifted back and lifted my dress to my nose, there was no scent except for mine. I put my bikini top on and couldn't seem to find my bikini bottoms. I looked in my backpack and they were not there either. Nothing else was missing, my phone and money remained untouched.

I slipped my sundress back on and would have to return to Athens commando. I should have brought some underwear with me, but I had simply tossed on my bikini this morning with a sundress over the top.

"Anyone missing anything?" I asked Rocky and Leo.

"No, nothing. Why?" Rocky asked.

"A piece of my swimsuit seems to be missing and my stuff was scattered around." I said.

"That's strange, I'm not picking up any scents, not

even an animal." Leo said as he sniffed the air.

"I don't think you two are the only ones masking your scent." I replied.

We returned to the dock to meet our ferry back to the mainland. I sat next to an open window and looked out at the other boats. A sleek black speed boat caught my attention as it headed back out to sea. A man with blonde hair was driving the boat, while a familiar looking handsome Alpha, wearing a white linen shirt and dark tinted aviator sunglasses looked in my direction.

Rae let out a low howl in my head and I could feel a need to be closer to him. I considered jumping out the window and swimming towards him, or maybe using my element to float his boat closer to me... what the hell is wrong with me? I was having irrational thoughts about a stranger who had snubbed me.

He stood up, reached into his front pocket, and pulled out a turquoise handkerchief. He pulled it to his nose and inhaled deeply. Wait a minute, that isn't a handkerchief, it's my bikini bottom! I could feel him looking at me as our ferry started to move.

Once the ferry made it past the wake zone in the ocean, it zipped into high-speed mode. The ferry was practically gliding on top of the water with the hydro skies under the boat extended out. I lost sight of the Alpha's speed boat and wondered if it was also heading to Athens.

Was he following me? Or maybe stalking me? Why would he steal my bikini? Maybe it was an Alpha thing? Goddess, he was hot! All these thoughts were floating around in my mind.

We arrived back at the dorm at about 7:00 p.m. and headed up the elevator to our rooms.

"I'm going to take a shower and order some delivery tonight." Leo said.

"Sounds good, I'm going to do the same." I said and we moved towards our doors. I unlocked my door and stepped into my dorm. I plopped down on my bed and looked through the binder of take-out menus.

I felt like eating something with extra spice and found the menu for an authentic Indian restaurant in central Athens. I called and placed an order for the chicken tikka masala dish with rice, garlic naan, and some spiced potato samosas. Then I headed into the shower to get cleaned up.

I was sitting on the bed wearing my pajama bottom shorts and a tank top while my wet hair was air drying. Picking up my phone, I passed the time waiting for my food by scrolling through my social media page. I found pictures from Zach's mating ceremony posted by mutual friends. Funny, with everything going on, I hadn't thought much about it. Sydney looked beautiful and Zach looked happy. I wasn't sure how I felt about it anymore and struggled with my own emotions.

I heard the elevator doors open and someone approached my door and knocked. I reached into my bag and pulled out a few euros to tip the delivery driver. I opened the door and a familiar face smiled back at me. "A delicious delivery for Miss Raven."

It was Niko! He stood smiling at me with his perfectly straight teeth and messy but stylish long hair. His olive skin tone made his green eyes pop. "What are you doing here?"

"Oh no worries, I already tipped the driver outside." He said as he sauntered into my room.

"Niko, what are you doing here?" I demanded.

"That's not fair, we haven't properly been introduced. You seem to know my name and I had to find yours out from a delivery receipt for Indian food."

"Hello Niko, I'm Raven." I said sarcastically.

"There, now we've been properly introduced. Are you following me?" I asked.

"No Lun—, I mean Raven, I'm just making sure you're okay." He smiled and opened up my food cartons.

"Why wouldn't I be okay?" I crossed my arms over my chest.

"Ohhhh SAMOSAS! I love samosas, can I have one?" He asked.

"Only if you tell me why you're following me." I said.

"Like I said, to make sure you're okay." He took a big triangular samosa and bit down into it.

"Mmm, these are the spicy potato ones, so good! You should try them."

"Put down my food!" He was starting to feel like one of my annoying younger brothers even though he was older.

"Do you have anything to drink?" He walked over to my refrigerator and helped himself. He opened up a bottle of coke and took a long drink. He stood in the middle of my dorm, just helping himself to my food and drinks.

"Oh, my Goddess! It was you! You ate the rest of my moussaka the other night. You were in my room! WHY?" I asked.

"I was checking on you and who wastes perfectly good moussaka, leaving it laying around? Didn't want it to go to waste." He smiled.

"But how did you get in?" I asked.

"Climbed up the tree and jumped to the ledge." He said.

"That's impressive." Rae said to me. "But, why?"

"Why?" I replied.

"We heard that a female had been abducted from here and my boss wanted to make sure you were okay?" He said.

"Did my father hire you to watch me? Is he your boss?" I demanded and snatched the samosa carton out of his hands.

"No. Who's your father?" He asked.

"None of your business." I snapped.

"He's obviously an Alpha, like you. He's got the re-sources and connections to hire my uncle, so he must be pretty powerful or important." Niko said out loud as if he was trying to connect the dots.

"Why does that matter to you?" I asked.

"I can't tell you." He said.

"I DEMAND YOU TELL ME." I used my Alpha voice. Niko tried very hard to resist it because I wasn't his Alpha, but then he bowed his head and exposed his neck in submission. Wow! I have never tried that on anyone before, especially not a strong Beta.

"Niko, please tell me what you can." I asked a little nicer this time. "Here, have another samosa." I offered and he took it. He sat down on the chair at my desk and looked up at me.

"Raven, someone very bad wants you. His goons have been following you and we think your friend was taken by accident instead of you."

"Someone abducted Angela? Is she still alive?" I asked.

"I believe so. We're working on tracking her exact location. It's complicated, there's an entire underground system that markets weaker omegas as slaves to packs but also humans as sex slaves to both packs and the human market."

"Please tell me Angela is okay."

"We think so, we're watching the possible locations and she will remain untouched so that her value is not decreased to the buyer. But, they were expecting to abduct you, which is strange they would even try to take an Alpha wolf." He said.

"Oh, Goddess! Why?" I whispered.

"We're not entirely sure yet." He said with a look of concern on his face.

"Who is it? Who do you believe is behind this?" I asked.

He replied with one word "Eros."

CHAPTER 10 – DIMITRI

Dimitri's POV

The last thing I ever wanted was a mate. I had always believed that if I found my mate, I would reject her. If I was unable to reject her due to the pull of the mate bond, I would simply have someone kill her and be done with all of that nonsense.

When my mother was taken and tortured, my father lost his mind. A mate is a liability to an Alpha and a weakness that could destroy him. We saw this happen with my father. I cannot afford to have a weakness in my armor in the form of a mate.

And then... she danced right into my life.

When I saw her at the club, my wolf Dom, actually tried to fight me for control. He wanted to run over and scent her. She was beautiful but young, I liked my women more experienced. I'm twenty-six and have enjoyed many mistresses in my years, but never had a real relationship. I certainly had no intention of getting attached to anyone, not even this raven haired kitten.

I watched her dance, the way her body moved, the way her long hair bounced. Maybe I was just attracted to her and nothing more. I tried to fool myself, but Dom was no dummy. I moved to the edge of the balcony and looked down at her. I just needed her to look up and make eye contact, then I would know for sure. I couldn't take my eyes off her.

That two-bit sleazeball must have noticed my reaction to her and tried to dance with her. I saw him lift her bracelet off her wrist and knew he was up to no good. Dom let out a growl and she must have sensed my anger, she fled with her friends.

I mind linked my Delta, who was outside with the car, her description, and instructed him to follow her home. Then I cornered Eros and reached into his shirt pocket, pulling out her bracelet. I resisted the urge to pummel him with so many humans around. He may have been an Alpha, but he was no match for me, and he knew it.

Eros is dangerous to humans and enjoys playing little mafia games in their world. He's as dirty and corrupt as they come. A real wolf in cheap clothing. Dom hated seeing him so close to her and I couldn't understand why. Perhaps it was because she was a young and attractive little thing. I should have just walked away and left well enough alone, but I just couldn't. I needed to know more about her.

An hour later, my Delta Spiro, had returned to inform me that she was a university student and living in the dorm. I gave him the bracelet and asked him to return it in the morning and find out what he could about her. The dorm advisor had recognized her description, taken the bracelet from him, and refused to give him any information on her.

I put my Beta Niko, on watch duty, and later that night he linked me to tell me she was out running with her friends. They ran towards the forest by the monastery and Dom demanded we go run. Something beyond curiosity was pulling me to her.

I shifted and ran through the forest trying to pick up her scent. I knew she was with two others, but I couldn't scent them. They must have been masking their scents with Evvie tea. I haven't had any in over a week, so my scent was strong in the air.

I found three sets of clothing near the tree line and her scent hit me like a ton of bricks! Sweet honeysuckle and vanilla. Dom wanted his mate and let out a loud howl as I fought him for control.

My Beta Niko, Gamma Alec, and Delta Spiro all rotated watching her. Alec had followed her to the museum and through the Plaka from the rooftops. Eros had a man following her too and Alec ripped his throat out before he could get his hands on her.

My father's old Beta and Niko's uncle, Kosta, took her home. I grew up with Kosta, he was a good man but left the pack when my father went mad. Kosta was a fighting legend in his prime and now worked as security. Anyone who hired him was either really important or royal.

The following day Kosta took her out to Delphi. Niko tried to coax an introduction but Kosta wasn't falling for it. Over the next few weeks, we watched as Kosta made frequent visits to the dorm advisor's apartment. Either she was working for him or he was sleeping with her. We also watched as Eros' men circled around, if Eros was so determined then he must have known something about her that we didn't.

Spiro was watching her when she left the university library late at night. He watched her enter a taverna and the other girl, with long dark hair, walked back alone. A car stopped abruptly and yanked her friend in. Spiro wanted to follow but needed to stay on his assignment.

Eros was getting bold, and the shifter's had become worried about his carelessness. In the beginning, packs traded or sold low ranking omegas into pack slavery. They would do the cooking and the cleaning for the packs. If they were extremely attractive, they might become a pack mistress. Then it expanded to humans and trafficking arms and drugs. Most shifter's have stopped dealing with Eros and would like to see the black market fold. But the money from human trafficking has allowed Eros and his boss to build an empire.

I was snoozing in bed when Alec mind linked me, she was going out for the day with her two friends and was at the boat docks. He watched her board a ferry for Agistri and I had him get the speed boat ready.

It didn't take us long to catch up to them. We also spotted two of Eros' men, wolves, following closely. Alec and I split up to watch from different places, fortunately, we had taken Evvie tea to mask our scents so Eros' wolves wouldn't pick up our scents.

I sat at the outdoor beach bar and watched them from a distance. She looked so hot in that little turquoise bikini and it bothered me that others could see her too. This was crazy, I just needed to get close enough, to look into her eyes, and then I would know for sure.

"What do you need to know for sure? That's our mate! I know it." Dom snapped at me. He was sure, but I still wanted to look into her eyes.

Alec sat under a shade tree on the other side reading a book and trying to look like he belonged there. "What are you reading?" I asked through the mind link.

"The only book I could find in the lost and found at the port information desk." He said.

"Yes, but you haven't looked up for nearly an hour, it must be good." I linked back.

"It's classical English literature." He replied.

"Good grief, you aren't reading Pride and Prejudice, are you?" I laughed.

"No." he laughed back. "It's Sense and Sensibility."

A few moments later, I was ready to order another beer, but they started getting up, ready to leave.

"They'll be heading your way to get some food," Alec linked me, and I moved.

"Have you seen the goons?" I asked.

"They're back in the woods, watching as well." He said.

I walked around the village and stopped at a tavern to use the restroom. When I came out, I had lost visual of them. "Where are they?" I asked Alec through the link.

"They're on the back patio at Raina's but she went downstairs alone. I don't see her, and the goons moved fast." He said.

If she stepped away from her friends, they could try and take her. Where the hell did she go? I heard a cat meowing loudly and I suddenly stood still inhaling her scent. She crashed right into me and my first instinct was to hold her to my chest.

Dom was howling in my head. What the hell was wrong with him, she can't be our mate.

"Then why are you so obsessed with her?" Dom snickered at me.

"Excuse me." She said, her voice was music to my ears. She looked right up at me with those beautiful blue eyes and I knew. FUCK!

I fought the urge to kiss her and felt myself getting annoyed at my weakness. Then I caught a glimpse of the two goons following her that stood watching us. I stepped away from her and quickly made my way to them. They ran behind the building, into a back alley-way.

A moment later, I had them both pinned to the ground with my canines and claws extended. One of them pulled a silver blade out and tried to stab me. I grabbed his arm and forced him to drive the blade in his neck.

"Who sent you?" I asked the other one still breathing.

"Fuck you!" He growled.

"I'm afraid you're not my type." I snarled back.

"But she is, isn't she? You can't watch her all the time!" He smiled before I snapped his neck.

"Alec, I've neutralized the goons. You can go and get something to eat before we head back." I linked my Gamma.

"You want anything?" He asked.

"I'm good, going to grab souvlaki at the stand on the corner and then go for a quick run." I replied.

I sat at the north end of the docks eating my chicken souvlaki pita. I couldn't stop thinking about her and it worried me. I never wanted a mate for this exact reason. Eros must have already figured out my connection to her and wanted her. Why did he want her? Eros and I usually stayed in our separate lanes.

"She's an adorable little creature." Dom practically purred at me.

"What the fuck, are you a cat all of the sudden?" I've never heard him sound so soft and I'm sure that was a purr.

My scent had been masked and my eyes were behind dark sunglasses, she might not be aware that she's my mate. I walked towards the forest and stepped out of my clothes before I shifted. I let Dom run off some steam and he really wanted to find his mate and claim her. "I'm picking up her scent." He told me.

"We can't approach her; she'll be with her friends. Let's see if we can find their things and get an I.D. on her." I told him.

Minutes later, I found her dress and backpack. I shifted to human form in the bush and quickly opened her bag up. Money, magazine, towel, sunglasses, cell phone, vanilla lip balm, and a lighter. Why did she have a lighter? She doesn't smoke. No identification, DAMN!

I shifted back and Dom started sniffing her clothes

and rolled around on them.

"ENOUGH!" I yelled at him. He then picked up a piece of her swimsuit in his mouth and we ran back to our clothes.

When I shifted, I noticed that Dom had grabbed her bikini bottom. I stared at it for a moment and then lifted it to my nose. Big mistake! Her scent sent a burning desire for her shooting through my body.

I'm in big fucking trouble!

CHAPTER 11 – PLAN

I felt anxious all day and couldn't focus on classes, I was thinking about everything Niko told me. Athens was full of beautiful young women; Eros could have his pick! Why me?

No one in Greece knew who I was, except for Kosta, and even he didn't know much about me. Maybe I should ask Kosta to help me with Angela? I considered this for a while but then decided against it because he will report back to my father and I'd be on the next flight out of here. No way in hell I wanted to be sent to school near home, I was finally free to do what I wanted, when I wanted.

I wasn't going to be able to do this by myself and I wasn't exactly sure how I felt about Niko or who he worked for. It was time to tell Rocky and Leo, they were my only wolf friends and might have some ideas. I texted both of them and asked them to meet at Richy's Temple of Sweets after class.

An hour later, I was standing in front of the ice cream shop. I looked into the window and Rocky wasn't there yet. "Raven." I heard Leo call as he walked down the sidewalk towards me.

"Hey, Leo." I waved at him.

"Is Rocky here yet?"

"No, I was just waiting."

"Her last class should have been over five minutes ago, I'm sure she's on her way. Let's go inside and check out Richy's specials for today." He said and we stepped inside.

"Hello, Hello!" We were greeted by the owner Richard, who was behind the counter in his apron.

"Hi Richard, what are the specials for today?" I asked.

"We have the Kaimaki, which is a chewy Greek ice cream with a sour cherry syrup and topped with chopped pistachio. We also have a new creamy and smooth banana ice cream topped with chocolate shavings." He said.

"I'll try the banana." Rocky said from behind us, she had just entered the shop.

"The Kaimaki sounds good." I said.

"Make that two Kaimaki's." Leo added.

I paid for all of our ice creams and we sat in the back corner booth that we regularly occupied at Richy's Temple of Sweets.

"Raven, is everything okay?" Rocky asked me digging into her ice cream.

What a loaded question. Where do I even start? I took a deep breath and just started telling them.

"Remember when we went to the club and the beast was there? Well, I recently discovered that the man dancing with me was indeed Alpha Eros, the mafia underboss."

"Oh, Goddess! I'm so glad we didn't stick around." Rocky said.

"I wish it were that easy. I think my father has someone watching me, maybe. That Niko guy I met at Delphi is Kosta's nephew and he told me that Eros was after me. He also told me that Angela was accidentally abducted by his men instead of me."

"What?" Leo said with a shocked look on his face.

"They were sent to pick me up, I was with her that night. Angela and I had just left the library and I stopped to get dinner at Cristopalous Taverna, she walked back alone. We both have long dark hair and we're about the same size." I said.

"Except she's human! How the hell did they miss that?" Leo said.

"So many wolves mask their scent around here, maybe they thought she had taken the same herb you take." I added.

"If Angela doesn't turn up, the inspector will be out any day now sniffing around. You'll be the first person they interview." Rocky told me.

"I doubt she will leave alive. If she finds out that she is being held captive by wolves, they will have to kill her." Leo said.

"I can't let her die because of me!"

"Eros is a very dangerous wolf, no one really knows who the head of the mafia is. Some people think it's him, that he's more than just the underboss." Leo added.

"Could the Beast of Greece be the mafia boss? I mean, he was at the club. Eros said the beast was watching me, maybe he wants me?"

"I wonder why he would go to such great lengths for you. You're Alpha born that would start a war among packs." Rocky said.

"Raven, which pack are you from?" Leo asked.

I paused for a moment and decided that I trusted them. "I'm from Crescent Moon Pack."

"THE Crescent Moon Pack? As in the largest power-house pack in the world?" Rocky asked.

"You're Alpha LaRue's daughter?" Leo asked.

"Yes, I am."

"Our Alpha Georgios sits on the shifter's council with your father." Leo said.

"I guess if anything happens to me, you'll know how to contact my family." I told them.

"Nothing is going to happen to you Raven. But, why didn't you tell us sooner?" Rocky asked.

"I didn't think it was important and Kosta had warned me to lay low. Maybe Eros has figured out who I am and now he wants me to hurt my father." I said.

"Shouldn't we let him know, he's got allies around the globe and we could probably get Angela back in no time." Leo suggested.

"You don't know my dad. I'm his only daughter of six children, he will bring me straight home."

"Okay, so what's the plan?" Rocky asked.

"I don't know. I thought about finding Eros and trading Angela for me."

"Are you crazy?" Leo asked.

"I'm an Alpha, I've been training since I was a pup, and I've got a few tricks up my sleeve."

"Tricks?" Leo asked.

"I'm elemental." I said.

"SHUT UP!" Rocky's eyes were wide open in shock.

"Elementals still exist?" Leo asked confused.

He had a water cup sitting in front of him and I willed the water to splash him in the face. Rocky burst out laughing, and Leo looked down at the water dripping off his face to his shirt in shock.

"Elementals are descendants of the Moon Goddess herself Leo, of course, they still exist, even if they are few and far between." Rocky told him.

"So, water is your element?" He questioned.

"Yes, and Fire." I said.

"I've never heard of a wolf that could control two elements." Rocky said.

"There was a prophecy before I was born, that a wolf

would eventually control all four elements and help win a great shifter war." I told them.

"So, you're thinking about trading yourself for Angela and then burning Eros?" Leo asked.

"Something like that, I don't know. I'd like to find where they might be keeping her first and then consider an escape plan."

"I'm in!" Leo said.

"Where do we start?" Rocky asked.

"We start at the Plaka district."

It's been three days now, the police inspector interviewed me yesterday. We've been out every evening trying to find buildings associated with Eros where Angela might be kept. Rocky and I have been walking through the Plaka district and the Monastiraki district, with Leo following from a distance trying to pick up a tail that might be following us.

We were currently in the Plaka and had found a waitress at a local cafe who was a wolf. Rocky had inquired where we might be able to purchase some Evvie, which could be found on the black market to help wolves mask their scent. This was our cover-up story for snooping around.

The waitress had informed us that it's very difficult to find but we should try looking at Howling Dogs night club. We went to the Howling Dogs, but the doors were locked.

"It doesn't open until later." Rocky said.

"They're closed until tomorrow, they've been setting up for the Dionysus festival." Said a familiar voice from behind us.

"Niko, what are you doing here?" I asked.

"I'm wondering what you're doing here. And why your friend is following you way back there?" He asked.

"That's none of your business." I replied.

"Third night in a row that you've been out wandering around. Are you looking for something or someone?" He raised a questioning eyebrow at me.

"Raven wants to mask her scent; we're looking to buy herbs." Rocky gave him our cover-up line.

"From the Greek mafia? Can't you just send her to your supplier? You're masking your scent right now aren't you, Beta?" He grinned at Rocky who looked like she was debating whether or not she wanted to punch him.

"Look Raven, you're making it difficult for us to focus on Angela when we're worried about your carelessness." He said.

"Excuse me? My carelessness? How long does it take to find and save one single human? I can't just sit around and do nothing." I snapped back.

"We expect to have her in the next few days, there's a lot of movement happening with the festival coming." He told us.

"Wonderful, then we will go back to the dorm right now, come on Rocky." I lied and just had another idea.

We walked back towards Leo and I noticed most places were already decorating and setting up for the three day festival. There's no way Eros would miss the festival, we could return in costumes tomorrow, with so many people it would be hard for anyone to really pick up my scent.

We slipped into a taxi and I waved goodbye to Niko. "We need to get some costumes for tomorrow." I told them.

"There's a plaza a few blocks ahead that will have some options." Leo said and instructed the driver in Greek.

"I think she's at the Howling Dogs. None of the other places were locked up and Niko must have been watching the place too. He seemed a little nervous that we had suddenly appeared there."

"I think you're right. That is a big building and I'm sure it has an underground level as well." Rocky said.

We reached the plaza and entered a store that was selling elaborate costumes. "Most people will be dressed as the ancient society dressed, in linen costumes, but we will need something to fully disguise us." Rocky said.

"How about this?" Leo laughed and held up a satyr costume.

"It's perfect for you!" I laughed.

Rocky and I also searched for costumes that would hide our heads and faces. Rocky found a Medusa costume with a big snakehead for herself and a wood nymph costume for me that covers the entire body and head with tree bark and vines. My costume also had a masquerade mask that matched the rest of the costume to hide my face.

We have our costumes and a mission for tomorrow.

CHAPTER 12 – FESTIVAL

I wiggled into my wood nymph costume, it was a layered dress with brown and green chiffon. It had leaves, bark, vines, and twigs were elaborately sewn into it. The headdress was beautiful and would hide my hair perfectly. It had vines and twigs intertwined in it and had a train that draped down my back.

I rubbed brown and glittery green body paint on the exposed parts of my arms and legs before I did the same to my neck and face. Once it was dry, I slipped the beautifully embellished masquerade mask over my eyes. The costume was sexy and fun, had I been wearing it for any other occasion I would have enjoyed it.

I grabbed my waterproof lighter and slipped it into my bra. My cellphone, money, keys, and another lighter went into a small brown pouch purse. I hung the purse over my neck and shoulder, and it blended well with my costume.

I knocked on Rocky's door and she opened it, the Medusa costume on her was fantastic. Leo was sitting in his satyr costume on her bed while she painted his face and nose with makeup.

"What the hell is that?" I burst out laughing pointing at Leo's satyr costume.

He looked down to where I was pointing and wiggled around a cloth penis that was sewn into his costume while laughing. "Satyr's were often depicted with an erect penis because they were horny little rascals. They spent their days chasing around nymphs and women, trying to seduce them. It was all about wine, sex, and partying; that's why they were always around Dionysus." He told me.

"We're saving these costumes for some real fun someday." Rocky laughed.

We made our way to the lobby and Karla was standing there watching everyone leaving in costumes.

"Off to the festival I see, be sure to stay safe and together." She waved to us and called out, "don't drink too much."

We took a taxi, but the streets were a disaster because some of the main roads were blocked. The parade route went from Monastiraki square, through the Plaka, and down to Kolonaki. We got as close as possible, then got out to walk the remaining blocks.

I could hear the traditional Greek klarino or karamuza horns playing and the drums pounding as we neared the festivities. People were linked in a line dance revolving in a circle in the streets, onlookers were clapping as they danced. We moved past them and into the Plaka towards the Howling Dogs nightclub. The parade was moving slowly and a float that instantly caught my eye had a big penis mounted on top. I laughed when I noticed someone on the float was tossing rubber penis' out into the crowd.

"Dionysus was also the God of sex and fertility." Leo smiled at my amused expression.

Most people were masked and there seemed to be a lot

of indecent costumes. Debauchery was definitely on the menu tonight for many. A float depicting Dionysus on a throne floated by us next and he was surrounded by many beautiful Greek Goddess looking women. A tall stilt walker was walking behind the float juggling hoops.

We were at a standstill by a wine booth and Rocky said something, but I couldn't hear her because of the loud music. She purchased some wine in large plastic goblets and handed them to us, I assume it was to help blend in. We continued to walk, and I could see the Howling Dogs come into view.

Two men were standing outside and looked like security, just then the door swung open, and Eros exited the building. We watched him walk down the block and then followed him. He walked with another man who looked like he was part of his security detail. They walked another block to a corner restaurant, and he entered the building.

We waited across the street and acted like party-goers. Leo grabbed a human girl next to him and they danced to the music. She was grinding against his cloth penis; everyone loves a horny old satyr I suppose. Rocky gave me the elbow and motioned her head towards the restaurant. Eros was being seated on the small balcony overlooking the festivities to dine alone.

"He's eating, maybe we should go snoop at the nightclub." I suggested to Rocky.

"That's a good idea, I'll mind link Leo to stay here and watch him. He can link me when Eros is on the move." She said.

We made our way back to the Howling Dogs nightclub; we saw a group of college kids approach the doors and try to enter. They were turned away by the guards and the club didn't appear to be open.

"If the nightclub isn't open, then why would two security guards be posted out front?" I said to Rocky.

"Something is very suspicious here." She said.

We walked around the block, down a narrow alleyway to the backside of the club. The lower level windows had bars on them. They had been blacked out so we couldn't see in or out. I was considering standing on top of the garbage can that was nearby and trying to see if the windows on the top level were open.

"Someone is coming." Rocky whispered.

"Quick behind here." I motioned to the garbage can.

We ducked behind it and crouched down in the shadows. One of Eros' security guards from the front had walked around the back. He pulled his zipper open and started to pee against the building. Rocky gave me a gagging look and I suppressed a laugh. I willed his urine, which was mostly made of water, to splash back up his shirt. He started swearing in Greek and pissing all over his shoes and pants.

"The coast is clear." I whispered to Rocky.

"That was brilliant." She giggled.

"I think I could reach the top window if I stand on the garbage can and look in." I said. We moved the garbage can in position and I climbed on top of it. I was about a foot too short to see in.

"I'll get on there too and give you a boost up." Rocky said.

I put one foot on each of her thighs and was able to look in. It appeared to be an office. I tried to lift the window open, but it was locked.

"The other window next to the office looks like it could be a bathroom window, there's a good chance it might be unlocked." I suggested.

We moved the garbage can over and did the same. This window was slightly higher and smaller, but it was unlocked. Quietly and slowly, I lifted the window open and tried to pull myself up. I had to step on Rocky's shoulder and my shoe got stuck on something and slipped off my foot. I pulled myself into the small bathroom and looked out the window at Rocky who had my shoe stuck in her Medusa head snakes.

"Be careful she whispered to me. If you're not back in twenty minutes, Leo and I will come in for you." Rocky said.

I gave her a thumbs up and closed the window but didn't lock it. I turned around and slowly walked out to the office and made my way to the door. Stopping at the door, I listened closely and heard nothing. I walked down the hall and tip toed down the stairs to the first level.

There was a door with a small window, and I peeked through it. It appeared to be the club but had been vandalized. Tables, chairs, and booths had been destroyed, glass smashed, claw marks on the floor, what the hell happened here I wondered. Then I heard a noise.

"I have to fucking change my clothes!" A man was yelling. "I'll be back in ten minutes, just go upstairs and stand watch, Marty went to go get some food and the boss wants the front door guarded."

I heard some footsteps coming from the basement and pulled the door open to the cleaning closet. The smell of chemicals was strong which would help mask my scent. Their steps were getting closer and they walked right by me and out through the club.

When I couldn't hear them anymore, I stepped out of the closet and dashed to the basement. I reached into my purse pouch and took out my lighter in case I needed it. I entered the small room at the bottom and found a recliner chair, laptop, and small table sitting by the door. Someone was spending time down here keeping guard.

On the opposite side of the room were a sink, microwave, and mini-fridge. I looked down at the table and found a set of keys, so I grabbed them. The other door seemed to lead into another room, I opened the door and found four cells. Three of the four cells had occupants and one was Angela.

"Angela." I called out.

"Who are you?" Her trembling voice asked. I was unrecognizable in the costume.

"It's me, Raven. Rocky is outside and we're here to get you out." I placed the lighter back in my purse and started inserting the keys into the locks, I finally unlocked hers with the fourth try.

"Raven, we can't leave them here." She said about the other girls and I nodded my head.

These guys were monsters, one of the girls couldn't have been older than fifteen, and they were going to sell her. They looked scared and nervous. I stood frozen for a moment and heard a noise thanks to my wolf hearing.

"Stay right here and work on unlocking the cells. Don't come out until I come to get you." I told Angela and she nodded.

I slipped out the door and went to the sink in the first room. "What are you doing here?" A wolf appeared at the door.

"Hello, I was thirsty and needed a drink." I turned on the sink.

"Well I'm horny and need a fuck, what do you say sexy wood nymph?" He smiled and adjusted himself moving closer to me.

"I say, you look thirsty. Have a drink first." I smiled.

I lifted my hands and willed the water to form a water bubble around his head and he thrashed around trying to knock it down, fighting for air. I focused to keep the water bubble in place. A few minutes later his lifeless body fell to the ground.

I pulled the door open and Angela had unlocked the other two girls, we quietly made our way back up that stairs and into the office. I opened the window in the bathroom and saw both Rocky and Leo.

"Thank the Goddess! Eros just came back. Hurry!" Rocky said with panic in her voice.

I lowered the young girl first and Leo grabbed her. Then I lowered Angela and the third girl. I lifted my leg through the window when an arm wrapped around my waist and pulled me in.

"Not so fast little wolf." A voice growled in my ear.

CHAPTER 13 – ESCAPE

"I've "I've been waiting to get you alone and now you just stumble right into the wolf's den. What luck!" Eros smiled at me.

"Why have you been looking for me, Eros?"

"Oh Raven, little Raven." He sucked his teeth. "Seeing you in this sexy little costume would make even the God Pan chase after this tempting wood nymph." He said as he lifted my mask from my face.

"What do you want from me?" I demanded.

He grabbed me harder around the waist and dragged me into his office. He threw me into an armchair, placed one hand on each side, and leaned his crooked nose inches away from mine.

"Tell me, why are my men disappearing when they get close enough to you?" He asked.

"I have no idea what you're talking about." I snapped back.

"I've sent some of my best warriors after you and most don't come back." He stared intently at me.

This must have been what Niko was talking about. "Those were your best? They couldn't tell the difference between a human and a wolf. They picked up the wrong girl." I snarked back.

"Some might not be the smartest, but they are the strongest of the warriors" his voice was annoyed.

I could feel Rae inside ready to attack. She hated having him so close to us. "Let's light his slimy ass up." She said to me.

"I need him alive for more information, I don't think he's working alone." I told her.

"There's a perfectly good toilet filled with water in the next room, let's water bubble him into talking." Rae suggested to me. It wasn't a bad idea, but I wasn't exactly sure how to control it yet, I'd probably just kill him, which was also not a bad idea.

"My men are disappearing because the beast is obsessed with you. He killed his mate and now he wants you." He said.

"And why exactly do you care if he wants me or not?" I said. "Do you work for him?"

"Bhahahaha." His laugh was maniacal. "What a ridiculous notion that I would work for him. Oh no, my boss makes the beast look like a kitten." He smiled and leaned back against his desk.

"So why do you want me?"

He reached into a cigar box on his desk and pulled one out. He held it in his hands and smelled it. There was a knock on the door and a man stepped in.

"The buyers are here, and the merchandise is gone." He said.

"Where are the girls?" Eros growled at me.

"What girls?" I asked in my most innocent voice.

"Marty is dead." The other wolf added. I assumed Marty must have been the wolf I water bubbled.

"The boss wants little Raven here dead, maybe I should let them have their fun with her. They came all this way and she let the merchandise go free." His eyes flashed with anger.

"What should I tell them?" He asked Eros.

"Tell them I'll be down in twenty minutes. I'd like to have a taste of this little wolf first." He said.

"Yes, boss." He nodded his head and left the office.

Eros lunged at me and I kicked him in the gut sending him flying backward. I made a run for the door and he grabbed the back of my headdress yanking it off. Then he grabbed a fist full of my hair and pulled me back. I looked up at his face and he still had the unlit cigar in his mouth.

He tugged the front of my dress down and it ripped down the middle. I could feel my bra and cleavage exposed.

"What is this?" He noticed my lighter and reached into my bra to pull it out.

"Guess I'm not the only wolf who likes to smoke." I said eyeing his cigar.

He pushed me back down in the chair and looked at me as if I was prey. Pacing in front of me, he looked at the lighter in his hand and flipped the lid open. The cigar was still in his mouth, he brought the lighter to the end of the cigar and flicked it on.

There was a loud commotion coming from downstairs and the sound of gunfire. Eros' eyes flared with anger and I knew it was time to make my exit. I willed the fire at the tip of the cigar to expand and burn. Eros let out a scream as the side of his face caught fire and the room filled with the smell of burning hair.

I bolted for the door and could hear the fighting downstairs. I ran down the stairs and heard the sound of guns firing. Before I could see what was happening, I was tossed to the ground with a heavy body laying on top of me.

"Be careful, those are silver bullets they're using." Niko told me.

"What are you doing here?" I asked.

"Rescuing you."

"I was doing just fine."

"Yes, I can see that. Come on, my bike is in the back."

We ran out through the back door and Niko jumped on his motorcycle and fired it up. I hopped on and we took off. Niko was bobbing and weaving between all the people at the festival.

"Hang on tight, we're about to take some stairs." Niko called to me and I squeezed my arms tighter around his waist. The stairs in the Plaka were narrow and made of stones. We weren't moving as fast as I wanted because of all the people and festivities. I looked back and caught a glimpse of a wolf running on the rooftops trying to keep up with us.

We took a turn and came face to face with some of Eros' goons who were also on motorcycles. "We've got company!" I yelled to Niko.

We turned back around and cut into the parade, riding alongside the floats. We accidentally knocked over some bobblehead costumed characters. I looked over my shoulder and saw they were gaining on us, but they couldn't shoot or shift without the humans noticing.

One of the floats had a fire baton twirling on it and I continued to look over my shoulder waiting for the perfect time. Just as the goon's bike got close enough under the float, I sent a flame shooting down from the baton to the top of his head. He lost control of his bike and skidded, the motorcycle behind him crashed into him and sent the driver flying off.

We made it out of the Plaka district and raced north, a black Mercedes swung out behind us and was joined by two more motorcycles. Someone from the car started shooting at us and Niko turned down a narrow street of food vendors that would not accommodate a vehicle. The two motorcycles followed us as we made our way north to Kotzia square by the city hall building.

There was a big water fountain in the square and Niko zipped right by it. I turned my head and willed the water from the fountain to rise and fall on the two motorcycles chasing us. They went slipping and sliding into each other.

"Suckers!" I heard Rae say.

We continued north on the main road and the Mercedes swerved out behind us again. I heard gunfire and a bullet zipped just past my ear. Niko pulled up next to the car ahead of us and passed it moving to the front. The black Mercedes squeezed next to the car behind us and bumped it out of the way.

Niko took a sharp corner, and the Mercedes did the same. Another gunshot ripped through the air and the mirror on our bike was hit. I spotted a restaurant up ahead with outdoor dining, which means that candles would be on the tables. I set my eyes on a flame willing it to grow larger and flying at the shooter hanging out the window.

He was soon engulfed in flames and the driver of the vehicle jumped out of the still moving car. The Mercedes hit another parked car and exploded in flames. Car alarms went off, people came rushing out from the buildings and Niko was completely unaware of what I had just done.

We continued riding north for another hour. I wasn't exactly sure where we were going but I knew that returning to my dorm wouldn't be a good idea. I had just killed several mafia henchmen and set the underboss on fire. Worst of all, these weren't humans, they were the most despicable and lethal wolves I've ever met.

I wondered if Leo and Rocky were okay, how Angela was doing and if the police were called. As much as I enjoyed my time in Greece, I knew these would be my last days here. As soon as my father hears about it, I would be on a plane home.

"Home sounds great right now." Rae said to me.

"I should have just picked the college in San Diego." I told Rae bitterly.

I pressed myself up against Niko's back for warmth, my costume was so thin, I was practically naked. The hum of the motorcycle was soothing, other cars had become few and far between. The further we got away from Athens, the safer I felt.

Niko turned the motorcycle down an old road in the woods, I wondered if he was taking me to a hideout or somewhere to kill me.

"If he wanted to kill us, he would have done it already, he's had plenty of opportunities." Rae reminded me.

A howl ripped through the air and several wolves ran in our direction. I was ready to reach for my lighter and start fighting when I realized that Niko was very relaxed. A few of the wolves came out and ran alongside the motorcycle as if they were escorting us. Niko continued to drive, and I could see a light come into view in the distance.

This was pack territory and we finally pulled to a stop in front of a huge mansion.

CHAPTER 14 – BEAST

We dismounted the motorcycle and Niko turned to me, "It's okay, you're safe now."

"Where are we?"

"We're at my packhouse." He answered. "I think you'll like it here."

"Does your Alpha know I'm with you?" I asked.

"Oh yeah." He smiled wide. "Listen, Raven, he could be a bit grumpy at first, but I know he will warm up to you." Niko grinned.

"I bet! I'm sure grumpy Alpha will appreciate a sassy, opinionated, female Alpha with a knack for getting into trouble." I groaned and rolled my eyes.

"He will love you." Niko laughed and led the way.

We walked up the stairs and entered the double doors of this stunning house. The dark wooden floors were a beautiful contrast to the light colored walls and decor. There was a double grand staircase with the same dark colored wood used for the railings. The chandelier was a gorgeous crystal and tied everything together.

"The Alpha is in his office waiting for us." Niko told me.

I nodded my head and walked with him down a long hallway to the big dark wooden door at the end of the hall. I looked down at my torn neckline and pulled up the costume to try and hide my bra. I'm not sure why, but I felt nervous meeting this Alpha. Niko pushed the door open and we entered. The office was so grand, it reminded me of my father's at the castle.

"Have a seat." Niko motioned to a leather armchair sitting in front of a really large, magnificently carved, wooden desk.

The occupant of the desk sat in a large leather chair and was turned around facing away from me. I could only see the back of his dark head, strong shoulders, and massive arms. He was wearing a long black sleeve dress shirt with his sleeves rolled up.

I could feel an extraordinarily strong and heated Alpha aura pulsing through the room. Rae was disappointed that she couldn't pick up his scent. Any minute now he would turn around to speak to me and the anticipation was growing.

There were two other wolves in the room with us that I did not know. One had sandy blonde hair with brown eyes and smiled at me. The other had dark brown short curly hair, brown eyes, a scar on his chin, and had a serious face. They both looked about the same age, mid-twenties maybe and they were cut with strong muscular builds. I tried to scent them, but only one seemed to have a scent.

"Why am I only scenting one wolf in a room with four wolves?" I asked out loud before I could stop myself.

It was quiet for a moment and they all stood with their eyes glazed, they were obviously mind linking. No one answered me.

"Where am I? What's the name of this pack?" I asked.

I looked at Niko who seemed to have a frustrated expression on his face. They were still mind linking and I wondered what was wrong. Maybe Niko was filling them in on our escape? Or maybe the Alpha was upset he had brought me here?

"I could just wait outside, give you more privacy, you know, so you don't have to mind link around me." I suggested and stood up to leave, I could feel Rae getting frustrated too.

"SIT DOWN!" I heard a growl coming from behind the chair.

"Not until you tell me what's going on." I snapped back. I felt myself getting annoyed because he hadn't even turned his chair around to look at me. As if I was insignificant, like a child in the room. How rude and disrespectful.

"I'm the only reason you're still alive and the only thing standing between you and a very angry Greek mafia. I'm not even sure if I want you alive." His deep voice was harsh.

Hearing those words was like a dagger to my heart and I wasn't sure why. Was this Alpha going to kill me? Rae was anxious and I considered if I could outrun them and leave. I wasn't feeling welcomed or wanted and wondered why Niko would even bring me here.

"Grumpy my ass! He's a jerk." Rae said to me.

I looked up at Niko and he gave me an apologetic look. "Can I at least use the restroom?" I asked.

"Sure, it's right this way." He said and led the way. We exited the office and Niko pointed to the door on the right.

"You weren't kidding when you said he was grumpy." I whispered to Niko.

"Hurry he doesn't like to be kept waiting." Niko whispered back.

"I don't think I caught his name." I said.

"It's Dimitri." He said in a hurry pointing to the restroom door.

I stepped inside and locked the door. Oh, Goddess! He said Dimitri, as in the beast of Greece. I was in the lair of the beast and he wanted me dead too. What the hell is going on here?

"Rae, we've got to get out of here." My heart was racing.

I removed my pouch purse and stripped off my nymph costume. Then I stuffed the only clothing that could fit into my small purse, which was my underwear and bra. I lifted the small window open and climbed over the toilet seat, out the window.

I shifted as soon as my feet hit the ground and took

off running. We had traveled north on the motorcycle which means Athens was south of here. Athens isn't safe at the moment either. I decided to keep moving north until I reached a town and then I would call my dad. I was running at top speed with my purse hanging in my mouth. I wondered if I kept running north if I would run into another pack's territory.

"Let's just focus on getting out of this territory first." Rae said to me.

An angry howl rang out from a distance as they discovered I was gone. I wish I had found some of those scent masking herbs. These wolves didn't play fair, and I wasn't exactly sure what I had done to piss them off. There was no place to hide in their territory that could mask my scent. I tried to listen for moving water, I could usually hear it from a mile away but heard nothing. Thank the Moon Goddess that tonight was nearly a new moon, which would help hide my black wolf better in the dark forest.

I could hear heavy paws running behind me and pushed Rae to keep running faster. Moments later I was knocked down and an angry roar came from above me. I flipped over and attempted to take off running again but this time I was knocked into a tree. The sound of other running paws approaching us could be heard.

I looked up to find a giant black Alpha. He was twice the size of a normal werewolf; I've never seen anything like it. My father is the largest Alpha I've ever set my eyes on, but he was even bigger than my father. He was a beast of a wolf.

I stood back and bared my teeth at him, my hackles

were raised. I wasn't going to let his size intimidate me, I may be smaller, but I could roast this beast if I wanted.

"We could even drown him." Rae said to me.

"Except we don't have any water." I told her.

The beast shifted back to human form and I continued to growl at him. "I will break you pup." He said with amusement in his voice.

Sweet Moon Goddess, he was naked! There was a shadow from the tree he was standing under that was hiding his face, but something felt familiar about him. His muscled body was perfectly sculpted, and I couldn't seem to look away.

"Mmmm, will you look at that!" Rae purred at me.

"Now's not the time Rae, he still wants us dead." I reminded her.

"He might actually be able to kill someone with *that* thing." She jested.

"Stop looking at him." I told myself and Rae but couldn't take my eyes off him.

"Like what you see?" He laughed at me.

Just kill me now. He caught me staring at his manhood. How embarrassing. His laugh sent a fluttering sensation through me.

I could feel other wolves nearby in the shadows, there was no way I could run for it now. I moved next to a bush and shifted back, I was naked and could feel his eyes on me. My purse was on the ground and I grabbed it. Then I stood up in all my naked glory and he let out a growl. The other wolves all dropped their heads to the ground. I reached inside my purse and pulled out the lighter.

"You shouldn't play with fire little pup, you'll burn yourself." He mocked.

"Come closer and you'll be the one that gets burned." I lit the flame.

"I will kill you before you can even flinch." He threatened.

I willed the fire to expand and aimed a big ball of fire near his feet as a warning. Before it even landed, a wall of dirt blocked it and smothered the flame.

He must have fast reflexes because I didn't even see his foot kick up the dirt. I willed another big ball of flames into my hand and stood proud. "You will let me leave and you will not chase after me."

"You're elemental!" He snarled at me.

"And I will not hesitate to use this." I expanded the flame.

The beast stomped his foot and the ground beneath me shook. A dirt clump smothered the flame in my hand and a rock shot towards me. I didn't see anyone actually throw it, but it knocked the lighter out of my hand. I bent down to grab it, and a big dust cloud hit me in the face.

"What the hell?" Rae snarled in my head.

"He's elemental too!" I told her.

I felt a hand reach down and pull me up by the arm. He grabbed me so hard, my arm was tingling. I just wanted to see his face, but I couldn't see anything because of the dust in my eyes. I stood quietly for a moment, with my eyes closed, wondering if he would just snap my neck or rip my throat out.

He was standing so close to me, I could feel the heat from his body. Oh Goddess, his naked body. He was still naked. He leaned down and I thought he was going to whisper something in my ear, instead, he took a deep breath. He was scenting me, and heat pulse through me. The proximity was driving Rae into a frenzy.

He pulled away and growled, "GET HER A SHIRT AND TAKE HER TO A CELL!"

CHAPTER 15 – TROUBLE

Dimitri's POV

"SHE DID WHAT?" I yelled at my Gamma Alec who was supposed to be watching Raven from the rooftops of the Plaka while she was at the festival.

We had suspected that she would be out again with her friends, getting herself into trouble. She certainly has a gift for finding trouble. The buyers for the humans would be arriving today and we wanted to make sure they were dead before they could leave with the girls. Then we would pick the girls up and release them.

If we can hurt his business, by hurting his clients, we would be able to draw him out in the open and finally send him to hell. Weeks of planning and it was all going to go to hell because of one little bird. She had broken into the building and would probably be captured by that bastard.

I called Niko. "Yeah, boss?" He answered.

"She went into the building, get her out." I ordered.

"Fuck! The buyers and their guns just went into that building too." He said and disconnected.

I knew my Beta Niko could handle it, but Dom wanted to rush over to that side of Athens and help. I was at the northern docks waiting for Eros' boss to make a move on a big arms shipment. He was also buying large quantities of silver bullets, which are fatal to wolves.

With the festival going on, the police would be too busy with petty crime and crowd control. This is a perfect night for the mafia agenda. No one knew who Eros worked for, but I had a feeling deep in my gut exactly who it was. The last mafia boss was murdered ten years ago and this monster, the real beast of Greece, is the head of the crime organization now.

The boat carrying the arms was docked and my Delta Spiro, was in the water attaching explosives to the boat. I waited and watched until he was done and swam back. Spiro put his scuba gear away and got in the car with me, and my phone rang.

"Yes." I answered.

"Niko has her. They're on his bike and just left the Plaka." Alec told me.

"Call the crew back to the packhouse, Eros will be out hunting wolves tonight." I ordered.

I pulled out of the marina and nodded my head at Spiro giving him the go ahead. He triggered the wireless detonator and the boat exploded at the dock. I looked in my rearview mirror and saw the raging inferno the boat had become.

I knew that Niko would be heading home with Raven on the back of the motorcycle. She was not going to be safe anywhere in the city. I could feel Dom getting excited to see his mate again. I wasn't exactly sure what I was going to do with her either, it's not like I wanted a mate.

"We need our mate." Dom huffed at me.

"Needing and wanting are two different things." I snapped.

"Who will give Olympus Blood Moon an heir?" Dom nagged me.

"I don't need a mate. Odessa can give the pack an heir."

We drove back in silence. I thought about how young and foolish she was going into that building alone. She was Alpha born, probably from America, and out to have a good time in Greece. With a stubbornness like that, she no doubt was daddy's spoiled princess.

"She's got kefi." Dom told me.

I mentally rolled my eyes at him. I'm not sure why he was so soft about having a mate all of the sudden. Six years ago, I was involved with Heather, she was over the moon for me. I never really dated anyone long term, but Heather was a favorite and I probably kept her around longer than I should. She was so in love with me, she started telling people she was my mate. I knew she wasn't my mate and had planned to break it off with her that night.

When I got back to my office, a box had been delivered to me. It was a similar styrofoam box sent when my mother died. I opened the box and found Heather's decapitated head, just as my father had eight years prior with my mother. Rumors circulated that I had killed my mate and my family was cursed.

"Nothing is going to happen to our mate." Dom said.

"You're right, nothing is. I'm going to send her back home, far away." I told him and shut him out.

We arrived back at the packhouse and the patrols let me know that Niko had returned with a female. I could hear the chatter through the mind link as they entered pack territory. They thought she was beautiful, they could sense her Alpha wolf and wondered who she was.

Spiro and I waited in the office for them to get here. Alec walked in and started filling us in on the details at the Howling Dogs. All three buyers had been taken out and Eros was severely burned though we're not sure how that happened.

I could hear Niko and her walking down the hall and approached my office door. I'm not sure how she will react when she finds out I'm her mate. She can't scent me and if we don't touch, she won't know, but she's an Alpha and her senses are stronger than most wolves. One look into my eyes and she will know.

I spun my chair around and looked towards Spiro who was standing behind me. Spiro was the only mated wolf in the room with us and his mate disapproved of him masking his scent. A mate's scent is very important to a wolf, it had the power to calm, excite and arouse.

As soon as she walked into the room her scent flirted with my nostrils. Dom was excited and it annoyed me.

"Have a seat." Niko told her, and she sat in the chair before my desk.

I could feel her gaze on my arms. Alec stood smiling like a fool and mind linked us. "Oh yeah, she's checking out the big bad Alpha."

"Why am I only scenting one wolf in a room with four wolves?" She asked with no hesitation.

"Because Spiro is pussy whipped." Alec laughed through the mind link.

"She's very observant." Spiro said.

"Alpha don't be rude, turn around and be nice." Niko told me.

"I am nice, I haven't killed her yet." I linked back.

"You couldn't hurt your mate and she's our Luna." Niko said to me.

"Where am I? What's the name of this pack?" She asked.

"I haven't claimed her, she's not the Luna." I snapped back. No one outside of this room knew that she was my mate. Niko, Alec, and Spiro were my best friends since we were pups, they knew how I felt about having a mate. It just wasn't for me.

"I could just wait outside, give you more privacy, you know, so you don't have to mind link around me." She said.

"SIT DOWN!" I heard myself growl. Where the hell was she going, she just got here.

"Don't scare her." Niko linked me.

"Not until you tell me what's going on." She sounded annoyed.

"I'm the only reason you're still alive and the only thing standing between you and a very angry Greek mafia. I'm not even sure if I want you alive." I told her.

"So much for not scaring her. I can feel her anxiety now." Niko linked me with frustration in his voice.

"Can I at least use the restroom?" She asked Niko.

"Sure, it's right this way." He said and took her to the restroom outside my office. "You guys talk some sense into him." Niko linked us.

"You know boss, maybe you should just give her a chance. The Moon Goddess mates us for a reason." Spiro said.

"She's too young and impulsive." I scowled.

"Look how happy Spiro and Adanna still are after four years together, that could be you." Alec told us.

"Yeah, no thanks." I said.

"Niko, what happened to the front of her costume, it was ripped?" Spiro asked through the link.

"What do you mean her costume was ripped? Did that bastard touch her?" I growled. I'm going to fucking kill him!

"Calm down, it was just a little rip, she could have done it climbing in the window at the Howling Dogs." Niko said. "You know, for someone who doesn't want her, you sure are possessive over her."

"What's taking so long?" I asked.

"I think she's gone." Niko said.

"What do you mean gone?" I stood up and moved across the room yanking the office door open.

"I-I think she went out the window." Niko said.

"FUCK!" I kicked the restroom door open and the window was open. I looked down and her costume was laying on the ground. She had shifted.

I jumped out the window and shifted mid-air, I sniffed around and caught her scent north. I let out a howl and let my patrols know to look for her. Dom was not about to let her get away and we took off running.

Where the hell did she think she was going? Eros was going to pump her full of silver and Athens would be crawling with his thugs. Rogue wolves always went to go work for him or lived free on the islands. He was going to have every one of them looking for her. We needed to keep her out of sight and prepare for a possible rogue attack. I may not want a mate, but I also didn't want to see her end up like Heather.

I could see a shadow of her raven black wolf; Dom was almost twice as big as her. He was enjoying the chase and pounced on her, no way she was going to escape him. He growled and she tried to run off again, he tried to push her down, but she fell back into a tree.

She stood up and bared her teeth at me with her hackles raised. She thought she could take me, I suppressed a laugh and shifted back to human form. She looked like she was seriously considering attacking me. "I will break you pup." I told her.

That's when I felt her eyes roaming my body. She was checking me out. I thought I saw a hint of lust in those beautiful blue eyes. Dom let out a proud howl in my head when she couldn't rip her eyes away from my cock.

"Like what you see?" I laughed.

She shifted back and what a beautiful naked sight she was. Dom growled possessively and the other wolves averted their eyes. She held up a lighter, what was she going to do with a lighter?

"You shouldn't play with fire little pup, you'll burn yourself." I joked.

"Come closer and you'll be the one that gets burned." She said threateningly and she flicked on a flame.

"I will kill you before you can even flinch," I told her. Then she made the fire jump near my feet. In a flash, I used my element to block it with the earth. She then held a big ball of flames in her hand, and I knew it wasn't black magic. Her hand wasn't burning from her flame because she was elemental.

"You will let me leave and you will not chase after me." She said.

"You're elemental." I meant to ask, but it just came out as a statement.

"And I will not hesitate to use this." She confirmed.

I shook the ground beneath her to distract her and smothered her fire with earth. Then I willed a rock to knock the lighter out of her hand. When she bent down to retrieve it, I hit her with dirt in the eyes.

Her eyes were closed, and she was crouched down on the ground. I pulled her up and when I touched her arm, my hand was tingling. We were still naked, and I fought the urge to pull her into me and kiss her all over.

Before I knew what happened, I leaned into her neck and inhaled. I almost kissed her. Raven was trouble, she was young and impulsive, and she would try to escape again. If she had continued running north past Mount Olympus, she would have run into Eros' pack territory.

She must have set Eros on fire! Fuck!! She should have made sure he was dead. Now it's going to be personal for him and he will stop at nothing to get her. She doesn't seem to have much control of her element and will probably set the packhouse on fire.

Fuck, Fuck, FUCK! Only one place to put her until I know what to do with her and keep her safe. Dom knew what I was thinking and was getting angry with me.

"You can't do that to our mate! Our job is to protect her." He said.

"We are protecting her." I told him. "GET HER A SHIRT AND TAKE HER TO A CELL!" I growled out.

CHAPTER 16 - HIM

"YOU WILL NOT PUT ME IN A CAGE LIKE SOME WILD ANIMAL!" I yelled at this Alpha jerk.

My eyes were still closed because they had dirt in them. I desperately wanted to wash my face and rinse my eyes out. I could feel him standing inches away from me and I couldn't help but think about his naked body.

"Look at you." He said and gently tucked a strand of hair behind my ear. "You're a wild animal." He said. Tingles shot down my spine at the sound of his voice. I was fighting an urge from deep down inside of me to lean into him and make contact.

I heard footsteps approaching and I was hoping it was Niko, but I could smell the she-wolf. "Here you go Alpha." She said.

"Thank you." He replied to her. He was being nice to whoever the strawberry sorbet smelling female was and I felt a pang of jealousy.

"I can't open my eyes, I need to rinse them." I said.

"You'll have to wait until we get back. Now raise your arms." He said and I felt a shirt being pulled over my head, so I raised my arms while he dressed me.

"I won't be able to see where I'm walking." I protested.

The next thing I know, I was being flung over his shoulder and he was carrying me. I was suddenly very much aware that my butt, which was barely covered by a long shirt, was right next to his face, while my upper body dangled like a sack behind his back. He had put on some shorts, but his upper half was still naked, my skin tingled everywhere we made contact. What the hell was happening to me, I wanted to touch him all over.

"Alpha, the patrols have picked up rogue scents near the southern border." A male's voice said.

"Get the warriors ready, I need to get Raven out of sight." He commanded. Wait a minute. Did he just say my name? Why was I so giddy over something so ridiculous?

He broke out in a run and I tried to steady myself to keep from bouncing around. Moments later he stopped running and I heard the sound of wolves shifting. He went up some stairs and into a house, the packhouse I assume.

"The pack doctor will be here in a few minutes with an eyewash." He said and set me down in a chair.

"Eros must know we're involved if he's sending rogues already." A voice that sounded like Alec said.

"They could just be scouting for her, we're the closest pack to Athens. They set foot on my land; they die." Dimitri growled.

"Raven, Eros was badly burned, was that you?" I heard Niko's voice ask.

"Uhhh, maybe." I wasn't sure what to say.

"What do you mean MAYBE? Either you set him on fire, or you didn't?" Dimitri asked annoyed.

I wasn't sure how to answer grumpy Alpha. "Eros said his boss wanted me dead, but first he wanted to have fun with me. He went to light his cigar and I expanded the flame to his face." I told them.

"Holy Fuck!" Alec said.

"Next time you burn someone trying to kill you, finish the job completely." Dimitri growled at me.

"Thanks, I'll remember that when you try and kill me." I said bitterly and Alec laughed out loud.

"Do you think he knows you're elemental?" Niko asked.

"I'm not sure, he used my lighter for his cigar. Maybe he thought there was something wrong with the lighter and it burned him?" I added.

"Of course he's going to know, he's a wolf. Normally a burn will heal, but he's going to be scarred. Elemental fire burns hotter because it's controlled by emotions. If he hasn't figured it out already, he'll know in the days to come." Dimitri said.

Great, just what I needed to hear. Eros was going to hunt me down to the ends of the earth. I wondered if he would try to hunt me down back to Crescent Moon. I needed to call my dad. Ughh, I must have left my purse in the forest with my phone.

"Where's my purse?" I asked.

"Odessa has it." Niko said. "Should I have her bring it down?" He asked.

"No, I'll be stopping at her room tonight and will get it." Dimitri said.

He was going to her room. It must be well after midnight. Was she his girlfriend or maybe a lover? Why do I even care? And why was I feeling jealous? Rae wanted to gouge out Odessa's eyes and we hadn't even met the skank yet.

There was a knock at the door. "Come in Dr. Vovos." Dimitri called out.

"Good evening Alpha, where is the patient?" She asked.

"This is Raven, she seems to have some dirt in her eyes." Dimitri explained.

"Hello Dear, I'm Dr. Vovos." She warmly greeted me.

"Is it just the dirt in your eyes? Or is anything else bothering you?" She asked.

"No just the dirt, it feels scratchy, like someone rubbed sandpaper on my eyeballs." I said.

"Mm-hmm, certainly not the first time I've treated people for this ailment, let me get the eye rinse ready." She said.

Of course, this wouldn't be the first time, Dimitri was also elemental and had the gift of earth. He probably has hit half the wolves around here with dirt in the eye. Outside of my family, I'd never met another elemental wolf before. I wondered if Dimitri had, if there were others.

"OK, we're going to do one eye at a time, I need you to bend your head down and then tilt it back and open your eye." She instructed. I did as she said with both eyes and felt them clear out.

"Now I'm going to apply a few drops of ointment to help the stinging. Then I will place some cotton and gauze on your eyes, you should be healed in about an hour and can remove the cotton." She said.

When she finished, I was left sitting in the chair with gauze covering my eyes. I could feel Dimitri move closer to me; his aura was dominating. Something inside of me wanted to rest my tired head on his chest, maybe even cry myself to sleep, but I'd probably be sleeping in a cell tonight.

"When did you get the gift of fire?" He asked me.

I wasn't sure that I wanted to answer him or tell him anything more about me. It's not like we're friends. "You need to let me go." I said.

"Where will you go? Do you have any idea how much trouble you're in?" Dimitri said.

"My father could fix it." Shot right out of my mouth.

"And who is your father?" Dimitri asked.

"None of your business." I said.

"Raven, no one is going to hurt you. We just want to help." Niko said.

"Right, after he leaves me to rot in a cell." I scoffed. "It doesn't matter, Kosta will realize I'm missing and call my father."

"Niko, call your Uncle in the morning, I'm sure he will be more cooperative than she's being." Dimitri said.

"How about we go pick up her two friends from Alpha Georgios' pack, at the dormitory?" Alec suggested.

"Leo and Rocky know nothing about me, leave them alone." I practically growled. How dare they try to use my friends as a way to scare me or coerce me into talking.

"We'll talk about this in the morning. Spiro is with the warriors, Alec, check on the patrols and trackers. Niko, I want an update every two hours from Athens." Dimitri said.

"Are you taking me to my cell now?" I asked.

"Can you control your element?"

"Yes."

"And do you promise not to run away again?" He asked.

"Yes." I responded, it's not like I had anywhere to go, my money and passport were back at the dorm.

"Little bird, if you break your promise to me, I will punish you and enjoy it." I probably should have been scared, but his words made me quiver.

"Okay love birds, I'll see you in the morning." I heard Niko tease.

Love birds? Did I miss something? I wasn't even sure this grumpy Alpha even liked me. As a matter of fact, I think he still wanted to kill me. I bet he just wanted to make sure I wasn't anyone important before he killed me.

"I'll take you to your room." Dimitri said scooping me up and carrying me bridal style.

"I could walk you know."

"But you can't see yet."

I could feel him going up a few flights of stairs as he carried me. Probably wanted me at the top level so I couldn't escape out of a window again. My body was completely relaxed in his big strong arms as if this was the most natural thing.

He opened a door and carried me into another room. I felt him bend forward and lower me onto a comfortable bed. The only thing I was wearing was a large baggy shirt with no underwear. I was worried about rolling around on a bed and waking up with the shirt pulled up around my waist. I was a messy sleeper.

I laid back on the pillows and there was a scent on them! Caramel and spice! I recognized this scent from the first time I went running with Leo and Rocky. It was him. The beast was in the woods that night and his scent was on my clothes. I turned my head into the pillow taking deep breaths. It was so heavenly I actually let out a moan, I couldn't get enough.

This was his room. I was in his bed. Rae was so excited; I could hardly calm her. I sat up and reached for the gauze on my eyes. Something inside of me needed to see him, to look into his eyes. I had to know.

His hands touched mine. "Are you sure you want to do

that?" He asked.

"Absolutely!"

I peeled the gauze back and slowly opened my eyes. I turned my head and saw his handsomely rugged face. I'd seen this face before when I was on the island. I stared into his light honey colored eyes and they seemed to pierce through to my soul.

Rae was howling and I managed to whisper one breathless word. "Mate."

CHAPTER 17 – REALIZATION

His lips crashed onto mine and the electricity exploded in my core. My hands reached for his face and I wanted more. His tongue traced my lips and a moan escaped me. Seizing the opportunity, his tongue made its way through my slightly parted lips to my tongue. I welcomed the invasion and kissed back. He deepened the kiss and I could feel his hunger for me. His big strong hand was suddenly cradling the back of my head.

His kiss was so delicious, my inexperienced mouth craved more even as I struggled for air. My toes curled and my heart was racing. I had only ever kissed one boy before, and that was Zach. Dimitri was no boy; he was a man with years of experience ahead of me. I suddenly felt so insecure, so little and inexperienced.

Feeling my hesitation, Dimitri pulled back and studied my face. He was several years older than me, an established Alpha. He probably has a girlfriend, several lovers, in fact, he was going to Odessa's room tonight. I felt vulnerable and I hated it.

I had just discovered he was my mate but wondered how long he knew. When did he find out? He wasn't even sure he wanted me alive, that is what he said in his office, wasn't it? He didn't want me!

"You knew! You knew this whole time!" I stared in disbelief.

"Raven, I wa—"

"When? When did you find out?" I demanded.

"My wolf, Dom, could sense you at the club. I watched you dancing from the balcony. Eros noticed my interest in you and started having you followed." He said.

"He's been following me because he thinks you're sweet on me or because he knows I'm your mate?"

"Something like that." Dimitri said and ran his hand over the back of his neck, which reminded me of something.

"Your neck, is there a mark on the back of your neck?" I asked.

"You mean this?" He turned around and I saw the same exact Crescent Moon mark of the Moon Goddess.

"It's identical to mine." I said.

"I've never seen anyone else with the mark." He told me.

I lifted my hair and turned my head so that he could see the nape of my neck.

"You were in the woods a few weeks ago when I went running with my friends, your scent was on my clothes."

"Dom really wanted to see your wolf. But I didn't know for sure until we came face to face last week on the island."

"Well, hellOooo Dom." Rae purred at me.

"YOU came face-to-face with me; I just saw my own reflection in your sunglasses. Why did you walk off so rudely?"

"Eros' men were on the island following you, Alec and I took them out."

I thought about what he was saying, but then I felt myself getting angry. If he was aware that I was his mate last week, how could he stay away from me for so long? He sent other men to protect me, but that is the job of the mate, to protect and care for you.

Did he not want a mate? I wanted to ask him but felt an uncomfortable knot tightening in my stomach. I wanted to reach for him, to wrap myself up in his comfort and put my worries to rest, but something was holding me back.

"On the island, you stole my bikini bottoms. I saw you scenting them." I stated.

A sheepish grin formed on his face. "That was Dom. Your scent calms him, he needs to be close to you."

"Is that why you wanted to throw me in a cell?"

"That was to keep you safe, I wasn't sure if you were going to run away or set the mansion on fire." He said. "You look exhausted, please get some sleep, we can talk about it in the morning."

"What if I leave in the middle of the night?" I asked.

"I will tie you to the bed if I have to little bird." He said with a tone of seriousness almost daring me.

"Excuse me?" I scoffed.

"We have a busy day tomorrow get some rest." He said.

"Where will you sleep?" I asked.

"Hopefully on top of us." Rae snickered in my head like a dog in heat.

"In this chair, making sure you don't get yourself into any more trouble." He stood up and turned off the light. Then he leaned back in the chair and closed his eyes.

I laid back on the pillows and pulled the covers up over me. I stared at his handsome face and noticed the full sleeve tattoo on his right arm. His long muscular legs were extended towards the bed and I felt an urge to curl up in his lap.

"Raven?" He whispered.

"Yes."

"What's your wolf's name?"

"Rae." I said.

"Rae." I heard him repeat back as he dozed off to sleep.

The sunlight was shining through the curtains and I turned my face to bury it in a pillow. His scent was all over the bed and it was like a warm cocoon of comfort and safety. I felt the pillow move and realized it wasn't a pillow after all. It was him!

Dimitri had climbed into the bed with me at some point in the night and I was shamelessly sprawled

PAULINA VASQUEZ

across his chest with my head buried in his neck. I climbed off him and he opened his eyes. He was shirtless and wearing nothing but shorts.

I jumped out of the bed and remembered what happened last night and where I was at. I wondered if he went to see Odessa last night, I didn't smell another scent on him, but the wolves around here regularly masked their scents.

"Good morning." He said.

"I thought you were sleeping in the chair?" I snapped.

"I was getting a neck kink." He grinned. "The bed is so big, I climbed on one side and you rolled over to my side."

"I need my phone; I have to check in on Leo and Rocky." I said.

"Okay, I'll have Odessa bring it up. She's charging it for you." He said. I glared at him. The thought of seeing his mistress was stabbing at my heart.

"Excuse me, who?" Rae growled in my mind.

"She's about your size, but a little taller. I'll ask her to bring some clothes for you too." His eyes glazed over, and he was mind linking her.

I considered wrapping a sheet around myself for the day, like a Greek toga. It's what the ancients wore, wasn't it? This was so uncomfortable, there's no way I was wearing her clothes. I had just met him; I wasn't even sure that he really wanted me. What if he picked her over me? He had killed his first mate, maybe he killed her so he could be with Odessa?

132

"If you're going to reject me, you should do it now. I have no intention of sticking around and watching you flaunt your girlfriend in my face." I said. Jealousy, anger, possessiveness, pride was pulsing through me at the same time.

He looked at me standing here, slowly taking me in, wearing nothing but a shirt, hair messy, fists clenched, and face red. The realization had just swept through him.

"You're so cute. A little maddening but adorable." He continued to smile.

"What?" I huffed.

He stalked towards me and I backed up into the wall. He placed both of his hands next to my head on each side and leaned in towards me. His size was intimidating, and he looked down into my eyes. His Alpha aura was strong and the heat from his body was causing all kinds of crazy reactions from mine.

"You're not jealous are you little bird?" He asked.

"Pfffft, jealous of what?" I rolled my eyes and tried to play it off.

"I will rip her eyes out!" Rae snarled inside of me.

"Look at me." He commanded.

I couldn't help myself, I looked at him. His eyes came closer to my face and the warm honey color was dazzling, his eyes shifted to my lips and I could feel his urge to kiss me. I bit down on my lower lip trying to restrain my urge. He brought his hand up to cup my face and lowered his lips close to mine.

There was a knock at the door that brought us back to reality. He stepped back and turned around. "Come in." He said and moved closer to the door.

"Good morning." Her voice rang out and she walked over to Dimitri.

"I'm sorry about last night." He said.

"What the fuck is he apologizing to her for?" Rae growled in my head.

"I was a little preoccupied last night." He chuckled.

"That's okay." She giggled back and wrapped her arms around him to hug him. An involuntary growl escaped me and they both turned to look at me. His smile widened and my reaction seemed to amuse him.

"Raven, I'd like you to meet Odessa, my sister." He smiled. "Odessa, this is Raven." He added.

I felt foolish for a moment, all this time, I thought Odessa was his girlfriend. I'm sure he has mistresses around, I saw him naked, how could he not have mistresses. I also noticed that he didn't introduce me as his mate to his sister. This did not escape me.

"I had your underwear cleaned, and I believe this dress will fit you properly. I wasn't sure about your shoe size, but these sandals are adjustable." She handed them to me.

"Thank you. It's nice to meet you." I said and stared into the same light honey colored eyes as Dimitri.

"I also charged your phone for you. I'm sure your friends must be worried about you." She smiled.

"I do have a few calls to make." I smiled.

"You can call after breakfast, Elaina will have breakfast at the table waiting for us." Dimitri said.

CHAPTER 18 – DESIRE

I was wearing a pretty cream colored dress that Odessa had loaned me, all eyes seemed to be on me. Most faces were warm and friendly, some were curious. Whispers from the other tables buzzed as speculation about me continued to grow.

I sat quietly at the breakfast table between Dimitri and Niko. Dimitri kept stealing sideways glances at me and his chair was inching closer and closer to me. I could feel his aura and the need to be closer to him was burning in my chest, like a pull. Niko and Alec were smiling at each other, their eyes were glazed over, I had a feeling they were mind linking. Elaina and the kitchen staff had prepared a big spread with sfougato, which is like a big Greek breakfast frittata. There were also, sausages, oatmeal, yogurt with honey, different breakfast breads, and fresh fruit.

"So Raven, how did you sleep last night?" Niko asked with a big suggestive grin on his face and Alec burst out laughing.

"Fine, thank you." My response was short.

"I don't see any signs of special bed bugs biting." Alec said laughing.

"Two grown men cackling like silly schoolgirls." Odessa rolled her eyes at Niko and Alec.

"Pay no attention to them. I don't think we've been

properly introduced, I'm Spiro, the Delta and this is my mate Adanna." He smiled.

"It's very nice to meet you." I said.

"Oh, your accent is lovely." Adanna told me with a Greek accent of her own. "Where are you from?"

"Western Canada." I responded without even thinking. The table went quiet, Dimitri and Niko exchanged curious looks. The silence was broken when Elaina came in and greeted me.

"Kalimera, it's so wonderful to have you with us. Please eat, eat." She said in that same thick accent as Adanna. "Whatever your favorite Greek food is, you tell me, and I will make it for you." She was an older plump lady; her hair was pulled back in a bun and she was definitely in charge of the kitchen.

"She likes moussaka." Niko chimed in.

"Wonderful! I will prepare some for dinner tonight." She smiled at me.

"I like her already." Rae said to me. Rae was always thinking with her stomach.

I wished her a good morning back. "Kalimera! The sfougato is amazing, thank you Elaina." I said.

"Ahh good, good, I'm glad you like it. It's the Alpha's favorite." She beamed at him. "I've been making it for him this way since he was a little pup." She said proudly.

She spoke of Dimitri with such fondness in her voice and had been feeding him most of his life. It was hard to believe she was talking about the same beast that killed his father and first mate. These were nagging thoughts I would get to the bottom of.

We finished breakfast and Dimitri leaned into me, "we need to talk." His breath was warm on my ear and sent tingles down my back. We headed back to his bedroom and I was hoping to have some privacy with my phone. First things first, I needed to check on Leo and Rocky, make sure Angela was okay.

Then, I needed to call my dad and get as far away from Eros as I could. Rae whimpered at the thought of leaving but I wasn't even sure that my mate wanted me. This isn't how mates are supposed to work, but I was a LaRue, and my family seemed to have its challenges when it comes to mates and rejection.

"Raven." Dimitri's voice pulled me from my thoughts. "What are you thinking?" He asked as if he could feel my anxiety building.

"I need to get back to the dorm and get my clothes and passport."

"I have a man watching your dorm, it's not safe, Eros' thugs have already been there. I can have him bring back your things tonight."

"What about Rocky and Leo? I need to call them." I said.

"Your phone is on the dresser." He said and sat in the chair by the bed. "Don't give away your location. If they want to join you, I can have my men pick them up at the Acropolis and safely escort them here."

I had hoped for some privacy, but I didn't want to

argue when I could be on the phone with Rocky now. I had four missed calls from her. I called her back but got her voicemail, I left a message.

"Hi, it's me, I know things got crazy last night but I'm okay and I'm with a-a friend. Call me when you get a chance, bye."

I dialed Leo next, I had two missed calls from him. "Hey Leo, I'm calling to check on you and Rocky. Hope Angela is doing well too. I'm with a friend in a safe place. Call me back please."

I paced the room for a minute. I debated on calling Karla, but I didn't want to worry her, there were still two more days of the Dionysus festival so she wouldn't miss me for a few more days. I thought about Kosta, my dad trusted him, but I wasn't sure I wanted my dad to know yet.

"So, I'm just a friend, am I?" Dimitri questioned, obviously he was listening to the messages I left.

"Isn't that what I am to you?" I shot back, remembering the way he introduced me to his sister. He moved at a speed faster than I could register, picking me up and tossing me back on his bed.

"Let's see ... what are you to me?" He said out loud as he crawled on top of me on the bed.

His hand roamed up my leg and to my thigh sending shockwaves of pleasure to my core. It moved slowly to the back of my thigh, caressing me as if he had done this hundreds of times to me. He pinned my wrists above my head with his free hand. I could smell his scent coming back and it was driving me crazy, the herbs were wearing off. I took deep breaths greedily inhaling his scent.

I ached for his kiss again and he leaned in to tease me. "Tell me, *friend*, tell me what you feel when I do this."

He moved to my neck and started kissing it gently, then licking it, then kissing and sucking more aggressively. I let out a moan when his teeth grazed my marking spot. My breathing was heavy, I had never experienced anything like this before. Heated pleasure bubbled down below, and I could feel his thigh resting between my legs. I had no control over my own body, without thinking I was grinding myself against his thigh. Almost begging for relief, begging for his touch.

Dimitri made his way back up to my face and inhaled deeply. "You smell intoxicating little *friend*." He liked this. He was enjoying my body's response to his. His eyes gazed down at my chest and I could feel his desire.

He took my lips hungrily, kissing me. I moaned into his mouth and he deepened the kiss. His hand roamed up the back of my thigh to my ass and pulled me closer to him. I wanted to touch him, to run my fingers through his hair and over his muscles.

My cell phone started ringing and Dimitri rolled off me. I wasn't sure if I was relieved or disappointed at being interrupted. I could hear Rae whimper. I looked at the screen and saw that it was Kosta calling me. Dimitri gave me a quizzical look and I answered it on speakerphone.

"Kalimera Kosta." I answered.

"Hello, I was checking to make sure you're okay. I

heard the young lady from your dormitory was found."
He said.

"That's wonderful news! I'm doing good, thank you." I
said.

"Yes, but listen to me carefully. Do not tell anyone
where you're at. There's some trouble in the city and
you should remain right where you are. Enjoy some
sfougato and lay low until it's sorted. Understand?" He
said.

"Yes, I understand." I said and he disconnected.

"I need to have Niko get in touch with his Uncle tonight. Kosta works independently and may have other
information. He knows where you're at." Dimitri said.

"How do you know that Kosta knows where I'm at?"

"He told you to enjoy some sfougato. Elaina makes it
every Saturday. Kosta used to be the beta of this pack."
He smiled.

"Kosta must know that Eros is looking for me." I said
out loud.

I wondered if I should call my father, but I knew he
would make me come home. I couldn't imagine leaving
my mate but then again, I wasn't sure what was happening in that department either. Most wolves would
have mated and marked in the first twenty-four hours.
He had found me last week and stayed away from me.

"Why don't you want a mate?" I decided to ask.

"It's complicated." That was all he said.

"Well, it's about to get more complicated because I need to leave." I said.

"You're not going anywhere." He growled.

"Did you really kill your first mate?" I figured I was going for it, may as well ask.

"I never had a first mate; you're my first mate. And the answer is no, I didn't kill her." He replied.

"So why don't you want me then?" I demanded.

"Damn-it woman! I'm fighting extremely hard here not to bend you over and mount you. **OF COURSE, I WANT YOU!**" Rae howled with excitement at his confession of raw desire. I was a little taken back but excited as well.

CHAPTER 19 – HISTORY

My phone was ringing again. "It's a video call from my cousin Clair." I said and sat on Dimitri's bed ready to answer.

"Hello, Clair." I smiled and waved into the camera. Clair is my Aunt Payton's daughter; she had the same LaRue bright blue eyes and black hair, as I did. We were often mistaken for sisters and had grown up in the castle together like siblings.

"Hey, what's going on? How's the Dionysus festival going?" She eagerly asked.

"It's been very interesting." I laughed. "How's everyone doing?"

"My parents are visiting Uncle Ranger. Your parents are in the city for a few days on business. Zach and Sydney are still on their honeymoon in Australia. Helga just made an amazing cheesecake, nothing too exciting."

"How are the boys?" I asked and Dimitri stood tense hearing me ask about boys. Guess I forgot to mention that the boys are my brothers.

"They're great, Peter found his mate at Dark Moon pack. Her name is Mandi, she's Gamma Blake's daughter, which is perfect because Peter will be taking over Dark Moon next year anyway." she said.

"Wow! Peter found his mate, I can't believe no one called to tell me." I said, feeling a little hurt.

"Well, it just happened last week, and they've pretty much been locked away mating and bonding. He's already marked her! They're going to have the mating ceremony next month."

"That's wonderful. How's Knox taking it?" Knox was the oldest and Peter's twin, he had yet to find his mate and has been searching for the last two years."

"Not so great. I was thinking that maybe we should come to visit you in Athens. The ancient city of the Gods might be a nice diversion for Knox, and we miss you." She squealed.

"You really want to come here?" What horrible timing I thought.

"Why not? You're loving it there, aren't you? The pictures of those beaches you sent are gorgeous." She said.

"Greece is full of surprises!" I said and my eyes moved to find a smiling Dimitri standing close to me which made my heart flutter.

"OH, MY GODDESS! Raven, you're glowing! What happened? What's his name? Is he a wolf?" Her eyes lit up like a child at a candy store.

"I don't know what you're talking about." I tried to smile normally and fake it.

"Girl, please! Who do you think you're fooling? Zach is but a faint memory now." Clair giggled at me. Dimitri raised an eyebrow at Zach's name.

"You better start talking! Is he a Greek God or what? Oh Goddess, did you lose your virginity?" She asked excitedly.

Oh no she didn't! Please just let the bed open up and swallow me whole. My face flushed and Dimitri gave me a wide eyed look at the mention of my virginity. She had no idea that he was standing in the room with me. He smiled and there was a mischievous twinkle in his eyes as he stepped closer to me.

"Hello, Clair." Dimitri's deep voice said, and he leaned in to kiss me on the cheek. CRAP! Visions of my entire overbearing family flying to Greece flashed before me. This can't be happening right now.

"Hi, I'm looking forward to meeting you. Knox and I will be making our way to Greece shortly." She squealed.

Clair leaned into the phone and whispered as if Dimitri couldn't hear anything, "Is he your mate?"

I nodded my head yes and she squealed again. "Oh my Goddess, oh my Goddess, oh my Goddess!"

"Please don't tell anyone yet Clair. I'd like to be able to talk to dad about it first." I begged.

"My lips are sealed." She grinned.

"Talk to you soon." I smiled and hung up.

"Oh, this can't be good." I said pacing the room.

PAULINA VASQUEZ

"Raven come sit down." Dimitri said as he grabbed my hand and pulled me to him. He leaned back in the chair and opened his arms to embrace me. I sat on his lap and he pulled me tight to him.

"I have a crazy mafia lord chasing after me and now my brother, whose the future Alpha of our pack, and my cousin are coming to Greece."

"We should have Eros neutralized in the next few days." Dimitri told me.

"But what about his boss, Eros said it was his boss who wanted me dead. I think they know who my father is, maybe that's why they want me? My father is part of the shifter's council."

"Will you please tell me who your father is?"

"I'm Raven LaRue, daughter of Alpha Diesel LaRue from Cre—"

"Crescent Moon Pack!" He said. "Of course, you said western Canada at breakfast, I should have known. That explains why Kosta has been watching you too. But I don't think they are after you to hurt your father."

"What do you mean?"

"I'm not exactly sure where to start." He said trying to focus.

"Just start at the very beginning." I told him.

"My family is said to have been descended from King Lycaon of Arcadia who was turned into a werewolf by

146

Zeus. The males in the Theodorus bloodline are usually twice the size as normal werewolves and the strongest of our kind. My father was the Alpha of this pack, he was strong and powerful, my mother adored him. When I was a pup, the Greek Mafia started stepping on pack toes, and my father pushed back. He made an enemy of the wrong person and my mother was abducted and tortured for weeks. She was his everything, his other half." He paused for a moment.

"My father lost his mind, he felt her pain through the mate bond, everything they did to her and it haunted him. They raped, mutilated, and beat her. He felt all of that and wasn't able to do anything. After he felt the bond break, they mailed her decapitated head to him in a box."

I let out a gasp and he squeezed me closer before he continued.

"I was twelve and Odessa was four. The next four years were awful. He was cruel and often ordered the execution of pack wolves for the most minor offenses. If he couldn't have my mother, no one was allowed to be happy. When Odessa turned eight, Elaina had made one of her special desserts for Odessa. He was so angry; he ordered a public whipping of Elaina's mate because she had wasted kitchen ingredients on foolishness. My father was insane, and the pack was falling apart. Kosta was his beta and best friend, he left the pack after my father raped and killed his mate." He said with sorrow.

His father was a real monster. I can't imagine the years of hell everyone suffered. I placed my hand on his chest to help calm him and he kissed the side of my head.

"I was sixteen and shifted early, so I challenged him. My wolf Dom was pretty feral, and we had the elemental gift of earth which my father didn't know about. There's a waterfall and river about eight kilometers east of here and we fought near the edge of the cliff. I had blinded one of his eyes with a sharp rock and beat him. I was ready to rip his throat out and put him out of his misery when he submitted. When I turned to face the bowing wolves of the pack, he lunged at me from behind. I sent him flying over the edge of the cliff to his death."

"That's when they started calling me *The Beast*. I killed my father at only sixteen and my wolf was even bigger than his. No one has ever seen a wolf the size of Dom. I spent the next few years building up the pack and expanding our family business. We own dozens of olive farms around Greece that are exported for pickling or pressing for olive oil. We also own two international labels of olive oil."

"What about the first mate rumor that you killed her?" I asked.

"Six years ago, I was seeing someone, she really wanted to be with me and told people we were mates. I was planning on breaking it off with her, but before I could, someone mailed me her decapitated head. Just as my father had received my mother's head. Whoever killed my mother is still out there and apparently, they have a vendetta with me. I suspect it's Eros' boss."

"That's why you didn't want me!" I said as I connected the dots.

"I had sworn to never have a mate and only short term

mistresses. I couldn't suffer like my father did and become a true monster. My pack has suffered enough."

"Short term mistresses? Great, our mate is a hoe!" Rae scoffed in my mind.

"Mistresses you say. Is the pack swimming with them?" I asked, not really sure I wanted to know.

"No. I haven't been with anyone from my pack since Heather was murdered. Now that I have my mate, I won't need a mistress." He smiled at me.

"No, he won't." Rae said.

"What if I'm not ready?" I asked. "Wil-will you continue to see a mistress?" I felt so anxious and insecure.

"Baby, the way your body reacts to me, you'll be the one begging for me soon." He grinned.

I did want him, but I felt like such a little girl compared to his years of experience. He was used to being with women, experienced women, and I wasn't sure that I could even kiss properly. He made me hot and nervous, the butterflies in my stomach wouldn't stop.

"Look at me." He said and my head lifted to meet those beautiful light honey colored eyes.

"I want you, more than anything. It's in a wolf's nature to take what he wants. As an Alpha, I should be able to take what I want, when I want. Dom wants to spend the day buried deep inside of you, claiming you. As a gentleman, I should be able to wait. It will not happen until you beg for it."

CHAPTER 20 - TRAP

"YES! She made the moussaka tonight!" Niko said as the kitchen staff placed the platters of food on the table.

"You will never move out of the packhouse so long as Elaina is here cooking for you." Odessa teased Niko.

Not only had Elaina made the moussaka for dinner, but there was also keleftiko, which is a traditional lamb dish, stuffed bell peppers, rice, vegetables, and a lovely Greek salad topped with feta.

I had spent the day napping and was hoping to get out and explore the beautiful pack lands here, but Dimitri insisted that I stay inside. He was concerned about the rogues that had been near the pack territory. We're not sure if their presence was coincidental or if they were looking to find me.

"You know, you'll have to make an appearance or two at the Dionysus festival, so it looks like business as usual. If you're not seen, it's going to look like you're hiding Raven and staying close to her." Spiro told Dimitri.

"I'm not leaving her alone if that's what you're suggesting." Dimitri looked up as he forked lamb onto his plate.

"It's only for a few hours, we get in, get noticed, look

like we're out enjoying the festivities, and get back." Alec said.

"Could we swing by the dorm so I could pick up a few things?" I asked.

"You're not going anywhere; Eros has men watching your dorm. Alexander, one of my warriors, has already collected most of your belongings that could be salvaged. He should be here anytime now." Dimitri told me.

"What do you mean salvaged?"

"Someone had already been in your room and trashed it." Niko said while shoving a fork full of moussaka into his mouth.

"Leo and Rocky are on the same floor, you didn't happen to see them or any sign of them, did you?" I turned to Niko.

"I don't know, Alexander went in. He used the rooftop door to sneak in and out." Niko continued to shovel food into his mouth.

"The Adonis tends to attract most wolves in the city for a good time, it should be pretty busy tonight. Perhaps we should start there? I could call Evelyn to help us." Alec asked.

"A night of debauchery at The Adonis." Niko chuckled.

Who the hell was this Evelyn I wondered? Spiro was seated next to his mate who gave him a stiff side glance at the mention of the Adonis. "I should probably stay here and make sure everyone is safe." He said.

I finished eating my moussaka and stuffed pepper. It was only my second night here and the thought of Dimitri going back to Athens and leaving me here alone bothered me. What was this night of debauchery Niko mentioned? Were they planning on going out to party? With women?

"Alexander has just returned and placed your things in our room." Dimitri told me.

Our room? Everything felt like it was moving so fast. Things seemed so surreal; my life had changed so much in the last week. I was destined by the Moon Goddess to be the Luna of this pack. Olympus Blood Moon was the largest pack across Europe with almost fifteen hundred members.

We made our way back to the room and I was eager to take a bath and get into some of my own clothes. "Alexander said your laptop was smashed, he dumped out your dresser drawers in the suitcase and grabbed the things from your closet."

"Are you really going out tonight?" My voice was just above a whisper.

"Yes, I need to. They will be watching for me. Promise you will not leave this house."

I wanted to see what they had done to my dorm room. I needed to make sure Rocky and Leo were safe, and I was going to be stuck here tonight, alone. What if Dimitri didn't come back tonight and he went to see some mistress to satisfy his needs? Maybe this Evelyn woman?

I sat on the bed and Dimitri went to shower and get

dressed. I tried to call both Leo and Rocky and received no answer. I had a text message from Clair telling me that she and Knox would be arriving in Athens in two days. I laid back wondering how I would break the news to my parents.

"You're a grown woman now. Stop worrying and enjoy what's in front of us." Rae told me.

Dimitri stepped out of the bathroom, his short dark hair was styled, and his well-groomed short facial looked so sexy on him. He walked past me with nothing but a towel wrapped low around his waist. I could see how shredded his body was and my eyes trailed down his abs. My face flushed remembering the sight of him naked.

"And what a sight that was!" Rae said to me.

He stepped into a large closet and started getting dressed. Moments later he emerged wearing dark blue jeans with a black shirt that seemed to complement his chest. He looked hot and now he was going out to the festival to be seen, flirted with, lusted after. My jealousy was peaking, and I couldn't understand what was happening to me.

"I want to go with you." I said a bit forcefully.

"It's too dangerous. We'll be stepping into a pit full of vipers. I can't do what I need to and worry about you. I need to be seen without you, give the illusion that I don't know or care where you're at." He said and placed a kiss on my head.

"How long will you be gone?"

"I should be back before you wake up."

"I could go and help, I'm not some weak wolf who needs to hide. I'm a gifted Alpha you know." I scoffed.

"If you're thinking about going anywhere, I will tie you to the bed! You need to promise me you will stay here." His voice was rough.

"You wouldn't dare."

"Oh, I would! And I'd enjoy punishing you too. Don't make me spank you, little girl." He looked at me with a smoldering look that told me he would definitely enjoy making me squirm and submit.

"Fine, go. I'll be here waiting." I huffed and sat back down on the bed with my arms crossed over my chest practically pouting.

"That's a good girl. Spiro will be downstairs if you need anything." He kissed me quickly before he left the room.

As an Alpha, he should know that it's not in the nature of an Alpha to sit down and do nothing. He had called me a little girl and suddenly I felt small. What kind of festivities was he going out to enjoy tonight?

My phone chimed and I looked down to find a text from Rocky that said "Where are you? We've been looking for you."

A wave of relief washed over me, and I picked up the phone to call Rocky. No answer. I texted back, "Is everything okay?"

"Everything is fine. Can you meet us at Richy's Temple of Sweets? I'll explain everything."

"What time?" I texted back.

"10:00 p.m." The phone chimed.

I grabbed my purse and ran downstairs to the kitchen looking for Spiro but found Elaina. "Has Dimitri left yet?"

"I'm not sure, he might still be in the garage downstairs." She said.

"Thank you." I called and ran towards the stairs leading down to the garage. They were already gone. I had less than two hours to get to the ice cream shop. I couldn't mind link Dimitri yet because we haven't mated, and I didn't have his cell phone number to call him.

I looked around the garage, there were several cars and motorcycles to pick from. When I was fourteen, Knox and Peter had received motorcycles for their sixteenth birthday, they taught me how to ride. I decided a motorcycle would be best because the streets would still be a mess with the festival going on. I flung my purse over my neck and shoulder. It had my phone, forty euros and my lighter in it. I slipped on a full-face helmet and rolled my hair in a knot to tuck it up inside of the helmet.

We had driven north to get here, so I knew that Athens was south. I paid attention to the roads and landmarks so that I could find my way back. An hour later, I could see the lights of Athens come in to view from a distance. Anxiety crept up inside of me, this city was crawling with henchman looking for me.

As I entered the city, I wondered what Dimitri was

doing and what kind of festivities he was enjoying. I tried to focus on the task at hand, which was to go and meet with Rocky and get back before Dimitri noticed I was gone. The university came into sight and I pulled up near Richy's Temple of Sweets. Strange, the shop appeared to be closed. It was usually open until eleven on the weekends.

"Maybe he closed early because of the festival." Rae said.

I reached into my purse to see if Rocky had texted me, nothing. My fingers were ready to dial Rocky when the phone rang. I pulled the face shield of the helmet up and answered on the speakerphone.

"Rocky?" I asked.

"Tisk, tisk, tisk. Is that how you greet an old friend?" Eros' voice sent a cold chill down my spine.

"Where's Rocky?" I demanded and the phone disconnected.

"GO, GO, GO!" Rae yelled at me.

I heard the sound of heavy footsteps running in my direction and dropped the phone back in my purse. I punched the motorcycle and started zipping and darting, not sure where I was going. I could hear other motorcycles speeding up behind me.

The palm trees at the National Garden came into view and I jumped the sidewalk and cut through the park. National Garden is a large and lush park in the heart of Athens. I wasn't sure where to go and continued to drive like a madwoman nearly knocking people over. I jumped the sidewalk and darted down the walkway through the park. I looked over my shoulder and didn't see anyone following me.

This was a setup. Rocky was nowhere and they had her phone. They probably had Rocky too. It was all my fault and I needed to find Dimitri.

CHAPTER 21 – DEBAUCHERY

I reached the east end of the park and scanned the area. Some of the floats were preparing for a parade at the park. I spotted a costume rack next to the float and parked the bike in between other scooters and motor-cycles nearby.

It was total chaos everywhere and people were rush-ing behind the float to change into costumes. No one seemed to notice when I walked over to the rack and quickly selected a Grecian toga looking costume and head wreath. I went behind the float to change and took off my jeans and burgundy shirt. Then I walked back to the motorcycle and stuffed my clothes in the saddlebag. These goons would be looking for a girl with a burgundy shirt on a motorcycle.

I wasn't sure how to get ahold of Dimitri, so I called the only other person I knew in Greece. I called Kosta, but he didn't answer. I considered taking a cab back, but I wasn't sure exactly where the packhouse was lo-cated or if I had enough money for a long cab ride. I was running out of options; Alec had mentioned some-thing about visiting The Adonis. I looked down at my phone and searched the location of The Adonis. It was located at the edge of the Monastiraki District, not too far from here.

I kept my head down and walked through crowds of people trying to blend in. Fortunately, most of the people were dressed the same as me. I looked up to make sure I wasn't being followed and something caught my eye in one of the balconies. A young woman was bent over the edge with her dress lifted, a man was standing behind her thrusting away. They were having sex!

"Debauchery indeed." Rae snickered.

I was so distracted by that interesting performance, that I didn't notice a man grab my arm and pull me to him.

"A Greek Goddess!" He said out loud. "Such beautiful blue eyes like the Goddess of wisdom and war, Athena."

"Excuse me, I'm looking for my friends." I said and pushed away.

"Not so fast my Queen, take a drink with you and when you find your friends, please come back and join us." He smiled, clearly having had too much to drink already.

I saw a motorcycled goon from the corner of my eye and ducked for cover, right into this stranger's arms, and hugged him. I pulled back and smiled at him before I took the large plastic wine goblet he handed me. "Thank you, good sir. I shall return when I find my friends." I lied.

"Don't drink that." Rae said to me.

"I'm not, it's more of an accessory." I told her and continued walking right by another couple kissing and dry humping against a light post. Everyone seemed to be uninhibited tonight and enjoying themselves. I wondered if Dimitri was doing the same.

I caught the scent of a wolf, one was near me. The good thing about having so many people around was that it made it hard to pinpoint a scent. As long as I stayed close to large groups of people, I would be hard to detect. I was about one more block away from my destination and saw a large man with a mate mark on his neck. He was a wolf and I tried to avoid him by standing next to a gyro stand. The scent of roasting meat might help mask mine. He continued walking and towering over the crowd in search of something or someone.

I walked quickly to the Adonis and there was a long line outside. I wasn't sure if I should stand in line or if I even had enough money to pay for the entrance fee. This place looked upscale and expensive. I didn't even know if Dimitri was here or not.

I walked around to the back of the building and noticed the back door was cracked slightly open. I tip toed in the shadows and saw no one. I peeked in the door and noticed it was the back of a barroom. I slipped in and slowly moved towards the door on the other side of the room.

The bartenders were busy, and no one seemed to notice when I slipped out and into the hallway with restrooms and showers. Showers? What kind of place was this that it had showers?

This was some kind of performing arts theater, I saw the stairs that led to the top level and figured I'd have a better chance of finding Dimitri from up there. I quickly went up the stairs and found myself on a small balcony. I stood for a moment and looked down at the stage. My mouth fell open in shock. Nearly two dozen naked people were on stage engaged in sex.

I dropped to my knees to hide on the balcony. The thought of Dimitri actually being here made me angry and jealous. I crawled to the edge of the balcony to look out, my eyes were glued to the action on the stage. Did orgies regularly happen here or was this a special event for the Dionysus festival?

A busty woman was taking two men, one underneath her and one behind her. Two naked women were laying on a stack of pillows kissing and caressing each other. A half-naked woman was perched over a man's face as he pleasured her. Another man was sitting in a cushioned chair, with his head thrown back, while a naked woman kneeled before him pleasuring him. His head moved and that's when I saw him. That wasn't just any man, THAT WAS ALEC!

"What kind of world have we been living in?" Rae whispered to me.

My eyes were wide open. I scanned the rest of the men on the stage for Dimitri and was relieved I didn't find him. I saw Niko at the bar drinking a beer with two women desperately trying to rub their half-naked bodies up against him. Was this their idea of getting noticed and looking normal?

My face was flush with anger and jealousy. I scanned the rest of the audience looking for Dimitri and couldn't find him. I remained on my hands and knees peeking like a voyeur. I had watched porn before on the Internet, but this was wild beyond anything I could imagine. It was kind of exciting for some strange reason.

"See something you like?" I heard a familiar voice say from behind me.

"Dimitri?" I whispered and my mouth went dry.

"You're in so much trouble little bird." His angry voice said.

"I can explain." I said.

"Lay still and keep your head down, we're going to have to sneak you out of here now."

"That's Alec on stage." I said.

"With his mistress Evelyn." He told me.

"Now stop talking and lie down. I know it's hard for you to follow directions but try, this place is crawling with Eros' men." He said and his eyes glazed over mind linking someone.

Ten minutes later, Niko appeared with a purple party wig and a cocktail waitress outfit. "Bring the car around to the side of the building, Alexander will create a diversion and we'll slip out the back."

"I don't think Alec is done." Niko smiled.

"He will be in ten minutes." Dimitri grinned. He tossed the wig, cocktail waitress outfit, and a drink tray on the floor next to me. "Put that on and stay low." He told me.

"Don't watch me." I said.

"Whom should I watch then? The women on stage?" He grinned.

"NO!" My possessive instinct responded.

I quickly wiggled into the dress and wig and felt Dimitri's eyes on me as I undressed and dressed again. A part of me was glad he was watching me instead of the naked women on stage. The other part of me was burning with jealousy thinking about him with other women here. I crawled out of the balcony and stood up once I reached the hallway.

"Act like a waitress and head for the back of the bar." Dimitri whispered to me.

We made it down the stairs and a naked man, with his semi-hard penis, walked right up to me and grabbed my arm. "Excuse me, I've been waiting for my drink."

In a flash, his face was met with Dimitri's fist and he slumped over against the wall. There was a loud commotion ringing through the theater that sounded like fighting but we didn't stick around to find out. We made it into the back of the bar and slipped right out.

Niko was driving the car and Dimitri sat in the back with me. "Raven, how did you get here?" Niko asked.

"I took a bike; it's parked at the east side of National Garden." I said and handed Dimitri the keys.

"I got a text from Rocky just after you left. I didn't have your phone number and needed to meet her. I took a bike and when I got here, it was a setup. Eros called me from her phone, and I got chased by his men. I remembered that Alec had said you would be at The Adonis, so I thought I'd come find you." I told them. Dimitri looked like he was struggling to control his wolf.

"Big mistake Raven. The Adonis is owned by Eros. The reason we went there was so they would see us out and about." Dimitri said.

"What was the diversion?" Niko asked Dimitri looking through the rearview mirror.

"I had Alexander grab Phillip's ass and come on to him. It started a fight." Dimitri chuckled and Niko laughed out loud.

"If they've seen Raven in the city, we can't go back to the packhouse. They're going to be watching the roads. Let's go to the penthouse. Kosta should have a lead by tomorrow on Rocky and Leo." Dimitri said.

"How does Kosta know?" I asked.

"Karla has been working for him, to keep an eye out on you. She told him that Leo and Rocky had been taken early this morning. If you had gone to Spiro, as you promised, you would have realized that it was a trap." Dimitri scolded, and I could feel his frustration with me.

We pulled into an underground garage and Niko dropped Dimitri and me off. I was wondering where he was going and if Dimitri and I were going to be left alone tonight. Dimitri used a key fob to access the elevator and stepped inside.

"Niko is not going to stay?"

"He's going back to keep up the charade, they'll be back after a few hours." The elevator doors opened to a hallway with one door at the end. Dimitri tapped in a code and the door unlocked.

We stepped inside and the window views of the city were breathtaking. It had panoramic views, I could also see the ocean and the Piraeus Port marina. Dimitri pressed a button on a remote controller and all the blackout shades on the windows rolled down.

Dimitri started unbuttoning his shirt and poured himself a glass of whiskey. He sat in a big leather chair eyeing me, I could feel his frustration and desire. He wasn't too happy with me at the moment.

"Take the wig off and come sit on my lap. I have a punishment to deliver to a naughty little wolf."

CHAPTER 22 – PUNISHMENT

I reach up and pulled the purple wig off my head allowing my long hair to cascade down my shoulders. He set his glass down and leaned back in the chair waiting for me. His eyes smoldering, and I couldn't decide if I wanted to sit in his lap or lock myself in the bathroom.

I moved towards him and stood between his legs. He set his glass down and looked up at me taking me in. I was a hot mess. His hand moved up to my waist and I sat down in his lap.

"You sure do have a gift for stumbling into trouble. Tell me, do you enjoy being disobedient?" He placed a kiss on my shoulder that sent a zing right down to my core. I shook my head no. His hands wrapped around my waist and in one swift movement, I was suddenly laying across his lap on my stomach.

"You not only put all of us at risk tonight, but you put yourself in grave danger. Are you trying to madden me?"

His firm hand caressed the back of my thigh and moved higher flipping the dress up to expose my ass. I heard a low growl in his chest as he moved his open palm over my bottom. He caressed my curves slowly and felt the roundness of each cheek in his strong hand.

"Ohhh yeah!" Rae purred in my head.

"I'm going to give you exactly what you need." He shifted and made me spread my legs apart, I felt completely vulnerable as sparks shot through my body under his touch. He pulled his hand back and suddenly his open palm slapped my ass.

SMACK! My left cheek stung.

SMACK! My right cheek stung.

SMACK, SMACK, SMACK! His hand continued to connect with my ass, and I yelped. My lace black panties provided no protection from the punishment.

He paused for a moment and gently rubbed my ass. "You're going to learn one way or the other, little bird."

SMACK, SMACK, SMACK, SMACK! He alternated between my left and right cheek. I was kicking my legs and my body was flailing around, my ass was on fire. His hand moved down between my thighs cupping my sex in his hand over my panties.

SMACK! SMACK! I whimpered and tried to roll off his lap. His other arm firmly held me down in place. I was at his mercy.

"I will fuck you into submission if you continue to fight me." His hand rubbed down my slit and I couldn't escape the tingling sensation.

"We should continue to fight him." Rae encouraged.

"I swear you're a horny mutt." I snapped at her.

SMACK, SMACK, SMACK, SMACK, SMACK! I was so confused, the pain was mixed with pleasure and I longed for more, more of his kisses, more of his touch, more of him.

"Beautiful, you're so beautiful." He said and paused to rub me gently. My heart was racing, my ass was stinging, and my core was throbbing with lust for my mate. *SMACK, SMACK, SMACK, SMACK, SMACK, SMACK!*

"Who's your Alpha Raven?" His dominating voice demanded. A sudden realization hit me, he was my mate and I belonged with him, which made him my new Alpha.

"Y-You are." I managed to utter.

SMACK, SMACK, SMACK! "And you will listen next time, won't you?"

I nodded my head yes and squirmed in his lap. When the hell is this going to end. I can't take much more. A whimper escaped me.

"Words Raven, use your words." *SMACK, SMACK!*

"**YES!** Yes, I'll listen." I barely recognized my own voice.

His fingers kept trailing up and down my slit, teasing me. I took a deep breath and his scent relaxed and soothed me which was a big mistake because he started spanking me again.

SMACK, SMACK! I continued to squirm and could feel his hard cock in his pants throbbing against me. I tried to shake the visions of his nakedness from my mind which just excited me more.

"I'm sorry... please, I'm sorry." I cried out.

He ran his fingers down my soaked panties. "Are you sure? This doesn't feel sorry." I could hear him inhale deeply. With just the thin fabric of my panties covering my heated core, I knew he could smell my arousal.

SMACK, SMACK, SMACK! My core was throbbing. I needed him, I needed his touch, and he knew that. He ripped my panties off, exposing me completely while his eyes feasted on my stinging red ass. His hand soothed as it continued rubbing and exploring my curves. He reached underneath and cupped my entire sex in the palm of his hand, squeezing and massaging it.

I was so lost in the moment that I gladly welcomed his finger when he slipped it into my heated pussy. He started circling my clit with his thumb and several moans escaped my lips. I felt completely submissive to my mate and that is exactly what he wanted.

I could feel the tension building in my core and the yearning to release. Dimitri slipped a second finger in and the strokes continued to tease me. I was on the edge of orgasm when he stopped. He just fucking stopped.

"You haven't earned it." He said and I whimpered at the loss of contact.

Dimitri scooped me up in his arms and carried me into the bathroom. He set me down, turned the water on in the shower, and started undressing. I tried not to stare at him naked. Or at least tried not to make it look so obvious.

"I'm having a newfound appreciation for the male

body just looking at him." Rae panted in my head.

He stood in front of me staring down into my eyes. He leaned down and kissed my lips gently before his hands lifted the waitress dress over my head. His arm reached behind me and unclasped my bra.

I looked up into his face and he was grinning at something behind me. I turned my head over my shoulder and saw the reflection of my glowing bottom in the mirror behind me.

"What a beautiful sight you are." He smiled back at me. I was sure my face was just as red as my ass with embarrassment.

We stepped into the shower and Dimitri stood behind me snaking his arms around my waist. I leaned my body back into his and we stood there for a few moments before he started soaping me up. I wanted to return the favor and soap him up as well, to take my time and explore his magnificent body but I suddenly felt self-conscious. This was all new to me and I wasn't sure what to do.

After the shower, he wrapped me in a large, heated towel and dried my hair with another. "I don't have any clothes." I said and blushed remembering my ripped panties.

"Alexander will gather your things from the packhouse and bring them here in the morning." He told me and scooped me up carrying me to the bed.

"Aren't we going back to the packhouse in the morning?" I asked.

"I think you will be safer on one of our islands. The

security makes it difficult for anyone to breach the island." He said. "You'll be able to go outside, and we can work on your element training."

"Does anyone live on the island we're going to?"

"We have three private islands with large olive groves. A few hundred pack members live on the islands, they tend to the olives and help run the pack businesses."

"My brother and cousin will be arriving in Athens on Monday." I told him feeling anxious about the timing of their arrival.

"We can bring them to the island too. The packhouse on the island is no mansion, but it has plenty of rooms to accommodate them. Elaina and some other staff will also join us there."

"What about Leo and Rocky?" I asked.

"We should have their location in the morning and work out the rescue plan. I need you to trust me, Raven, don't worry, we'll get them back." He assured me.

"I'm sorry I didn't finish Eros off; I've only had my gifts for a few months." I said feeling like I had failed.

"It's okay. He's a walking dead man!"

Dimitri stepped over to the closet, handed me one of his shirts, and put on black boxer briefs. My eyes trailed across his chest and I longed to feel it pressed up against me.

"Do you need anything? Something to drink? Are you hungry?" He asked.

"Hungry for you." Rae snickered in my head.

"I'm good, thank you." I said.

He climbed into bed with me and turned the lights off with a remote controller by the bed. Dimitri pulled me into him and spooned me. I felt his body relax and his breathing became even as sleep started taking over. Without thinking, I pressed my backside into his crotch; I could still feel the sting and heat of my ass from the spanking.

"Don't start something you can't finish." His husky voice said.

That was it, I hadn't finished. He had brought me to the edge and then denied me my orgasm. I couldn't sleep. I needed to release the built-up tension and he had promised I would beg for it. Was this what he had planned all along? To tease me until I couldn't stand it anymore.

I shifted around pretending to accidentally bump my ass into him again. I'm sure he could hear my heart-beat quicken as I felt the heat pooling between my legs thinking about the spanking I had received and how he touched me. The thought of being laid across his lap with my ass completely exposed to him nearly made me moan. I wiggled back into him again.

Dimitri let out a growl and before I understood what was happening, he was hungrily lapping at the wet-ness between my legs. His tongue felt amazing and I started bucking my hips. Complete madness took over me when he plunged his tongue deep inside of me. He wrapped his arms around my upper thighs holding me in place and continued to give me the most amazing pleasure I have ever felt. My body started shaking, my head spinning and the fireworks in my body exploded. A half scream, half moan ripped from me as I released into his hungry mouth.

When he was done, he laid his head on my hip inhaling my scent and calming the beast inside of him. I could feel him struggling to control his wolf and I moved my hand to his head. I stroked his head and ran my fingers through his hair. I felt him completely relax at my touch. We laid like this for a while before I felt my eyes getting heavy with sleep. Dimitri moved next to me and pulled me onto his chest sending me to dreamland.

CHAPTER 23 – BONDS

Dimitri's POV

I couldn't believe she had set foot in The Adonis, which was a live sex show theater that attracted lots of swingers. When I saw her on her hands and knees watching like a peeping Tom, I had to hold Dom back who wanted to mount her on the spot. To dominate and claim her.

She is just as much stubborn as she is beautiful. I had to keep reminding myself that she was much younger than me and would make a few foolish, impulsive decisions. I don't know what I would have done if those bastards had gotten their hands on her.

Dom could sense that she was a powerful wolf, but because of her young age, she may have not received much of the training she needed. We need to work on developing her elemental gift too. I could cause earthquakes, sinkholes, landslides, bring trees and buildings down with my gift. She should have been able to torch Eros from head to toe with very little effort.

Judging from her phone call with her cousin, Raven was indeed daddy's girl and may have been accustomed to getting her way. Her training might have been far more relaxed because she was the Alpha's daughter. She's my mate now and the future Luna to our pack, I need to claim and mark her soon. I don't want to rush her into mating because she's still a virgin, but that makes Dom even more anxious to have her.

Raven had a stubborn pride about her, and I needed to get her attention, make her realize that she belongs to me now. That I was now her Alpha and I needed her to obey me. The mate bond would make her submit. The more time she spends near me, the stronger the mate bond pulls.

Wolves are naturally sexual creatures. Our genetic makeup and instincts revolve around territory, food, mating, and dominance. Right now, Dom wanted to mate, and I wanted dominance.

"Take the wig off and come sit on my lap. I have a punishment to deliver to a naughty little wolf." She obediently came to me and sat in my lap, which pleased the Alpha side of me.

Before she could register what was happening, I had shifted her across my lap and flipped her dress up. Her ass was begging to be spanked and it was exactly what she needed. Her wolf completely submitted, and Dom was in a frenzy to claim her. Raven tried to resist with the first dozen spanks and then the scent of her sweet arousal hit me. She was enjoying it as much as I was, she was putty in my hands. I teased her to the brink of orgasm and was on the verge of losing all my self-control when I pulled away and stopped.

I took her into the bathroom with me for a shower and she didn't resist at all. She seemed completely at ease around me in the nude. The mate bond was working fast. I could feel her eyes on my body and the heat of desire coming from her. My self-control was being tested.

After our shower, we headed straight to bed. My naughty little wolf teased me when she kept rubbing her backside into me as if extending an invitation. Her heart was racing, and I could sense she was still tense with need. Dom took control of me for a moment, when I regained control, I found myself buried between her legs satisfying her. After her deliciously sweet release, she drifted off to sleep across my chest.

"You're welcome." Dom quipped and was content at having his mate so close.

I was pulled out of my sleep when Niko mind linked me early in the morning with bad news. A growl escaped me, and I realized I had woken up my mate.

"What's wrong?" She looked up to find me pulling my pants on.

"Alec was taken last night when he took Evelyn home. Niko is downstairs. Kosta was watching the docks and believes they are holding Alec with Rocky and Leo."

"Are you leaving?" She asked.

"Yes. I need you to listen to me carefully. You need to stay here, don't open the door for anyone. Alexander should be here shortly with your bags and my sister. He has a key and access code. When Odessa gets here, stay in the penthouse, it's practically impenetrable." I told her.

I went to the dresser, pulled out my gun, and shoved a clip full of silver bullets into it. Raven looked at me with wide eyes and shock. "Eros' men don't fight fair." I explained.

"Are you sure I can't come with you?" She asked.

"Baby, Alec is one of the best fighters we have, and they have him. They will not hesitate to use silver bullets and you are the main target. I need you safe and I need you to help keep Odessa safe with you. I was planning on taking you both to the island this morning, but I have to go deal with this. Now give me your phone."

"My phone?" She asked.

I took her phone and dialed my number. I hung up when I felt my phone vibrating, registering her cell phone number. "That's my number. Call me if you need anything. I'll be back as quick as I can. Raven, you are *not* to leave this penthouse."

"Be careful." She responded.

"I'm considering tying you to the bed, don't make me regret not doing it."

"I promise I'll be good." She assured me.

I kissed her goodbye and quickly moved to the door. Niko was waiting in the car when I stepped into the parking garage.

"How long until Alexander and Odessa are here?" I asked.

"They're about thirty minutes away." Niko said.

"Do we know what time they picked Alec up?"

"He left with Evelyn shortly after the fight Alexander triggered. They were ambushed in front of her home.

She was found dead on her doorstep with her neck snapped. Kosta believes Eros' men carried Alec onto a boat just before sunrise."

"Let's get to the marina and have a look, but first I want to stop by Evelyn's place." I told him and he drove to our first destination.

We arrived and the place was already crawling with police. Evelyn was human and her body had already been removed, but I wasn't here for that. I was here to scent the other wolves who did this. To find the one or two who might still be hidden nearby watching things unfold.

My eyes scanned the crowd of onlookers, the buildings nearby, and the cars in the area. I got out of the car and Niko circled around the block. A figure nearby turned and started walking in the opposite direction at an unusually fast pace. I followed and picked up his scent as I got closer, he was a wolf. He turned a corner and took off running. Bad move. Running triggers chase and he couldn't outrun this Alpha.

"Niko bring the car to the east end." I mind linked him before I tackled my target. He wasn't a rogue which means he belonged to Eros' pack. I picked him up and threw him in the back of the car with me. I took my gun out and held it to his head.

"It's loaded with silver bullets." I flashed a dangerous smile. Dom wanted to rip his heart out and eat it for breakfast.

"I don't know anything." He said.

"And you just happen to be an innocent bystander at

the scene of a crime? WHERE HAVE THEY TAKEN MY GAMMA?" I snarled.

"I told you, I don't know anything." He snapped back.

"Oh, it's not going to be that easy for you. I see that you're marked. Is she a nice she-wolf? Would I like her?" I threatened and could see the rage in his eyes.

"You've heard the rumors about my wolf, haven't you? Why he's so much larger than other wolves? It's because he loves to snack on pups. Tell me, do you have any pups?" I smiled wide.

"You're a sick bastard." He snarled back at me.

"You know, my Beta over here prefers males instead of females. Would your mate be able to feel your rape and torture through the mate bond?" I asked.

"I am not fucking some guy." Niko mind linked me, and a laugh escaped me.

"Easy there virgin, I know you're waiting for your mate. Pullover at the park up ahead so I can plant him there." I linked back.

"You have two minutes to talk before I put a bullet in your head and then hunt your mate down for fun."

"I don't know where they are." He growled.

I dragged him out of the car behind a small wooded area at the park. He took off running and I opened up a hole in the ground under his feet. He fell in.

"Stop playing with your food and let's go. He's not going to talk." Niko linked me.

I walked to the edge of the hole he was laying in. "Last chance, where's my Gamma?"

Nothing, he just glared at me. I pulled the gun out, shot him in the head, and used my element to fill the hole back up with dirt.

We pulled up to the marine biology and research lab which had great views of everything going on at the marina. Kosta also worked in the security business and was able to gain access to the building. Niko and I went inside to meet with Kosta who was on the rooftop looking out at something through his binoculars.

"Kosta!" I greeted him.

"Alpha." He responded and shook my hand.

"Which building are they in?"

"They're not in a building, they're on a boat." Kosta told me and handed me his binoculars. "It's the big yacht docked in the cove out there." He pointed out and I looked.

"The one named *Basileus Lycaon*?" I asked.

"Basileus is Greek for King!" Niko said.

"Yes, King Lycaon. Can you think of anyone who would name a yacht after him?" Kosta said.

"It would have to be a werewolf." Niko said.

"Not just any werewolf. No one from our kind would

be bold enough to do something like that knowing the true descendant of King Lycaon is still alive and the most feared in all of Greece and Europe." Kosta said looking at me.

I knew in my gut what Kosta was saying. It was something I had felt deep inside, something I dreaded. Something only those closest to him might know because of the strings that tie us, the bonds are still connected. Kosta was his Beta and best friend, I was his only son.

"MY FATHER!" I growled.

CHAPTER 24 – WHAT?

Alexander had stopped by with Odessa and my bags. I was in the bedroom digging through my bags for something to wear. My hands found fresh underwear and a denim sundress. I changed my clothes, brushed my hair and teeth, and went back out into the living room to find Odessa. She was in the kitchen warming up kreatopita, a Greek meat pie, that Elaina had sent over.

"That smells delicious." I said.

"Elaina is the best cook in all of Greece." She smiled.

"Does she share her recipes?" I asked.

"Nope. Though I imagine she will with you since you're the Luna."

"You know?" The question seemed to slip out of my lips before I could even think about it.

"Of course I know, my wolf may be young, but she recognized you as Luna right away. Dimitri's wolf can hardly contain himself."

"How long have you had your wolf? I mean, how old are you?" She looked about the same age as me.

"I just turned eighteen a few weeks ago." She said.

I knew it. "I turned eighteen three months ago just after high school graduation."

"Wow, and your parents let you come so far to attend a university. I guess it was destiny because the Moon Goddess paired you with my brother." She told me.

"Believe me, it took a lot of convincing." I laughed. "As a matter of fact, today is Sunday, I'm going to have to call my parents and pretend everything is going well."

"Do they know about Dimitri yet?" She asked.

"No, not yet. If I tell them, they'll be on the next flight over." I smiled.

We ate and spent the next few hours getting to know each other. Odessa had the same olive skin tone as Dimitri, dark hair, and warm honey colored eyes. She was beautiful and funny. I felt an instant connection to her.

The door opened up and Dimitri walked in followed by Niko. Niko headed straight for the food while Dimitri pulled me into his chest and buried his head in my neck. Scenting me seemed to calm him. He pulled back and kissed me, I had missed him in those few short hours he was gone.

"Come on, I'm trying to eat over here!" Niko groaned.

"Pay attention, you might learn something." Odessa teased him.

There was a knock at the front door before it opened, and Alexander came in with two other warriors.

"Alpha." They bowed their heads in submission. Then they turned to me and did the same. "Luna."

I looked over at Dimitri and he gave me a quick smile. I haven't been claimed and marked yet, but maybe their wolves recognized me as their Luna like Odessa's wolf had. Rae was bursting with pride at the level of respect being shown to us.

"Where's Alec?" Odessa asked.

"We're still working on that, there's been a complication." Dimitri told us.

There was a knock at the door. "That would be my uncle." Niko said. Kosta entered the room and we all sat down around the dining table. Dimitri pulled me to his lap, as strange as this would look to me when my parents did it, it felt completely natural and comfortable.

"Congratulations on finding your mate Raven. Have you shared the news with your parents yet?" Kosta asked.

"Err no, not yet. We've been a little distracted." I smiled.

"Your brother and cousin are arriving tomorrow morning, one of my men is picking them up. Where should we take them?"

"I had planned to take them out to the island this morning while we sorted out this mess. But now I'm rethinking." Dimitri said.

"Let's just storm the yacht and get them back tonight." Alexander suggested.

"The yacht sails at night back and forth to Santorini and refuels at the marina. Eros' pack doctor has boarded the yacht a few times and I believe Eros is on the yacht." Kosta informed us.

"Are we sure that Alec is on it too?" I asked.

"Yes, he was carried onto the boat. Our contacts on the island of Santorini have not seen anyone leave the boat. Unless they threw Alec overboard at sea. The same two men who boarded the boat in Santorini have gone on and off within an hour. They never stay long and then the yacht sails back." Kosta said.

"Do we know who the men are in Santorini visiting Eros?" Niko asked.

"We believe one of them is Stefanos." Kosta said.

"Our father?" Odessa asked with a sudden look of panic in her eyes. I could feel her anxiety and fear in the air.

"I thought he was dead!" Niko said.

"That's what we all thought, but he's been building an empire as the head of the Greek mafia for the last decade." Kosta said.

"Your father is actually Eros' boss?" I asked as realization hit me.

"That explains why I never felt the bond fully break." Odessa said in shock.

"Oh, Goddess! Your father is the one who wants me dead! Why?" I asked.

"He went mad when he lost my mother." Dimitri said.

"That's part of it." Kosta said. "You also challenged him

and blinded one of his eyes. What you did was the best thing to do for the pack. The pack is thriving as the strongest pack on this side of the world. He's looking for revenge. The best way to ensure a wolf suffers is through its mate. He's not planning on killing you right away, he's planning on torturing you for a long time so that Dimitri suffers." Kosta told me.

"That sadistic bastard!" Dimitri growled.

"Stefanos had crossed the former mafia boss Athos, who took your mother to break your father. You saw what it did to him. His heart for everyone turned to stone the day he lost her. After you defeated him and took his pack, he killed Athos and became the new mafia boss. He sent you Heather's head believing she was your mate. He's been waiting for you to find your mate and destroy you from the inside."

"How is such a cruel and evil person our father?" Odessa said.

"So, are we going after the yacht tonight or in the morning?" Niko asked.

"You won't be able to board the yacht so easily, it has wolfbane misters that are motion triggered all around." Kosta said.

"So, we wear masks." Niko responded.

"It also has wolfbane dart triggers and guards armed with silver bullets." Kosta added.

"Maybe we should sink the boat?" Alexander said.

"We might kill the people we are trying to rescue if we sink it." Dimitri said.

"Rocky is the future Beta of Alpha Georgios' pack and Leo their Delta. If we don't get them back tomorrow, we need to notify Alpha Georgios." Kosta said.

"Alpha Georgios sits on the shifter's council with my father. He's going to tell my father." I said nervously.

"Your brother will be here in the morning, I'm pretty sure your father will know by this time tomorrow." Kosta said.

"What's the problem with her father?" Niko asked.

"She's Alpha Diesel LaRue's only daughter." Kosta said as if that would explain everything.

"As in Crescent Moon pack?" Niko looked at me wide eyed.

"Raven is my mate, I have the utmost respect for her father, but my mate belongs with me. No one can interfere with the Moon Goddesses pairing." Dimitri was struggling to keep his cool.

"The longer we wait, the greater the chances are of not finding them alive." Alexander chimed in.

"We need a plan to get on that yacht." Niko said.

"Dimitri, can I speak to you alone for a moment. It's kind of important." I whispered to him.

"Excuse us for a moment." He said and we moved into the bedroom.

"Dimitri, I want to help." I said.

"I can't have you—"

"Just listen to me, please." I said. "I can help with the yacht, I think. I have an idea."

"What do you mean?" He raised a brow.

"Let me show you." I walked into the bathroom and turned on the sink. He stared at me curiously. I took a deep breath and focused on the water, I willed it to float in the air and circle around his head before I sent it splashing back into the sink.

"WHAT?" He stared at me in shock.

"Water element." That was all I could manage to say.

"You have the gift of water too?"

"Yes."

"You have both water and fire?" He asked again, as if not believing what he just saw.

"Yes."

"Do you have another element or talent that I don't know about?"

"No, just the two." I smiled.

"Is that even possible?" He was asking himself in disbelief.

"I can help with getting people on the yacht, I can lift a person up with water onto the deck." I suggested.

"Can you shipwreck the boat with high waves and bring it to shore?" He asked.

"I-I'm not sure. But my brother can, he's had a few years of training with his element." I said.

"Your brother? He's elemental too?" Dimitri asked.

"Yes, my older brothers are, we're not sure about the younger ones, they're not of age yet."

"What? Raven, just how many brothers do you have?"

"Five. Knox and Peter are the twins. They're older than me and also have the water element. Roman, Seth, and Levi are my three younger brothers."

"Do they have fire as well?" He asked.

"No. My father has water, and my mother has fire. My brothers have water, I'm the only one with both."

Dimitri stood in shock trying to process what I just said. "I've never heard of the Moon Goddess pairing two elemental wolves together. We're so rare and yet you've got a family full of them." He said as he ran his fingers through his thick hair.

"I wonder if our pups will have all three?" I said without even thinking.

"Our pups!" Dimitri said grinning wide and pulling me closer to him sending a blush over my face. "I like the sound of that, shall we get started now?" He joked, at least, I think he was joking.

"He can make me howl anytime." Rae snickered in my head.

"We've got bigger things to worry about right now." I reminded him and ignored my horny wolf.

"Do you think your brother will be willing to help with the yacht?" He asked.

"Are you kidding? He will insist on helping." I said.

We left the bedroom and returned to join the rest of the group.

"Lovers quarrel already?" Niko smiled at us and Odessa smacked him on the back of the head.

"We've got a plan; we move in the morning when Raven's brother is here." Dimitri said.

My phone started ringing, everyone looked at me as I pulled my phone out of my pocket to answer it. The caller ID flashed a photo. "It's my dad." I said as I walked back towards the bedroom for privacy.

"Dun, Dun, Dun!" Niko laughed.

"It's not her father I'd be worried about, it's her mother! Her aura will bring even the strongest Alpha to his knees." I heard Kosta tell them.

CHAPTER 25 – FAMILY

It was just before sunrise when I felt the bed moving and stirred awake. Dimitri headed into the bathroom and I heard the shower turn on.

"Girl, what are you doing? Follow his sexy ass in there! He might need someone to help soap up his back." Rae barked at me.

I rolled out of bed and pulled off the shirt I was sleeping in. The shower had started to steam up and I stepped right in with Dimitri. He smiled at me and I saw his eyes drop down at my chest making me blush. His lips met mine and the warm tingles pulsed through me. I moved my hands around the back of his neck to pull him closer and deepen the kiss.

"Goddess I want you." He moaned lifting me up with one arm and I wrapped my legs around his waist.

"I want you too." I replied. I could feel my wolf panting for his as he kissed and licked up and down my neck. He stopped for a moment and let out a frustrated groan.

"Alexander just linked me, Kosta's man has left the airport with your brother and cousin. They should be here in about thirty minutes; we'll have an hour to explain what's happening and eat breakfast before we leave for the marina."

"Breakfast! Oh no, I forgot about breakfast." I had a

moment of panic. I'm sure Knox and Clair will be hungry, and I hadn't planned anything.

"I asked Niko to pick some up." Dimitri told me.

I watched him rinse the shampoo from his hair and admired his magnificently chiseled chest. "Keep looking at me like that and we won't be going anywhere today." Dimitri grinned.

We finished with our shower, got dressed, and packed up our belongings that will be going to the island with us. The island was about two hours away with the high-speed boat and was owned by Dimitri. He wasn't sure how long or short our stay on the island would be, it all depended on the outcome of today's rescue mission and developments. Greece has nearly six thousand islands ranging from tiny to mega sized, only a few hundred are inhabited. Being on a private island will make it very difficult for anyone to find us.

I was pacing the living room waiting for them to arrive. Dimitri sat in the leather chair watching me and Odessa was in the kitchen making coffee. I was worried about Knox calling our parents right away and wasn't sure how he would react when he meets my mate. I heard the elevator doors open in the hallway and Dimitri walked over to the door to open it.

"Eeekkkk!" I heard Clair squeal as she wrapped her arms around me.

"Clairy Fairy!" I squealed back and hugged her. It was my nickname for her because she always wore her black hair in a shoulder length A-line cut which reminded me of fairies.

"Hey, trouble." Knox smiled and hugged me.

"This is a pretty fancy dorm you're living in." Clair said admiring the room and views.

"This isn't the dorm." I laughed.

"Are you going to introduce us to your friends?" Knox asked eyeing the other Alpha in the room.

"Yes, but you can't tell mom and dad yet." I said.

"Tell mom and dad what?" Knox looked confused and Clair was trying to contain her joy for me.

"This is Alpha Dimitri Theodorus, from the Olympus Blood Moon Pack and this is his sister Odessa Theodorus. Alpha, this is my oldest brother and future Alpha of Crescent Moon Pack, Knox LaRue, and my cousin Clair LaRue Taylor." They shook hands.

"Knox, Alpha Dimitri is my mate." I added.

"You have GOT to be kidding me!" Knox looked at me wide eyed.

"What's that supposed to mean?" I asked.

"First Peter, now you!" Knox said.

"You'll have to excuse my cousin, he's got mate envy." Clair giggled.

"My brother had to wait eight years before he finally found Raven. Who knows, your mate could be on the opposite side of the world." Odessa told Knox.

"Well Knox, now that you're on the opposite side of

the world, look into Odessa's eyes, she might be your mate." I said laughing at their wide eyed embarrassed stare. I knew Knox couldn't resist. He turned his face and looked at Odessa, they both laughed at each other, but nothing happened.

The elevator door dinged, and Dimitri opened the front door again. Niko walked in holding a large bag of take-out in one hand and eating a Gyro with the other hand. It's a good thing Niko is a wolf because if he was human, he wouldn't be able to maintain his physique with as much as he eats.

"You're always eating! And where did you find Gyros this early in the morning? I thought you were getting breakfast!" Odessa said.

"It's okay, we love Gyros, plus it's dinner time back at home." Clair smiled and Niko stood frozen on the spot.

"Oooh, I could go for some Gyros." Knox said practically salivating as the room filled with the smell of delicious Gyros.

"Hello, Clair?" I called out to Clair who was smiling and frozen like a statue.

"Good grief Niko, you've got tzatziki sauce on your face." Odessa said grabbing the bag full of Gyros sandwiches from Niko's arm.

"MINE." Niko growled and we knew he wasn't talking about the bag full of Gyros.

We stood quiet for a moment watching Niko and Clair embrace. Niko buried his face in her neck, and she giggled. Seeing them together made my heart happy. They were perfect for each other.

"OH COME ON!! ARE YOU FOR REAL?" Knox seemed to be staring up towards the sky as if asking the question to the Moon Goddess.

"Congratulations to the both of you. Clair, we are honored to have you as our Beta female at Olympus Blood Moon." Dimitri smiled.

That's right! Now that Niko and Clair are mates, I would have my cousin and best friend with me in Greece. I was starting to feel bad for Knox, he's dreamed of finding his mate since he was a pup. He wants to be someone's knight in shining armor like my dad was, although my dad still swears that it was my mom who rescued him. This reminds me, we need to fill them in on Eros.

"Let's sit and eat. We have some important business to take care of and need your help." I said to Knox and his head perked up in interest.

Dimitri turned to close the front door and Knox noticed the same crescent moon mark we had on the back of Dimitri's neck.

"You're elemental?" Knox asked out loud.

"I am. Please sit down, we need your help with your element." Dimitri motioned to the table and we all moved to sit.

I explained what happened with Eros and how he became obsessed with me. How Eros figured out that I was Dimitri's mate, had a human girl abducted by accident, and how I set him on fire. Then I told him about my friends from Alpha Georgios' pack, and how Alec was abducted. Dimitri explained the history behind it all and his father's involvement.

"You're the one they call the Beast!" Knox said. I can't believe he said that out loud to Dimitri. I was a little worried about how he would receive that comment and wanted to kick my brother under the table.

"My wolf is abnormally larger than any Alpha and strong, I'm a descendant of King Lycaon. The reputation was built by distorted rumors because of my wolfs size, my earth element, my shifting so early and beating my father to become Alpha."

"My family vacationed in Greece a few years ago, my father wanted to meet with you. The shifter's council typically seeks out the strongest pack Alpha's in each region, you should have been selected but they picked Alpha Georgios instead because you had a dangerous reputation."

"What better way to keep others away from your pack. No one would dare challenge or attack someone they believe to be a ruthless and dangerous Alpha." Dimitri said.

"Wait, you have the earth element?" Clair asked and looked at Knox. I knew exactly what they were thinking. They were thinking about the prophecy.

"Yes." Dimitri answered.

"He can cause earthquakes, split the ground open, bring down trees, cause landslides and other cool stuff." Niko said excitedly.

"Just the earth element?" Clair asked.

"No one has more than one, do they?" Niko asked confused.

"Our father has water and our mother has fire. My twin and I have water, but Raven has both." Knox said.

"So, the Moon Goddess *has* paired two elemental wolves together before!" Odessa said.

"Yes, except our parents were second chance mates. Our mother was paired with our Uncle Ranger at first, he did not have a gift. It's a long story, but after he rejected her, she found our father." Knox explained.

"There's an old prophecy about it, well actually I guess it would technically be a future prophecy. Our parent's cousin is Alexis Ivy and she foretold—"

"THE ALEXIS IVY?" Odessa asked wide eyed and looking at Dimitri. We know her!

"Tell me about the prophecy." Dimitri asked.

"We should discuss the prophecy later; we've got to get going." I reminded them.

"What the hell are we waiting for, we can control three of the four elements, let's go save our friends." Niko said.

"Well that's the problem actually, I've only had my gifts for three months and haven't trained as much as I probably should. Knox, we need your help with a yacht and your water talents." I said.

"I'm in!" Knox said.

"Thank you, Alpha Knox." Dimitri said and I could feel Knox swell with pride because Dimitri addressed him with the Alpha title even though Knox had not taken over Crescent Moon yet.

"I'm in too." Clair said.

"No you're not" Niko growled, and we all laughed at his possessiveness over his new mate and his strong urge to keep her safe.

"We've got plenty of men in place already. Clair can wait with Odessa in the car nearby with a *mated* warrior." Dimitri emphasized the word mated to calm Niko down.

"But I've got Alpha blood in me and I'm one of our strongest warriors. I'm the next Beta of Crescent Moon." Clair tried to justify.

"Then you'd be perfect to help guard Odessa. My father wouldn't mind capturing her to hurt me. I would greatly appreciate it if you stayed with her, she's one of the most important people in my life." Dimitri managed to coax Clair into agreeing. I was certain Odessa could easily defend herself and had probably trained her whole life.

"Raven, Knox, and I will go out on the water to get closer with the fishing boat charter we've secured."

"Raven, do you have your waterproof lighter with you?" Knox asked.

"What's she going to do with a lighter?" Odessa asked.

"Roast some bad wolves." Knox smiled.

CHAPTER 26 – SINKING

Dimitri's POV

"Put the fish down Niko." Raven whispered to Niko.

We were crouched down on the stern of Poseidon's Trident fishing boat and Niko was being Niko. I hope his new mate will appreciate the sense of humor he has. The fishing boat belonged to a local fishing company that was owned by a friend of Niko's. The barrel of fish up on deck would certainly hide our scents if the wind picked up. I just hope Niko doesn't start playing with the barrel of squid next to my mate; she might consider setting his hair on fire.

"What are you grinning at?" Raven asked me.

"You, you're so cute." I told her and kissed her delicious lips.

"Ugh, I think I'm going to be sick." Knox groaned.

"Motion sickness?" Niko asked.

"No, all this mushy kissing." Knox laughed and we all tried to hold back our laughter. I liked Raven's brother, he was open and willing to help his sister the moment she asked with no hesitation. I would do the same for Odessa if she ever needed my help.

The marine biology and research lab boat was docked near the yacht. A dozen of our warriors had boarded the boat late last night and docked it near the area where the yacht preferred to anchor each morning. When the yacht returned from its sail to Santorini in the morning, it dropped anchor without suspicion.

We slowly made our way closer towards the yacht and I mind linked the warriors into position. The warriors slipped into the water next to the research boat and waited. There was a good chance that the yacht was equipped with a fish finder and would be able to pick up the movement from anyone swimming near the boat.

I gave Knox the cue and he pulled a massive wave of water up over the bow of the boat. Knox continued to rock the yacht with crashing waves. An armed guard came into view on the deck and Raven lifted him up with a water bubble and dropped him in the water next to our warriors.

Another giant wave came over the bow of the yacht and another armed guard stepped out. Knox hit him with a big wave that sent him falling over the edge and triggered a wolfbane mister. Wolfbane had a purple hue to it and we could see the misters that wrapped around the yacht. We've got to take them out to prevent our guys from getting misted.

"Raven, do you think you can take out the misters on our side of the yacht with fire?" I asked.

"I can certainly try." She said.

"Knox once she burns out the misters, extinguish the fire so it doesn't burn down the entire yacht just yet." I said.

Raven pulled out her lighter and lit the flame. She looked like she was holding a ball of fire and threw it in the air. The fire hit the mister and Raven continued to do the same to a few more until we had a safe point to pass by. Once the misters were disabled, Knox put the fire out with seawater.

An alarm sounded on the boat and it started to lift anchor to sail. If this thing started moving, we would lose it. Our fishing boat wasn't fast enough. We needed to get on that boat now.

"We need to get on the yacht now!" I called out.

Knox and Raven started lifting warriors with water and dropping them on the deck of the yacht. The yacht blew its horn and started moving. Three more guards who shifted into wolves started fighting with our warriors.

"Raven, get Alexander on the yacht" I pointed to him in the water and she lifted him right up with the water and dropped him on deck.

"I could push the boat towards shore with water." Knox said and I gave him a nod. There's no way I could let this boat escape.

The yacht was trying to move at full throttle and Knox was grunting and fighting pretty hard to hold the yacht there. A wolfbane dart was triggered from just below that mast of the yacht and Raven sent a big ball of fire to take it out.

"Our mate is brilliant." Dom said full of pride.

Knox was struggling to keep the yacht in place with

wave after wave. I had an idea, but I haven't done this before in such deep water. I focused on the seafloor which was made up of earth and willed all my energy into pulling up a sea stack of rock beneath the yacht. A roar escaped me as I focused my strength and a massive sea stack rose right up causing a collision. I heard Niko let out a whoop of excitement as the yacht became disabled.

"The yacht will be taking on water, we need to hurry. Raven, transport me to the yacht, and Knox, transport Niko." I said.

"Be careful." Raven called out as I jumped down into the water below. Niko landed beside me and we were lifted with the water and dropped on the deck of the yacht.

A guard came running onto the deck firing his gun and a moment later he was covered in a ball of fire. His screams echoed off the sea and he fell overboard. I was so proud of my little bird; she was getting better with her elements. We made our way into the lower cabins of the yacht and it was filling up with water fast.

"Niko get down to the lowest cabin first and make sure they're not there, this thing is going to sink quick." Niko went down lower, and I searched the rooms on the central level. I found no one. I could still hear fighting going on between my men and Eros' men.

Someone had to be trying to sail the boat, so I went up to look in the cockpit. I heard sounds of rustling and found a badly burned Eros standing there. He wasn't alone, he held a gun to Leo's head who appeared to be beaten and possibly drugged.

"We found them. I've got Alec and Knox has Rocky, but Leo's not here." Niko mind linked me.

"I'm with Eros and Leo in the cockpit." I quickly linked back.

"That's a very talented *mate* you have Dimitri!" Eros sneered at me.

"She is, isn't she!" I smugly replied.

"She will die for what she did to me." He roared.

"You don't look like you're getting out of this alive." I said.

"This isn't plastic!" He waved his gun and brought it right back to Leo's head. "It's loaded with silver bullets and there's plenty to go around for you too!"

"She's going to roast you the second you step off this yacht."

"We'll see about that, Leo and I are going to go for a swim, aren't we Leo. If anyone comes after me, I kill him." He pointed the gun back to Leo's head.

"Hurry up this thing is sinking quickly; water is almost to the top deck." Niko linked me.

"You're a dead man Eros!" I snarled.

"Your father says the same thing about you." He growled back.

"The fool with one eye hiding on Santorini. I'm going to finish him when I'm done with you" I said dangerously and could see a flicker of fear in Eros' eyes. "Oh yes, I know where that sadistic bastard is hiding." I continued.

"He'll find you first, he's got the city crawling with men. You will pay for everything." Eros said.

"He's known for a decade where to find me. I haven't been hiding under some rock. I've built the strongest pack on this continent and I'm going to take your pack in the north too. I'm going to challenge and kill your bastard son when I'm done with you scarface." I growled.

"You're a walking corpse." Eros snarled.

"Only dead man here is the one I'm looking at. If I don't kill you, my father will, he hates when you mess up." I said.

Eros backed slowly out the cockpit and water was starting to flood in, the boat was almost fully submerged. Raven pulled a water bubble up over Eros' head to drown him and the gun fired. I ducked as the bullet grazed my shoulder.

Leo dropped to the deck with Eros still struggling to breathe behind him. Eros gave me a final look of rage, aimed the gun back at Leo, and pulled the trigger. Leo fell forward and the life left his eyes. Raven let out a scream, breaking her focus. Eros dropped on the deck, coughing for air. Proving evil doesn't die so easily, Eros was still alive.

I was standing knee-deep in water and picked Eros up by the neck. We were sinking fast. Dom would have liked to torture him a bit, but the water patrols would be heading our way soon and we had a few dead bodies in the water. Eros made a feeble attempt to escape my grip, but I just dug my hand right into his flesh, my claws extended, and I ripped out his throat.

I dropped Eros' lifeless body into the sea and picked up Leo's. Leo deserved a proper burial. He was so young and got mixed up in all of this because he was a good friend to my mate. Knox lifted me back up onto the fishing boat and Alexander took Leo's body. Raven ran to me and buried her sobbing face into my chest. I wrapped my arms around my mate to comfort her and kissed the top of her head. Dom howled in my head at the grief his mate was feeling.

My eyes met with Alec's who was leaning on Niko to help him stand up. He looked horrible. A wolf has quick healing, but Alec looked like he was struggling. "Are you okay?" I asked.

"Yes, just a little wolfbane injections to keep us weak. They gave them to all of us." He said.

I found Knox still holding Rocky, she appeared to be in the same shape as Alec, but distraught over the loss of Leo. He held her close into his chest while she sobbed.

"Rocky, we're going to need to take Leo back to your pack. I'm going to call Alpha Georgios and explain everything." I said.

"Rocky, oh Goddess Rocky." Raven said as she lifted her head off my chest.

She had just realized that Rocky was on the boat with us. She turned around and walked towards Rocky, when she reached out to hug her, Knox let out a possessive growl.

CHAPTER 27 – CONFERENCE

The sinking yacht attracted lots of attention from surrounding watercrafts and the water patrols raced past us to the location. We returned to the marina on the research institute's boat with our warriors and Leo's bodies. Kosta was waiting for us with a few men of his own, he directed us inside the research lab.

"I've brought Dr. Homer with me, in case he was needed." Kosta told Dimitri.

"Thank you Kosta. I'm afraid we've lost Leo and need to make arrangements to transport him back to his pack. Dr. Homer should look over Rocky and Alec first, it appears they've been injected with wolfbane." Dimitri instructed.

"Of course, Knox, please take Rocky into the next room, so Dr. Homer can evaluate her." Kosta said.

Knox just clung tighter to Rocky, his eyes dark, and growled, "MINE."

"It's okay, I'm a mated wolf." Dr. Homer told us and pulled his shirt collar down exposing his mate mark on the lower neck.

"Knox, I'm sure you can go with her. Dr. Homer only wants to help her." I told Knox.

"Rocky, this is my oldest brother, the future Alpha of Crescent Moon pack, Knox LaRue. Knox, this is Rocky Onassis, future Beta of Zeus' Howlers."

Rocky looked up at Knox with tears still glistening in her eyes. "It's actually Raquel, but I prefer Rocky." She told him.

Knox's eyes filled with so much emotion when his mate spoke to him for the first time. "What's your wolf's name?" He asked.

"It's Reign. What's yours?"

"Knight. As in your Knight in shining fur." He smiled silly and Rocky managed a faint smile.

It was a really sweet moment that calmed Knox down. He picked Rocky up and followed Dr. Homer into the other room with her. Knox was a replica of my overprotective father.

"It's probably time to call my father and explain everything." The room stood silent for a moment.

"We also need to call Alpha Georgios." Dimitri said breaking the silence.

"There's video conference equipment upstairs we can use. Once Rocky is done we can get started. I'll go call Alpha LaRue and Alpha Georgios so they're ready for the video conference." Kosta said.

Twenty minutes later, Knox carried Rocky upstairs to join us. "Dr. Homer said the wolfbane will work its way out of her system in the next day or two, she just needs to rest." Knox told us.

"Are we ready to connect on the conference call?" Kosta asked.

Clair was sitting next to Niko, Knox was holding Rocky on his lap, Odessa stood by Kosta and I sat next to Dimitri. The equipment connected and the monitor showed my father in a room with my mother, Aunt Payton, and Uncle Max.

"Good evening Alpha LaRue, Luna, and Beta's. I'm Alpha Dimitri Theodorus, from Olympus Blood Moon. We're just waiting for Alpha Georgios from Zeus' Howlers to connect and we'll get started." Dimitri said.

"Knox! Is there something you want to tell us?" My mother asked with that knowing smile on her face. She was looking at Knox possessively holding Rocky on his lap. Alpha Georgios connected before anyone could answer my mother.

"Alpha Georgios, thank you for joining us." Dimitri said. He was about the same age as Dimitri, I wasn't expecting him to be so young for some reason. He had light brown almost blondish hair with striking hazel eyes.

"I apologize for the delay, I'm actually in Athens on business right now and there's been a great deal of commotion going on at the marina. It appears that Alpha Eros of Moon Warriors has been found dead." Georgios told us.

"That's great news!" My father said.

"It certainly is! That scum was a disgrace to our kind. Kosta, I didn't know you worked for Alpha Dimitri." Georgios said.

"Kosta is the Uncle of my Beta Niko Stamos and a former pack member of Olympus Blood Moon. He may be living and working independently in the city, but he will always be a trusted liaison. I believe his admirable qualities are exactly why Alpha LaRue trusts him as well." Dimitri said.

"You are correct Alpha Dimitri, please begin the meeting, I'm assuming my son and heir, Knox, has found his mate from your pack?" My father said.

"Raquel?" Georgios said suddenly understanding that Rocky was sitting in Knox's lap.

"Actually dad, it's a long story. Alpha Georgios, I'm Raven LaRue, from Crescent Moon. I should probably start from the beginning, so you understand exactly what has transpired and the current situation we're in..." I continued from the beginning. When I came to Athens, meeting Rocky and Leo and Eros' obsession with me. Dimitri filled in the parts about his father and the mafia connection.

We told them about the human trafficking and Angela's abduction. Then we told them about Rocky and Leo's disappearance, the arrival of Knox and Clair, and the rescue that went wrong this morning. We explained how we believe Stefanos is not only the mafia boss but also the Alpha of rogues and how he is possibly controlling Eros' pack.

"And now the mighty beast of Greece seeks our help?" Alpha Georgios said smugly, and I could hear Dimitri trying to control a growl in his chest.

"How dare you speak to my brother that way Georgios!" Odessa roared her eyes livid. "Eros was an evil monster and my brother ripped his throat out, which you seemed to be very happy about moments ago. Let me remind you, Olympus Blood Moon is nearly three times the size of your pack and far more powerful. We are not seeking your help, only your understanding for the loss of your future Delta and OUR FRIEND. Leo cared very much for his friend Raven, who is our LUNA."

Well, that's one way to tell my parents!

"What? Luna?" My mother gasped.

"Yes, Raven is my mate." Dimitri replied.

"LIKE HELL SHE IS!" My father growled and chaos seemed to erupt, everyone was talking over each other.

"EVERYONE CALM DOWN!" Kosta called out.

"Yes, it's true. The Moon Goddess has paired Raven with Alpha Dimitri. Alpha LaRue, before you say something else you might regret, you should remember the prophecy, something bigger is at work here and no one can stop it. Also, my nephew, the Beta of Olympus Blood Moon, is the mate of your niece." Kosta explained.

"Clair? Is this true? Why didn't you call me?" My Aunt Payton squealed. She was always the cool supportive one.

"Mom, I just got here a few hours ago and found him." Clair said blushing.

"What about Knox?" My mother asked.

"Raquel Onassis, Rocky, from Zeus' Howlers, is the mate of the future Alpha of Crescent Moon. I'm sorry Alpha Georgios, it looks like you're going to lose your future Beta as well." Kosta smiled.

"And who is this little ball of flames?" Georgios asked.

"This ball of flames is my sister Odessa Theodorus, and you will respect her." Dimitri said.

"I'll have the jet fueled and ready to go in the morning. We're coming to get you." My father growled.

"Dad, I'm not going anywhere." I snapped back.

"We'll sort it out when we get there, honey." My mother said. Which was code for, I'll calm your father down.

"Alpha LaRue, we'll be retreating to one of our islands while we establish a plan to take care of the bigger threat. There are too many rogues on the mainland, and I need to keep my mate safe." Dimitri said.

"Do you expect us to find you among thousands of islands?" My father growled.

"Of course not Alpha. When you and the Luna arrive, please call Kosta, he will arrange for our high-speed boat to bring you to the island." Dimitri graciously said.

"I need to return with Leo, for his funeral." Rocky said softly.

"Alpha Georgios, I will escort my mate with Leo back to your pack lands." Knox said.

"We're at the marina, the arrangements have been made to take Leo back." Kosta said.

"I'm nearby and will meet you at the marina to travel

back with you. Alpha Dimitri, I would like to request your sister escort your new brother-in-law and Raquel. To attend the funeral tomorrow on your behalf." Alpha Georgios said.

Dimitri looked at Odessa who nodded her head in agreement. "Very well, Odessa will accompany them on my behalf."

"We will attend the funeral as well Alpha Georgios, we have some things to discuss. Then we will join Alpha Dimitri and my daughter on the island." My father said and hung up.

"I will be at the marina in fifteen minutes." Alpha Georgios said and disconnected.

"Are you going to be okay going alone?" Clair asked Knox.

"Of course I am. We'll join you on the island after the funeral." Knox said before he turned to Dimitri. "Take care of my sister." Knox added.

"I will. Take care of mine too." Dimitri said as Odessa hugged him goodbye.

"The boat is ready to take you out to the island Alpha." Alexander said.

"Niko and Clair will be coming with us. Alexander, return with the warriors and take Alec back to follow up with Dr. Vovos." Dimitri instructed.

"I'd like to go out and have a moment with Leo before they leave with him." I said and Dimitri took my hand, leading me to the car to say my final goodbye to my friend.

CHAPTER 28 – ISLAND

We zipped across the Aegean Sea on the high-speed boat. I was seated on Dimitri's lap with my head nuzzled in his neck. My thoughts were swirling around with the stress of everything that transpired today his scent seemed to calm my wolf. Rae was perfectly content in the arms of her mate. The only thing that could make her happier was to finally be claimed.

One of our warriors was driving the boat, the further we got away from Athens, the better I felt. We passed dozens of islands in all shapes and sizes. I peeked over at Clair and Niko, they were seated in the same position as us. I thought about how lucky Clair was to have parents who were so easily accepting of her finding her mate. At this moment, I was very much envious of Clair having Aunt Payton and Uncle Max for parents.

When Clair turned eighteen, nearly a year and a half ago, she was heartbroken when she didn't find her mate. Of course, Knox had also been looking for his mate for two years. He took it harder than any of us when he turned eighteen and his mate was nowhere to be found. I'm happy for both of them and wish my parents would have been just as happy for me as they were for Knox and Clair. I was thrilled and thankful that Clair would settle down in Greece with me in the same pack. This would naturally mean more visits to Greece from our family.

It's strange, I never imagined myself as a Luna. Perhaps it's because I spent the majority of my life hoping Zach was my mate and he was a gamma. All those years, all those wishes on shooting stars, hoping and praying for Zach, and that now seemed so silly. In the three days that I have known Dimitri, I have felt so much more for him than if I had spent a lifetime with Zach. I wasn't about to let anyone take that away, not even my father.

I love my father very much, some would even say I was his favorite, but I wasn't looking forward to seeing him tomorrow. His reaction to Dimitri wasn't good, he even threatened to take me home tomorrow despite knowing that he shouldn't interfere in the work of the Moon Goddess. Dimitri had handled himself admirably and kept his cool. I continued to rest my head in his neck, and he continued to stroke my back.

A short while later, I heard our driver call out, "land ho." I turned my head to see an island in the distance that got bigger and bigger as we got closer. The waters had floating navigation buoys that were marked *private property* and *no trespassing*. I could see the island was covered in trees and olive groves. From the sea, a few houses scattered across the island were slightly visible. A small marina came into sight with two docks. It had a few boats of different sizes already docked. We slowed down and docked in an open spot.

"Welcome back Alpha!" A man in his early forties said as he helped tie the boat down.

"Thank you, Dumas. I'd like you to meet my mate and Luna, Raven LaRue. Raven, this is Dumas, my lead on the island and business manager." Dimitri said.

"How wonderful to finally meet you." He bowed his head. "Is this your sister?" He looked at Clair.

"This is the Luna's cousin and Beta Niko's mate, Clair." Dimitri said.

"Excellent news!" He smiled warmly at us and a realization swept across his face. "Did you say LaRue?"

"Yes. She is Alpha LaRue's daughter." Dimitri grinned and continued, "Have the others settled in?"

"Yes sir. Elaina and a few other members arrived yesterday. She has lunch all set for you at the main house. The carts are ready as well unless you want to let your wolves stretch their legs out." He said.

"A run sounds wonderful." Clair said.

"Let's get to lunch first and then I'll give you a tour around the island." Niko told her, always thinking with his stomach first.

We drove in golf carts towards the packhouse and Dimitri pointed out the sights. A large building came into view and Dimitri explained how it was a water treatment facility; it desalinated water for the whole island and irrigation of the groves. The south side of the island had a huge solar power system that created and stored energy. The island had about two hundred inhabitants that belonged to the pack.

"It's a highly profitable business. We have seven different kinds of olive varieties growing on this island and the ancient groves on the north end of the island live for hundreds of years. We produce some of the world's finest premium olive oils." Dimitri explained to me.

"This is absolutely stunning." I said.

We approached the packhouse and it was much bigger than I would have expected for an island. It was a large, single level, villa-style home that was surrounded by trees. I suppose a multiple level house would have attracted unwanted attention to the island from out at sea. This was a beautiful layout, complete with a swimming pool and a picturesque vegetable garden.

Elaina greeted us and nearly cried with joy when Niko introduced his mate. She had prepared a wonderful smelling lunch and we sat outside on the back patio, enjoying an ocean breeze. We had a tomato Greek salad, freshly baked bread, kalamarakia appetizer, and a lobster pasta dish. Elaina explained the tomatoes had come fresh from the garden. There was something amazing about the tomatoes in Greece, they tasted better than any I've ever had.

"The lobster was caught just this morning; the north end of the island is filled with them. We should consider exporting lobster." She laughed. "Save some room for dessert, I've made the Alpha's favorite cookie, it's a chocolate and salted caramel. They've just come out of the oven!" I almost laughed out loud at the idea of the big bad Alpha having a favorite cookie.

Lunch was delicious, and we laughed at the stories Clair told about us growing up. Dimitri has such a swoon-worthy, weak in the knees laugh, while Niko had a deep cackle. When we finished eating lunch, Clair turned to Niko with a smile, "Cleo is begging to go out for a run."

"Nyke will be very happy to take his mate out and show her the island, just as soon as I have one of these cookies." Niko said and grabbed three cookies before they left.

"And what would my beautiful mate like to do?" Dimitri asked and kissed my hand.

"I think I should lay down; I'm feeling exhausted." I said.

"Anything you want." Dimitri scooped me up and carried me down a corridor. "The Alpha suite is at the end of the western corridor of the house."

We entered a big, open, and airy feeling room with white walls and a massive bed in the middle of the room, surrounded by windows. Dimitri pressed a button on the wall and the room darkened as the blinds rolled down. I removed my dress up over my head and dropped it to the floor. I had intended to take a nap, but something had come over me. The only thing I wanted more than anything right now, was to have my mate claim me.

I looked into his eyes and he stood motionless in front of me as I reached behind my back to unhook my bra. As soon as my bra dropped to the ground, I heard a growl rumbling inside his chest. His eyes darkened and he struggled to maintain control. Rae was panting and needed her mate. I also wanted to complete the mating process. It seemed to be an urgent goal I didn't even know I had.

I reached down and slid my panties off and stood for a moment breathing in his scent. I reached for Dimitri and lowered his head to meet my lips, he closed his eyes and gently kissed my lips. I kissed him back with need and could feel his desire growing. My mouth moved to his neck and I started kissing and sucking on it.

"You're playing with fire." He groaned and closed his eyes.

I stepped back and turned to bend over the bed, so I could pull the covers back. I was suddenly pressed down on my stomach by the weight of Dimitri on top of me. His chest was on my back. He was fully clothed, and I could feel his hard cock rubbing against the back of my ass. My hair was all over my face and the only thing I could see was his forearms on each side of my head.

He leaned his head next to my ear, "tell me little bird, are you begging me to mount you?" His deep voice asked.

I'm naked, how much more obvious do I need to make it, I nodded my head yes. I needed him more than anything right now. I felt heated and my core was throbbing.

"Words, use your words." He cooed.

"Yes! Yes, please." I practically panted. I could feel Dimitri struggling, why was he resisting me? Was I not woman enough for him? Something deep inside suddenly felt rejected and a sob escaped me. I could feel

Rae getting anxious and wanting to be with her mate as well.

"Why the sudden hurry?" He rolled to the side and looked at me.

I had no answer, I didn't know what had come over me. Something inside of me, call it instinct, call it hormones, call it anything you want, needed him. I wanted to kiss him all over and erase the memory of all the other women he had been with. I felt like I was going to heat up and die if I didn't have him. Maybe it was the fear of my father taking me away?

"Raven look at me." Dimitri said as he pulled my hair out of my face. "I can hardly hold Dom back any longer and you're making things challenging. I don't want to pressure you into anything. There are a few things I suspect are going on here. You've had a long and stressful day with the arrival of your family, the rescue, and the loss of your friend. Then the reaction from your father who threatened to take you away from me."

"I'm not leaving." I said.

"I won't let you leave either. But you should also know as the moom gets fuller, it pulls mates together. Your scent is getting stronger, and Dom is about to lose it. I'm starting to suspect that since you've met your mate, you might be starting to go into heat." He said.

"Heat? As in ... HEAT HEAT?" I said with panic in my voice. Female wolves went into heat about once a year and the pull to mate would be so strong, it could become very painful if you resisted. Also, the scent of a female in heat would attract unmated males if her mate did not mate with her. This crazy animalistic pull ensured the survival of our species. I had just met Dimitri this week, how could this be happening so soon? Why didn't Rae warn me?

"Are there unmated males on the island I need to worry about?" I asked.

Dimitri grinned at me for a moment before he spoke. "The only unmated male that you need to worry about is the Alpha in front of you."

CHAPTER 29 – SUNSET

Dimitri's POV

As a dominant Alpha male, I've never second guessed myself. It seems these days, around Raven, I was second guessing my every move.

I should have been able to claim what was mine without hesitation. The animal inside was genetically wired to understand raw sexual needs and dominance. While the human side of me wanted to make sure everything was right for Raven, who is the other half of my soul. If you had told me a few weeks ago I would feel this way about my mate, I wouldn't have believed it. I had no intention of ever claiming a mate. Yet here I was, my body and soul completely owned by that little raven haired girl I was planning to turn into a woman.

Dom could feel her heat starting and was begging to be let out. After her father threatened to take her back home, Dom made several attempts to take control and mark his mate. I knew this was something I couldn't force, I needed to be sure Raven was fully ready.

"Looks like we're going to get some help from the Moon Goddess." Dom Snickered at me.

Raven had asked for some alone time to take a cold shower and get some rest. Dom wanted to stay by her side and comfort her. Reluctantly, I agreed and left her alone in the suite. I know she's got so much to think about with everything going on, but I wish she would have talked about it with me.

"The sooner we mark her, the sooner we can read her thoughts." Dom reminded me.

There's a soft sandy beach on the western side of the island which makes the perfect spot for watching sunsets. I will take her there tonight and have Elaina set up a picnic dinner for us. We need to spend some alone time with her and keep her away from the unmated males on the island. I mind linked Dumas and asked him to make sure the western beach was off-limits to everyone this evening. Then I decided to set up the picnic spot while she was napping.

A few hours later Raven emerged from the suite wearing a short sundress. Her sweet scent was strong and filled my nostrils. I was sitting on the sofa in the living room and motioned for her to come to me. She walked over and sat, not on the sofa next to me, but my lap. This made Dom howl with joy.

"Did you have a good nap?" I asked.

"It was a little restless." She said and buried her head in my neck.

"I told you she needed our comfort." Dom scoffed in my head.
"I think maybe Rae could use a run." She told me. I ran my hand over her legs and could feel how hot her skin was, she was definitely starting to go into heat.

"Dom will you be able to control yourself for a short while longer?" I asked him.

"I can try, but no promises." He huffed at me.

"We can take Rae for a run; would she prefer I run next to her in wolf form or follow in human form?" I asked.

"She's looking forward to running with Dom."

"Okay, let's get going." I said and Dom was yipping with joy.

We walked outside, passed the pool, and into the trees. I stripped off my clothes and shifted. A small gasp escaped her as she took in the sight of Dom for the second time. I realized the first time she saw him was when he chased her down and she may have not been as focused on all the details.

She looked a little taken back and unsure. Dom was Alpha black but much bigger than an Alpha. He could sense her fear and dropped his head down with a low whine. Raven stepped forward with her hand outstretched moving very slowly. I could sense her fear and hear her heart racing. I wish I had been able to mind link her and talk to her.

Most Alpha's are the size of a donkey, Dom is the size of a horse. Dom laid down on all fours to try and make himself look less intimidating; he really wanted our mate's approval. When Raven reached us, she stroked Dom's head and he closed his eyes. He was enjoying her attention and touch. She continued to rub and stroke our back and Dom turned his head to lick her face. She let out a giggle and the big bad Alpha was wrapped around her finger.

She took off her clothes and prepared to shift when

Dom gave her another quick lick on the back of her leg and then her butt. "DOM!" I shouted at him. Raven let out another giggle and shifted.

Dom yipped with excitement and Rae started rubbing up against him. We took off running and Rae kept pace next to us. Her coat was a deep shiny raven color, like Raven's hair. Her eyes twinkling with the same blue color as well, she was absolutely beautiful. Dom leaned over and nipped at her ear affectionately and she playfully returned a nip on my tail. We let the wolves play for a while and they chased each other through an olive grove.

I let out a bark and motioned my head for her to follow me. We headed to the western side of the island where our sunset picnic was waiting. We arrived at the beach and her eyes found the picnic surprise. I had laid out multiple blankets and pillows on the beach surrounded by candles earlier. Dumas had delivered the picnic basket moments ago and lit the candles.

Raven shifted back. "This is beautiful." She smiled.

I shifted back before Dom could lick her cute little butt again. "The sunset is stunning from here."

"Is it ok if I take a quick swim, I need to cool off? The run must have overheated me." She said practically panting.

"Of course, I have some towels and extra clothes here." I could smell her scent getting stronger teasing me with the scent of arousal.

We entered the ocean and Raven hunched over in pain.

She let out a low whimper and I moved towards her. She wrapped her arms around my waist and buried her head in my chest. "Dimitriiiii," she cried out.

The water isn't working, her body was burning up and the need to mate had become painful for both of us. Her need triggered my own. My erection had become so hard, it practically hurt and was begging to be buried deep inside of her. I scooped her up and carried her to the pillows on the picnic blankets.

Her head was thrashing from side to side as she trembled in pain. She reached for my hand and placed it between her legs. FUCK! She was burning hot and slick with wetness. Another cry escaped her beautiful lips and the only way to extinguish her heat was to mate with her. Her need was intensifying with every passing moment.

I spread her legs, exposing her fully naked body to me. My hungry eyes took in every inch of her, ready to make her mine. My body took over and my hands started roaming over hers. Her beautiful blue eyes locked with mine and she reached for me. I positioned my body on top of hers and kissed her lips.

"Please." She panted.

I reached down and slipped in two fingers, she cried out at the contact and I started moving my fingers in and out of her sweetness. She was so tight; I was worried about hurting her with my size. Her body was quivering, and I could hardly think clearly anymore. I pulled my fingers out and rubbed the head of my cock at her opening, I moaned at the sensation.

I gently thrust half my length into her and she stiff-
ened beneath me when I tore through her innocence.
"Breathe... breathe baby, it will pass." I whispered in
her ear. I peppered kisses on her face and neck, and she
let out a low moan. When she finally relaxed, I pulled
out and pushed back in. I continued to gently rock in
and out of her, stretching her to fit me one inch at a
time. Her body trembled beneath me, the feel of her
tightness gripping me caused me to curse in Greek.

This woman under me was a Goddess and she was
mine. The sounds of her moans were music to my ears.
I wanted to spend the rest of my life buried deep inside
of her. My hand caressed her breasts as I kissed and
licked up and down her neck. I sucked on her marking
spot and could feel her walls squeezing my cock.

I started moving faster, claiming more and more of her
as I moved a little deeper. Her nails scratched at my
back possessively and I felt Dom swell with pride. Her
cries of pleasure possessed me. I kissed her deeply and
continued to pound away into her, taking every last bit
of her. She felt amazing, the sensation pulsing through
my body was like nothing I have ever experienced before. She belongs to me.

"Oh, Dimitri." She frantically panted on the brink of
orgasm. She wrapped her legs around my waist allowing for deeper penetration. The look on her face was
so beautiful, her mouth open, the vulnerability in her
eyes as she squirmed and moaned. Taking me, all of
me. A growl rumbled in my chest and the beast inside
was ready. I returned to her neck and felt my teeth
elongate as I prepared to mark her. I continued to drive
my cock deeper into her and sunk my teeth in her neck,

claiming her. She cried out with pleasure and Dom howled in my head.

Raven wrapped her arms around my neck, pulling me to her. She kissed and sucked on my neck, earning her another growl from me. Her teeth rubbed against my neck and I came undone. She bit down on my neck and I roared as my orgasm exploded. She had officially claimed me as hers.

Everything finally seemed right, and I felt complete. The entire island could burn down right now and all that mattered was the Goddess in my arms. Raven nuzzled into my chest and I could feel the heat from her body had subsided.

"You were right." She said.

"About?"

"The sunset is stunning from here."

I picked her up in my arms and headed back into the ocean to rinse off. When we were about chest-deep in the water, she wrapped her legs around my waist and rested her head on my shoulder. I held her to me and breathed her in as we watched the sunset. When the sun had finished setting and I carried Raven back out to the picnic blanket and set her down.

"Are you hungry? I had Elaina pack dinner for us."

"I'm hungry for you." She smiled at me.

I leaned in to kiss her delicious lips and could feel her temperature rising again. I knew we would spend most of the night here quenching her heat. My cock stiff-ened in response to her need and the urge to mount her, right here, right now, took over me as I pictured her on all fours with that beautiful ass in the air.

Raven smiled up at me, as if reading my thoughts and rolled over. She stood on her hands and knees with her hips pushing back in the air, swaying before me. A smile swept across my face as I realized that naughty little wolf had indeed been reading my thoughts.

CHAPTER 30 – PARENTS

The night sky was starting to lighten which indicated that sunrise was fast approaching. We had spent most of the night lost in pure bliss on this sandy little beach.

Dimitri was laying with his eyes closed but wasn't sleeping. He held me tight to his chest under a blanket. I could feel his heartbeat and it seemed in sync with my own heart's rhythm. I inhaled his scent deeply and it had changed, both of our scents had changed and blended together.

"How are you feeling little bird?" His voice was gravelly.

"Perfectly content and exhausted." I giggled.

"The patrol will be resuming its run to this side of the island at sunrise." Dimitri stood up and slipped some shorts on.

"Are we running back?" I groaned remembering the long distance we had run in wolf form to get here.

"Dom would be thrilled to have you ride back on him." Dimitri grinned.

"Is he going to lick my butt again?" I joked and Dimitri laughed. He slipped off his shorts again and shifted. Dom was a spectacular sight, yet also frightening if you weren't accustomed to seeing him. I stroked his head for a moment and planted a kiss on the top of his head. He seemed to want to rub his wolf head all over me. It was sweet.

"Climb on." Dimitri said through the mind link and Dom laid down for me. I wrapped the blanket around me and laid down on Dom's back with my arms around his neck. He moved his head down and picked up Dimitri's shorts in his mouth. He stood up gracefully and started running at an easy pace back towards the packhouse. I was thankful for the easy pace as I felt the soreness between my legs.

"Kalimera Alpha. Kalimera Luna." A man with a young boy and fishing gear called out as we passed them. I waved and smiled at them.

I laid my head down on Dom and felt his strength and power beneath me. Rae was radiating pride and joy. "Mate is amazing!" She cooed at me.

Dom let out a joyous howl when he heard what Rae said to me through the mind link. "We think you're pretty amazing too." Dimitri replied to us.

We reached the packhouse and Dimitri shifted back. He carried me into the house, back to our suite, and into the bathroom. The tub started filling up with water and Dimitri squeezed a purple bottle of Lavender bath suds into the tub.

"A warm bath should help ease your soreness."

He leaned down and kissed my lips before he pulled the blanket off me. With very little effort, he scooped me up and stepped into the tub with me. I sat facing him, straddled over his lap. He took the loofah and soaped me up, I was so relaxed, I dropped my head into his neck and drifted off to sleep.

I heard a phone ringing and stirred awake. I was sprawled out in my favorite position across Dimitri's chest sleeping. The last thing I remember was getting into the bathtub with Dimitri. I looked at the clock on the nightstand and it was just after two in the afternoon. We had slept the morning away recovering from a night full of mating. I tried to climb down off Dimitri, but he wrapped his arms around me pulling me back down to him.

"You're not leaving me already, are you?" He joked.

"Of course not. You're stuck with me Alpha." I replied and kissed his neck. I only hope my parents won't put up a fight or be angry. I wasn't a pup anymore, but I knew my father would have a hard time letting me go. It's not like I was going to be at a neighboring pack, I was going to be halfway around the world.

"Worried about your father?" Dimitri asked.

"How did you know?"

"The mind link and I could feel your emotions." He grinned.

I need to learn how to pull up my wall and keep my thoughts private, I reminded myself.

"Don't do that." Dimitri said to me.

"Do what?"

"Block your thoughts from me and keep things private. We're mates Raven, please don't hide any part of yourself from me." He said.

"Only if you promise not to block me out from your thoughts. I want to hear the good, the bad, and the ugly." I replied.

"Sounds like a deal." He kissed my lips. "Now, what would you like for breakfast? I can have Elaina send it to our room."

"It's way past breakfast. We should get up and check in with Niko and Clair, besides, my parents should be here for dinner."

We got dressed and made our way into the kitchen. Niko was seated eating a sandwich stuffed with Greek sausage, peppers, and onions. Elaina greeted us and started preparing sandwiches for us as well. She set down a platter of Domatokeftethes, which is a delicious fried tomato fritter developed in the Greek islands.

Clair joined us and sat down next to Niko kissing him. "Sorry that took so long, my mother video called me." She smiled.

"How are they doing?" I asked.

"Wonderful, they'd like to come visit as soon as possible but need the approval of your—" she stopped midsentence and sniffed the air. She must have noticed the change in my scent and her eyes landed on Dimitri's mark on my neck.

"OH, MY GODDESS! YOU DID, DIDN'T YOU!" She squealed and ran to my side of the table to hug me.

"I'm surprised it took so long." Niko chimed in.

"Congratulations! I'm so happy for you both!" Clair said while we hugged.

"Thanks, let's hope my parents share the same sentiment." I said.

We finished eating while Clair raved on about the island. Niko had taken her on a tour, and they even took a catamaran sail around the island. "It was amazing seeing the entire island from the sea. The cliff and rocky sides make it nearly impenetrable. The only two points of entrance are at the little beach on the western end and the boat dock area." Clair said.

"I moved the rocks and cut the cliffs with my element for that exact reason. I can easily seal off the opening to the beach and boat docks to make it difficult to breach the island if I needed to." Dimitri said.

"Wow! You've really developed your element!" I said with a hint of envy.

"Raven, you barely had time to train yours before you ran off to Greece." Clair added sensing my envy.

"We can go out and work on your element if you're feeling up to it. Maybe it will help get rid of some of your jitters before your parents get here." Dimitri said.

"Sounds like a great idea." I smiled.

"I've got to see this." Niko said.

We stood at the northern cliff side of the island that had a large open area. It was the highest point on the island. Dimitri held a torch in his hand and drove it into the ground before lighting it.

"Elemental power is usually fueled by your energy and emotion. The more you use it, the more energy is drained from you. Fortunately for us, being an Alpha born wolf allows you to heal faster and replenish your energy quicker. Emotions that fuel control can be happy or sad, jealousy, anger or anything in between." Dimitri said.

"Think about last night's happy thoughts." Clair laughed.

"Can you pull up ocean water from this far up?" Dimitri asked.

"I've never tried." I said.

He stood behind me and placed both his hands on my waist. I could feel the butterflies and tingles shoot through me. "Focus on the ocean below and pull the water up to the cliff's edge. Then, try to hold it there for as long as possible." He instructed me.

I willed the water to rise, and it did. A moment later, it splashed back down into the ocean, I couldn't hold it there for very long. "That was very good baby. It's just like exercise, the more you do it, the more you push yourself, the better you get." He said.

We practiced with the water and the fire element. I

tossed fireballs at Dimitri who quickly extinguished them with earth. "Use both your hands and see if you can throw two fireballs at once." He called from across the field. Niko and Clair were seated on the ground watching the show.

A helicopter came into view and seemed to be heading straight for us. We all stood frozen and looked up into the sky. "I just got a mind link from Knox, they're on the helicopter. It was much faster than taking a boat and your father was getting impatient." Clair told us.

The helicopter hovered overhead, and we moved back. Kosta was sitting in the co-pilot seat and waved down to us. I gave a nervous wave back and tried to smile as best as I could. My heart was racing, and Rae was also anxiously stirring.

"Here come the in-laws." Niko teased us even though he could sense everyone's tension.

The helicopter touched down in the open field and the blades powered down. The doors opened and the anxiety pulsed through me. I reached for Dimitri's hand and found comfort and calm.

My father was the first to step off the plane and he reached back to help my mother down. They were followed by Knox, Rocky, and Kosta. My father was wearing a dark charcoal two piece suit, his fists were clenched and his blue eyes icy cold. My father was a very intimidating Alpha, but Dimitri seemed unfazed.

My brother stood just behind him with Rocky. My twin brothers, Knox and Peter were exact clones of my father, except in this moment, I could see sympathy in

Knox's eyes. They stood in front of us and I knew this was not going to go well. My mother stood next to my father and placed her hands on my father's arms to calm him.

"Hello, mom. Hi dad." I called out, my father growled, never taking his eyes off Dimitri. "This is my mate, Alpha Dimitri Theodorus." My father shot me a quick look, his eyes landed on my mark and he sniffed the air. A loud roar ripped from my father and he pulled his hand back and punched Dimitri right in the jaw. **"DAD!"** I screamed.

Dimitri growled and stood with his fists clenched. I could feel him trying to calm Dom down who wanted to take control. Dimitri kept reminding himself that Diesel LaRue was my father, and he didn't want to hurt him.

"You took advantage of my little girl, **YOU FUCK-ING BEAST!**" My father landed another punch across Dimitri's face. Dimitri let out a thundering growl and both Alpha's shifted, clothes ripping to shreds.

"Oh shit!" Niko managed to utter and pulled Clair behind him.
Knox also did the same with Rocky and stepped back.

"DAD STOP THIS!" I called out but he growled at me.

Duke had the same shiny deep raven colored hair and blue eyes that were prominent in LaRue Alpha's. Dom had the same honey colored eyes as Dimitri and black fur, but he was bigger than my father's wolf Duke. They circled each other snarling and snapping. My father lunged at Dom and Dom was able to throw my father off. My father pulled up a massive water bubble from the ocean and tried to bring it down on Dom's head.

Dom's front paw stomped the ground and a sinkhole opened up beneath Duke, who fell in. This broke my dad's focus on the water bubble, and it splashed to the ground. Moments later, Duke jumped out of the hole and was snarling with rage. "Diesel that's enough." My mother called out to her mate.

My father lunged over my mother and ran straight at Dom. Dom and Duke rolled onto the ground biting and snapping at each other. My father jumped on Dom and tried to sink his teeth into his neck. Dom let out a yelp and rolled over. He managed to kick my father off, sending him flying over the edge of the cliff. My father came floating back up on land using his water element. He was furious and ready to attack again.

We heard an earth shaking growl and my mother shifted.

"WHAT THE FUCK?!" Niko said taking in my mother's wolf, Lia. Her golden fur was radiating in the sun. Rocky's jaw dropped at the sight too.

My mother moved between the two Alpha's and growled out. My father lowered his head in submission and Dom bowed down to her as well. I looked around and everyone had their head down in submission, even Kosta.

My father's wolf Duke looked up at me and then at my mother, a low whine escaped him before he turned around and ran towards the tree line. My heart ached for him and I wasn't sure what to do. I had never disappointed my father, and I don't feel like I've done anything wrong. He couldn't possibly expect me to remain mateless my whole life and live at home. My mother stared at me for a moment before she turned to follow her mate.

CHAPTER 31- INTERTWINED

Dimitri's POV

"Well, that went better than I expected!" Kosta said.

"Why didn't you tell us sooner that they were arriving early?" Niko asked.

"I called, but Dimitri didn't answer his phone, so I left a message." Kosta said.

"Sorry Kosta, we slept in." Raven told him.

"I have to get back, call me if you need a ride back. Niko, send for a few men to take the luggage to the packhouse." Kosta said as Knox was unloading the luggage from the helicopter.

"Thank you, Kosta. Do we have to worry about Karla noticing the three of us gone?" Raven asked.

"No, I've taken care of Karla. It's your father you have to worry about. Being part of the shifter's council has exposed your father to some of the most vicious and cruel rumors about your mate. This won't be easy for him." Kosta told her and then looked at me. He nodded his head to me before he turned to leave. I was still in wolf form and stood next to my mate.

Kosta got back in the helicopter and the blades started spinning. Knox and Rocky moved to stand with us, and we watched as the helicopter lifted off and headed back towards the mainland.

"Are you okay?" I asked Raven through the mind link.

She couldn't manage an answer and I could feel her sadness. Her father's heart was broken, he knew he had lost his baby girl the second he saw the mark. He also didn't seem to approve of the Moon Goddess's pairing for her. A sob slipped out of her and she was suddenly overcome by sadness, guilt, and relief.

Dom licked her hand, and she wrapped her arms around his neck. "It's okay baby, it's going to be okay." I told her through the mind link.

"Raven, is ... is your mother an actual golden wolf? I mean, I know what I saw. Like ... WOW! Her roar! She's really a golden wolf, isn't she? It's not just a legend or myth, right?" Niko asked still in complete shock.

I heard a chuckle from Knox. "Yes, our mother's father, was a descendant from Apollo. A golden wolf from that line is born once every century. Our mother's mother was a descendant of the Moon Goddess and had the fire element that was also passed to our mother, Lucy. Not only is our mother the strongest of our kind, but she can tap into the power of the Gods and generate her own fire."

"Wow! Your pups will certainly be something special! It's like super wolves in the making." Niko said to Raven.

"With Dimitri being a descendant of King Lycaon and elemental, it looks like the prophecy is coming to life. I'm sure Aunt Lucy sees this." Clair said.

"Prophecy?" Niko asked and gave me a raised eyebrow look.

"I think my Aunt should explain it. It was before we were even born." Clair said.

I mind linked Dumas to send two carts up to get the luggage and we all shifted to run back to the pack-house. Niko opened the double doors and Dom trotted down the hall to our suite to shift and change. I slipped on some linen pants and a black short sleeve button up shirt then went to join the others.

"Should we go look for them?" Raven asked Knox anxiously.

"No, I linked mom already. Dad is just cooling down a bit. I left some clothes for them on the back veranda." Knox said.

Elaina served us refreshments, chilled glasses of ouzo lemonade, and meze appetizers. Niko reached for a small saganaki fried cheese square and popped it in his mouth without checking to see if it was cooled enough yet. "OWWWWW! HOT, HOT, HOT!" He danced around like a fool, fanning his open mouth with his hand, and reached for a glass of lemonade to chug down. The girls burst into laughter at him.

We continued to sit and wait for Raven's parents to return. Raven and Clair told Rocky all about Crescent Moon. Two hours later, I heard some movement outside and sensed a strong aura. I walked over to the double doors that went out to the veranda and came face to face with Raven's mother.

"Hello, Luna." I nodded my head.

"Good evening Alpha. My mate and I have just been out admiring your beautiful island." She responded.

"Thank you. Your belongings have been taken to the guest suite. It would be an honor to have you and Alpha LaRue join us for dinner, but if you would prefer a quiet dinner in your suite, we can arrange for that. I understand you may be fatigued from all the traveling."

"That's very kind of you." She smiled at me.

I could sense Diesel was still in wolf form just beyond the trees, he was listening to us. "My mate is anxious, and it troubles me. I understand you may have some preconceived notions about me, Alpha, and I hope to have the opportunity to set things right with you." I said and the black wolf stepped out of the shadows.

He stalked towards me and I could feel his angry aura radiating. He stopped next to his mate and bared his teeth at me. Obviously still upset. Lucy reached over and placed her hand on his back to calm him. We stood for a few moments staring into each other's eyes. Raven had the same blue eyes and dark shiny fur as her father.

"Alpha, I'm not going to apologize for loving my mate or reject what the Moon Goddess has done." I said. Diesel growled at me and looked like he wanted to attack, but his mate was holding him back and mind linking with him.

"Kosta was right, there are greater forces at work here.

I'd like to hear about your prophecy and share with you the prophecy I also received many years ago." I told them, this seemed to get Alpha LaRue's attention.

"Prophecy?" Lucy asked.

"Yes, Luna. The Greeks have long believed that an Oracle of the Gods still exists, the most notable Oracle of our time is Ms. Alexis Ivy, who was a friend of my mother's." I told her and noticed the sharp inhale of breath when I mentioned the Alpha's cousin.

"Please, come in. Your daughter wants to see you and I don't like seeing my mate upset. We also need to talk." I bowed my head and stepped back inside.

Twenty minutes later, Elaina and the kitchen staff started setting up dinner. We left the living room and took our seats at the round table. Alpha Diesel and Luna Lucy walked into the room holding hands.

"Mom, Dad!" Raven said and quickly moved to her parents for an embrace. I could feel her happiness which brought a smile to my face.

"At least he's not trying to rip your head off." Niko mind linked me laughing. Platters of grilled lobster tails, Greek mussles, fried fish, potatoes, saffron rice, zucchini, cucumber, and tomato salad, were set on the table.

"Wow, those lobsters are huge!" Knox said.

"That's because they're Greek." Niko smiled at him.

"This looks wonderful, thank you Alpha." Lucy said.

"Kali orexi!" I raised my glass to start the meal. Dinner went surprisingly well; Diesel didn't say much but Lucy seemed particularly interested in the olive business of the pack. She inquired about the ancient olive trees and the special reserve of fine olive oils they produced. She enjoyed cooking and was familiar with our premium and fine labels of oil.

"And the revenue from the family business, it generates enough income to sustain your pack's needs?" Diesel asked.

"I admit our humble little business is dwarfed when compared to the LaRue Enterprises empire Alpha. However, the table olive exports, for consumption, generate nearly twenty million euros in profits annually. Our olive oil labels, which hit the global market seven years ago, generate nearly twice as much."

"And your labor? Pack members or slaves?" He asked.

"Neither. The pack members who choose to live on the islands we own, caring for the groves, are also paid. The employees who work at our two large processing facilities and warehouses are well paid humans and wolves." I told him.

"What happened to the wolves from the small packs you've destroyed?" Diesel asked.

"I see you may be confusing me with Eros. The only packs I've destroyed are the ones where I may have killed an Alpha because he was engaged in slavery and trafficking. Or the ones that tried to attack my pack after I took over. I was young, a few other Alpha's thought they could pick me off easily. It's true, Greece once had a dozen packs and now we have five. Some of the smaller packs that were engaged in illegal or unethical activities have been destroyed, and I would gladly do it again."

"Why not seek the help of the shifter's council?" Diesel growled.

"You've been on the council what, ten years now Alpha? Have you not noticed that the council doesn't seem to show much interest in smaller packs? No, they're more interested in the larger packs, the ones that could disrupt the flow of order on a large scale."

"That's not true." Diesel said.

"It's not? Forgive me, but I recall both you and Alpha Georgios seemed to welcome the news of Eros' death. He was knee deep in illegal activities, trafficking omega wolves and humans as slaves on the black market. Running the human mafia business, drugs, guns, and sex. And what did the council do about it? NOTHING. Eros' pack, the Moon Warriors, is about six hundred members, not including the slaves. Alpha Georgios' pack, Zeus' Howlers, has about seven hundred members and mine is nearly three times the size. My pack, who runs a respectable business is the one the council is worried about." I said feeling the tension in the room.

Lucy broke the awkward silence. "Alpha, you said you had received a prophecy from my mate's cousin, can you share that with us?"

"Yes. My mother was friends with Ms. Alexis Ivy, I'm

not exactly sure when or how they met. When I was twelve, my mother, our beloved Luna was murdered. Which is what drove my father mad. Ms. Ivy attended my mother's funeral. Niko, Alec, and my sister were in the kitchen of our packhouse with me when she entered. Her eyes had lost color, they were white, and she walked as if she was in a trance. She placed her hand on my shoulder and spoke the prophecy."

"Do you remember what she said?" Lucy asked.

"The greatest of your kind will flourish in your hands to save us from the hells of war. Follow the dark bird to your destiny for they are intertwined." Elaina's voice said and we all turned our heads to look at her.

"I was in the kitchen that day too." She smiled.

"I thought the prophecy was about overthrowing my father, so the pack could flourish. My father was destroying the pack from the inside with his madness. Four years later, at sixteen, I shifted for the first time, which was two years sooner than normal wolves. I also discovered my elemental gift that same evening. I assumed it was a sign and challenged my father."

"Is Earth your only element?" Lucy asked.

"Yes. But I'm also a descendant of King Lycaon, who was the first werewolf turned by Zeus, so my wolf is much bigger and stronger than most." I said.

"What was your prophecy?" Niko asked.

"It was given to me when I was pregnant with the

twins, just before the Luna ceremony. I thought it meant one of the boys, they both inherited the water element. When Raven turned eighteen and discovered she had both elementals, I knew the prophecy was her destiny. I think I've always known it was her destiny. Her eyes would flash amber colors when she was a pup and experienced extreme emotions. The same thing happened to me when Alexis gave me the prophecy." She paused in thought before she continued to recite the prophecy.

"There is a war coming and a lost wolf. Only the one born from Gods can set the course. In a hundred years, a descendant will possess the power of all four and save us in the Great War to come."

Lucy took a drink of her wine. "We had a pack war and lost the most beloved wolf in our family shortly after the prophecy. As you may have noticed today, I'm born from Gods. I believe I have set the course; intertwined destinies are now coming together."

"Yours talks about war too." I said thoughtfully.

Diesel let out a low growl. "And yours talks about a dark bird with intertwined destinies ... a Raven is one of the darkest of birds."

CHAPTER 32 – TWIST

I woke up early in the morning, sprawled across Dimitri's chest. This seemed to be my favorite sleeping position. Even if I fell asleep on my side of the bed, I always seemed to wake up on top of him. Like some mysterious magnet that just drew me to him.

"Don't blame me, I sleep when you sleep." Rae said to me.

"I don't mind being your pillow baby, it makes Dom happy." Dimitri said as he opened his beautiful warm honey colored eyes. I kissed his chest and I'm almost certain I heard a purr from deep within. I ran my hands across his chiseled abs and heard a low growl in his throat. I wanted him.

"I'm trying to behave; your parents are under the same roof. If you keep that up little bird, they won't see us until dinner." He groaned at me.

"I wouldn't mind." Rae purred at me.

"Ughh, you're right. We should probably get showered and dressed. I needed to talk with my parents and find out how long they intended to stay. Surely they won't insist on me returning with them now." I said.

"Your father wouldn't dare upset his mate. Hell, I don't even want to upset her." Dimitri laughed.

We went into the kitchen to find my mother helping

Elaina with breakfast. Niko, Rocky, and Clair were already seated and eating. They had a platter full of delicious looking omelettes ready to be devoured. "Good morning, can you believe all the eggs are fresh from the chicken coop. I got to help gather the eggs this morning." My mother said enthusiastically, she enjoyed cooking.

"Dumas keeps a lot of chickens on the island for meat and eggs." Elaina told us.

"Fresh eggs make the best omelettes." Niko said stuffing his mouth full.

"Where's dad?" I asked.

"He's already had breakfast. Knox and your father went down to a little beach on the western side of the island to train with the sea. I guess it's not the same as training with the water from rivers or lakes." My mom said.

"Well, why didn't I get an invite? If anyone needs more training it's me." I scoffed.

I don't get it, my dad always did this! He spent more time training with my older brothers and only taught me the easy things. Just because they would both be the Alpha's of our two family packs, doesn't mean my training was any less important. For crying out loud, I'm standing in the middle of a shit storm with a deranged mafia boss who wants me dead; but at least I can perform a simple water bubble while my brother learns to part the fucking sea!

I ran out the back door fuming and could hear my

mother call out my name. I ignored her, ran into the trees, then slipped my clothes off and shifted. Rae picked up the dress in her mouth and ran to the only beach on the island.

When I reached the beach, my father and Knox had pushed the ocean back about five yards. They were both using their water element and holding it back like a wall of seawater. Rae let out a bark and they both turned to look at me. They lost their concentration dropping the wall that splashed back up to the shoreline. I went back behind a large bush and put my dress on, then I marched back to the beach to talk to my father.

"You know, Knox and Peter are not your only gifted children. Why do you only show me the easy stuff and they get to learn the big stuff?" I asked.

"Raven, we haven't had much time to develop your gift." My father told me.

"That's right and yet here you are, training Knox and completely forgot to invite me. Just because I'm not going to be an Alpha of a pack, doesn't mean I don't need the same training. I can do party tricks with water while my brothers can kill people with their gift." I snapped.

"And is that what you want? To kill people?" My dad asked.

"Of course not, but I still need to know how to defend myself and my pack." I replied.

"Well you have a very strong mate who will protect

you now, won't you Alpha?" My father said and I turned around to see Dimitri walking towards us on the beach.

"What's the problem here?" Dimitri asked me.

"My father was just training my brother how to hold the sea back." I tried not to sound like I was whining. "I haven't had as much—"

A popping noise rang out and Dimitri threw me to the sand before I registered what happened. A whizzing sound flew just over us, and my father roared out. Someone was shooting at us.

"NO, DON'T SHIFT! You'll be an easy big target on this beach. GET DOWN!" Dimitri called out to my father and used his element to lift the sand in the air to give us some cover. He also created a trench-like ditch in the ground to sink us into with his element.

Dimitri was still laying on top of me and looked out at the ocean. "There's two boats, wolves and they have silver bullets. Now would be a good time to try the sea wall, high waves, or better yet a whirlpool!" Dimitri said.

"Ohhh, I've never tried a whirlpool before." Knox said with longing in his eyes to try a whirlpool.

"They just tried to shoot someone we all love, with a silver bullet. Focus your angry energy on the water beneath the boat. Picture the water moving in a big vortex, a whirlpool pool that will suck them down." Dimitri told us.

"Did he just say he loved us?" Rae asked me.

251

I looked out at the water and did as Dimitri instructed, how the hell did they find us so quickly? A silver bullet would have been deadly to me, and it pissed me off! I thought about what happened to Leo and what they just tried to do to us, rage started to build inside of me. The water started spinning and their boats moved in a circle.

Dimitri floated around a few big boulders, to look like moving shadows. A few more bullets zipped at the floating boulders. These wolves were sent here to kill. Dimitri got angry and sent a massive boulder tumbling down from the edge of the cliff at one of the boats and it capsized into the whirlpool.

"Knox, are you making the water spin?" My dad asked.

"No!" Knox replied. They both looked at me with recognition in their eyes.

"Well? Are you going to gawk at me or help?" I said.

My father looked out at the spinning water and channeled his energy into it, the whirlpool started spinning faster. Moving river or lake water was so much easier than ocean water. The ocean had a mind of its own, with its own energy, forces, currents, and rip tides to work against. Knox also joined in and the boats were still spinning out of control. Dimitri sent another massive boulder flying at the boats and the second boat was on its side.

The power of the whirlpool pulled everything to the bottom and when we finally stopped, we sat waiting and watching for any survivors. Dimitri had mind linked Niko and the island warriors, they arrived at the beach.

"We've just had an attempted breach. Two boats, about a dozen wolves total, armed with silver bullets. I need the entire island fully patrolled now and everyone on high alert." Dimitri instructed.

"No one knows the location of this island. How did they find us?" Niko asked.

"I think you may have a traitor." My father told Dimitri.

"Maybe. Or possibly a tracking device of some sort." Dimitri said.

"Raven, you almost got hit with a silver bullet. You're not immune to silver and could have ended up like your grandfather. I think you should come home until all of this is sorted out." My father said.

"I am home!" I snapped back. What the hell is wrong with my dad? I needed to be with my mate, especially during this difficult time. I wasn't about to crawl into some hole and hide.

"That's not a bad idea." Dimitri said.

"Excuse me?" Rae popped off in my mind.

"Excuse me?" I echoed her sentiment out loud.

"None of these men survived. We don't know if they belong to Stefanos or possibly Hades. We can send you back with your parents and put the word out that you had been attacked and killed with a silver bullet."

Dimitri said.

"I'm not leaving." I said.

"I need you to be safe, I can't do what I need to do if you're in danger. If anything happens to you Dom won't be able to function." Dimitri said.

"What are we going to do, fake my funeral? I'm not hiding! We know where Stefanos is, we need to plan his takedown. If Hades is seeking revenge for his murdering father, I will burn him alive and send him to the underworld where he belongs." I said nearly growling.

"Who's Hades?" My father asked.

"He's Eros' only son, just turned eighteen, and will be Alpha of the Moon Warriors now. Their territory is north of mine, just past Mount Olympus and Georgios is east of it. I've been considering taking that pack, Eros was a terrible Alpha and his son will probably be worse." Dimitri said.

"If we help you with Stefanos, will you help me take that pack from Hades?" My father asked.

"Wait, what?" I asked.

"You want another pack?" Knox asked in disbelief.

"Yes. It's a small pack but perfect for Roman. I'm sure Raven has mentioned her five brothers. Knox is the heir of Crescent Moon and Peter is set to take Dark Moon from my brother. They will be twenty-one soon and have been training for the last three years to take over their packs. My brother and I will have more free time now. Roman will be eighteen in less than nine months and I'm sure he would love his own pack. My older brother Ranger and Clair's parents could also rotate and travel back and forth to help Roman with the pack. Plus, it will give us a good reason to be close to our daughter and niece." My father said.

"What about LaRue Enterprises?" I asked.

"What about it? We can easily open up a branch in Athens. I still expect you to be my CEO someday." My father smiled as if he had given this some thought already.

"You don't need an excuse to visit with your daughter Alpha, you are welcome anytime. If you want Eros' pack, I'll be happy to help you take it. The last thing Greece needs is another corrupt pack run by Eros' son. I don't think the shifter's council will care." Dimitri told my dad.

"I'll handle the shifter's council." My father said.

"I like the twist! Let's get back to the packhouse and make sure everyone is Okay. I also need to call my Gamma and Delta to warn them, Stefanos may send men to the pack as well." Dimitri said.

We shifted into our wolves and ran back to the packhouse. Rae enjoyed running with Duke, Dom, and Knight. When we reached the packhouse, my mother was sitting on the veranda with Clair. "Well aren't you quite the sight to see, four black Alpha wolves." She smiled.

CHAPTER 33 – DOLOS

"A vast sea, thousands of islands, and they found us that fast?" My mother asked when we explained what had just happened.

"Stefanos must be working with Hades now." Niko said.

"Maybe we should take the pack from Hades first and cut off a resource to Stefanos?" I suggested.

"But it still doesn't explain how we were tracked to the island. When I purchased the islands, my attorney did it with sole anonymity as a shell corporation. The island is also off the grid with its own water and electric supply." Dimitri said.

"Do you have scramblers on your internet?" My father asked.

"Yes." Dimitri said.

"Any new additions to your staff or pack brought to the island?" My mother asked.

"The same loyal members from our mainland pack." Dimitri looked lost in thought.

"Alpha, I've got Alec and Spiro on the phone." Niko said.

"Put them on speaker." Dimitri said. He explained what

had just occurred on the beach and Alec also suggested taking out the northern pack. Eros' son, Hades, was bad news. Spiro was going to double the patrols but reported nothing out of the ordinary. I reminded everyone not to trust scent alone because many wolves in Greece hide their scent.

"When should we expect Odessa to return?" Alec asked.

"What do you mean? She came back after Leo's funeral, didn't she?" Dimitri asked.

"No, she didn't." Alec responded.

"I thought you knew." Knox said.

"Knew what?" I could feel Dimitri's tension rising.

"Alpha Georgios said he would talk to you about it. He's Odessa's mate." Knox told us.

"WHAT?" Dimitri, Niko, and Alec all responded in unison.

"It's true, she asked us not to say anything until Alpha Georgios had the chance to speak with you." My mother added.

"I'LL FUCKING KILL HIM!" Dimitri growled.

"You can't interfere with the Moon Goddess' plans." My father suppressed a laugh at Dimitri's overprotective reaction. My mother gave my dad the eye and the smirk from his face disappeared.

"Where's your mate, Knox?" Dimitri asked my brother.

"Rocky wanted to sleep in and then take a long warm bath. I can go get her if you want." Knox said.

"Please do." Dimitri told him and Knox left the room to fetch Rocky.

"Alpha, should I get Georgios on the phone?" Niko asked.

"Yes."

I could just imagine how this was going to go. Odessa was Dimitri's only family; he had practically raised her himself. If they thought my father reacted poorly, wait until they see Dimitri's reaction. I could feel his emotions and he was ready to explode.

"It's a very nice pack and can easily be reached in five hours from your pack. She's still going to be fairly close to you." My mother tried to calm Dimitri.

"Hello, Alpha Dimitri." Georgios voice came out of the speaker phone.

"Where's my sister?" Dimitri skipped the formalities and got straight to the point.

"Ahh, I was hoping to speak with you about that tomorrow, when you returned to the mainland."

"What makes you think I'd be returning to the mainland tomorrow Georgios?" Dimitri asked and I could feel his suspicion.

"I-I assumed you would make your way home or to my pack once you heard about your sister and I being mates." Georgios said.

"You assumed wrong. However, if you don't put my sister on the phone, I will not hesitate to come rip your throat out." Dimitri growled.

"How are your in-laws doing? Has Alpha LaRue taken a liking to you?" Georgios quickly changed the subject.

My father opened his mouth to speak but Dimitri raised his hand and placed a finger to his lips to tell him to be quiet. We all got the message and stood quietly.

"I'm afraid Alpha LaRue is not very fond of me. Must be all those beast stories he's heard. He refuses to be in my company and has threatened to end me. I believe they left the island last night. I'm not sure what he's planning, but I don't trust him." Dimitri said and we all exchanged puzzled looks.

"I'm sorry to hear that. Families can be difficult sometimes, especially when they are overprotective of their females. I wonder if Alpha LaRue will reach out for my help? You have his daughter and I have your sister." Georgios said.

"Well Georgios, it seems that you and I are practically family now, surely you will not stand with LaRue." Dimitri said.

"And how is your mate? Have you claimed her yet?"

"I need to talk to my sister, *now!*" Dimitri emphasized the now.

"I'm afraid MY MATE is a little tied up at the moment and can't come to the phone." Georgios said.

"TIED UP? YOU HAVE ONE FUCKING HOUR TO HAVE HER CALL ME BACK. IF YOU HAVE HARMED HER IN ANY WAY, I WILL KILL YOU!" Dimitri roared and discontented the phone.

"You suspect Georgios?" My father asked.

"Yes, other than you and him, no one else outside of my pack knew we would be retreating to an island. His assumption that I would be returning so soon, is very suspicious. As if he knew about the attack." Dimitri said.

"Does he actually know where the island is?" My mother asked.

"No, but he may have a way of finding the location." Dimitri said.

"Kalimera Alpha, you wanted to see me." Rocky said as she and Knox entered the room.

"Kalimera. Rocky, do you have a cell phone here with you, on the island?" Dimitri asked.

"Yes."

"Did you contract the phone yourself or is it a pack cell phone?"

"No, Alpha Georgios provides them to all the top ranked wolves." She said.

"He pinged the location of her phone!" My father said.

"That treacherous bastard!" Dimitri growled.

"Has Alpha Georgios tried calling you since we left?" My father asked Rocky.

"Yes, last night. He wanted to check to see how I was doing and asked if Alpha LaRue and Alpha Dimitri were getting along." she said.

"And what did you tell him?" Dimitri asked.

"I told him that it wasn't going well and that Alpha LaRue was not happy."

"Excellent. Knox, I need you to destroy her phone. We'll get you a new one when we're on the mainland Rocky." Dimitri told her.

"Okay, but what happened?" Rocky asked.

Dimitri quickly explained what happened on the beach and his suspicion. Rocky confirmed that Alpha Georgios was connected to Eros' son Hades, whom she had seen meeting with Alpha Georgios the day they returned with Leo's body. I had a bad feeling about Hades.

The phone rang and everyone stood still for a moment. Niko nodded to Dimitri who gave him a nod back to answer it. Niko clicked the speakerphone and Dimitri said. "Hello."

"Hello brother!" Odessa's voice rang out.

"Is it true?" Dimitri asked.

"Yes, the Moon Goddess has blessed me with Alpha Georgios as my mate."

"Why didn't you call and tell me immediately about your mate?"

"I've just discovered my mate and wanted to spend time getting to know him. Alpha Georgios has been without a Luna for the six years he's had the pack. I've so much to learn and take care of for my new pack. We're planning to visit you soon, please don't worry about me. I think you have bigger things to worry about."

"Is everything okay? Is he treating you well?" Dimitri asked.

"Absolutely, as wonderful as Imara and Alec! One can only dream of being this lucky."

"I'm happy to hear that." Dimitri said, but he certainly didn't look happy. "I'll be seeing both of you real soon."

"Dimitri, don't forget, I found Dolos and he's mine. Please remember to have someone feed him for me." Odessa said.

There was an awkward silence as Niko and Dimitri exchanged glances. "Of course, your cat Dolos is in good hands, we'll take care of him." Dimitri said.

"See, she's doing great Alpha." Georgios was back on the phone.

"Take care of my sister Georgios. If you happen to see my in-laws, I'd appreciate a phone call." Dimitri said and disconnected.

"What was that all about?" My father asked.

"Did she say Imara and Alec? I didn't know that Alec had a mate?" I inquired.

"He doesn't. Alec was the first to find his mate. He met Imara the week after he turned eighteen, she was a year older than him and in love with a human in the city. She rejected Alec and he's never been the same since."

"So, Odessa was sending us a secret message!" I said.

"Are we sure it was a secret message?" My mother asked.

"Yes! She spoke about Dolos." Niko said as if that would make sense.

"When Odessa was a pup, she had a little black cat named Dolos. He was a mischievous, sneaky little thing, so the name suited him. There's an old Greek God named Dolos, who was the master of trickery, deceit, lies, and traps."

"Is Dolos still alive?" My mother asked.

"No. He's been dead for a long time now. What she actually said was, I found Dolos, he's *mine*." Dimitri emphasized the word mine.

"Mine, as in her mate! As in, Georgios is Dolos and planning something cunning!" Niko said.

"My sister is in trouble and she's discovered some deceitful plot. That's why Georgios is acting weird and is probably hoping Alpha LaRue will want me dead or help overpower me." Dimitri said.

"With Georgios thinking that we're not on the island and disapprove of you, he may believe that we could be allies." My father said.

"Do you believe that Stefanos is working with Hades or Georgios?" My mother asked.

"Without a doubt! Eros was Stefanos' right hand man. There's no way Hades, as his only son and heir isn't involved. Now that we know of Georgios' connection to Hades, Stefanos must be pulling the strings." Dimitri responded.

"And don't forget his control of the rogues. Those two packs, combined with rogues and silver bullets, may just be the small army he needs to take us out." Niko said.

"Our pack struggled financially for a few years. Georgios liked to gamble on the stock market. Then we started getting more purchased slaves, omegas I'd never seen before. Something felt suspicious but no one ever questioned him, he's on the shifter's council, so we assumed he had received aid of some kind." Rocky told us.

"And the slaves?" My mother practically growled. She's always been sensitive to slave labor and even suffered for a few years at the hands of her stepmother when my Uncle Ranger first became Alpha. Those were the worst four years of her life and she would never knowingly allow anyone to be treated like a slave.

"They're still there. He keeps them well dressed and clean, to look like hired servants. They have small rooms and bunk beds, down in the basement." Rocky said.

My mother let out a snarling growl. "Alpha Dimitri, please send for Kosta, my mate and I will be returning to Georgios pack this evening." We all stood paralyzed for a moment and looked at my mother. Her aura was dangerously strong, and her amber colored eyes came to life with rage and fire!

CHAPTER 34 – BLAST

Dimitri's POV

"Kosta should be landing with the helicopter in about ten minutes." I informed Diesel and Lucy. We stood at the northern peak of the island waiting for Kosta. Lucy was insistent about returning to Alpha Georgios pack right away.

"I'll see if I can speak with Odessa alone first. I'll call Knox when I've spoken to her, so he can update you. We'll let Georgios believe that Knox has returned to Crescent Moon with Rocky, and that we've remained in Greece because Alpha LaRue isn't convinced that Raven wants to be with you. That he's considering taking your head for stealing our only daughter and forcing her to mate with you." Lucy told me.

"Mother!" Raven protested at the idea of forced mating.

"We'll see if Georgios will lead us to Stefanos or if he lets anything slip. If we hit a dead end, I'll light Georgios up and send him straight to hell." Lucy said.

"I can position my warriors just outside his pack territory to lead an attack and help if things get sticky for you." I offered.

"I don't think his pack will put up much resistance, all they have to do is see your wolf. Greeks are taught wolf history and legends from a young age. Everyone will know you are born from Gods with just one look at you. This puts you at a much higher level than an Alpha. No one will dare defy you." Rocky said.

"I wouldn't say no one, some have tried before and failed." Lucy replied with a smile.

"Wait until they see her in action." Diesel grinned.

"Georgios seemed really interested in our reaction to Alpha Dimitri and Raven. He was acting strange; something was definitely off. If he's dealing with Hades and Stefanos, he's going to have wolfbane and silver like Eros' yacht." Lucy said.

"I'm not sure I like this plan anymore." I told her. I couldn't possibly let them walk into that trap. Wolfbane and silver is a lethal combination, Georgios would also use it if needed. I can't let Raven's parents take that risk.

"Oh, don't worry about my mate, she can take out a small army by herself. Besides, she's the only wolf on this planet who's immune to silver and wolfbane." Diesel told me.

"Really? She's immune?"

"Golden wolf!" He smiled.

"Mate will give our pups the strongest genes ever." Dom told me.

"Alec has already ordered trackers to locate Hades. Are we going to deal with Georgios first?" Niko asked.

"We'll return to the pack in case they're planning to

attack our pack first. Georgios is definitely dirty, he had to have tracked our location. I'll wait for the update from Alpha and Luna LaRue, then decide the next course of action from there." I told Niko.

The helicopter came into view and got louder as it got closer. Wolf hearing is so sensitive, we could hear noises at greater distances or noises others couldn't. We stood back and watched the helicopter land. When the blades stopped, Kosta stepped out.

"Alpha Dimitri. Alpha LaRue. Luna." He extended his hand and shook each of ours. "Our sources tell us that Stefanos left Santorini last night and headed towards the mainland. We believe he's in Athens." Kosta added.

"We need to return to Alpha Georgios' pack, I'll explain everything on the flight back." Diesel told him.

"Alpha Dimitri, will you be staying or need a ride back as well?" Kosta asked me.

"Thank you, but we're leaving in the next hour with the speed boat. I'll call you in a few hours when we're back at the pack. I have something I want you to look into for me." I told him.

"Of course." Kosta nodded his head and prepared for takeoff.

Raven finished packing her things and sat on the bed lost in thought. I had hoped we would have had more time on the island alone. Dom also needed some time alone with Rae. Everything was moving so fast and my mate was worried about her parents, my sister, and possibly being attacked. I could feel all of her thoughts, she even felt guilty about Leo's death. I sat next to her and held her for a while to help calm her.

"Can we come back soon?" She asked.

"Of course, this is one of our homes." I kissed her.

We left the luggage out in the foyer; Dumas was going to send it back with staff this evening. Elaina and the staff that came with her would be returning this evening as well. Rocky and Knox
would be returning to our pack with Elaina; disguised as staff, in case someone was watching the marina.

We took the golf carts back down to the dock and boarded the boat. Niko sat at the driver's seat, with Clair at his side. Raven sat beside me, she put her head on my chest and it made Dom happy. We drove back to Athens; the water was a little rough and slowed us down a bit. The sky was cloudy, and rain was in the forecast for this afternoon. I could see the marina approaching and Niko dropped the speed of the boat when we entered the no wake speed zone.

We slowly cruised to our dock and I scanned the marina. I saw the car that Alec had sent for us in the distance waiting. I picked up the anchor rope, and leaned over to the dock, ready to step out and tie the boat down. The boat gently bumped the dock and Niko turned the engine off. I heard a strange beeping sound coming from beneath the dock and realized what it was. Niko also recognized the faint beeps and quickly tried to shield his mate with his body.

BOOM! An explosion erupted and the dock was blown to bits. The impact from the blast sent our boat flying upside down and we were thrown into the water with debris falling around us. I swam up, my head broke the surface of the water and a big cloud of smoke surrounded us. The smell of fuel was strong and a moment later, there was another loud **BOOM** as our boat exploded.

Raven was by my side and I could see her mouth moving but I couldn't hear anything. There was a ringing in my ears from the sound of the explosion, I was closest to the blast. Niko motioned to the dock and I could see people looking at the fiery mess. Clair was clinging to him and noticed blood in the water. That was a lot of blood, someone was bleeding badly. Raven said something and pointed but I couldn't understand what it was.

"I can't hear anything. My ears are ringing." I said or maybe I yelled, I couldn't tell. I tried to mind link Niko, but it didn't seem to work, the ringing in my head was loud.

Raven moved us in the water towards shore quickly using her element. We stumbled up onto the shore and I felt a little disoriented. I looked down and found a large piece of metal had pierced my abdomen. My other cuts had already started healing but the metal would need to be removed quickly and would require treatment. Raven grabbed my arm and motioned for us to move. Thank the Goddess she appeared to be unharmed.

Clair looked pale and shaken but okay, Niko refused to set her down and carried her to our waiting car. Our pack warrior, Gus, had been sent with the car to get us, he started running towards us. I could feel the warmth of blood running from my abdomen down my leg, it was trickling on the ground pretty fast and left a trail behind me.

Gus' lips moved but I still couldn't hear anything. Raven said something to him, and he nodded his head. We reached the vehicle and I slid in the back. Raven sat next to me and her worried face started swimming in my vision. She put her hand on my face. Goddess, she is so beautiful! I hated seeing her so worried it was just a minor scratch, I'll be okay. My vision darkened and my eyes closed, I fought to keep them open, but the darkness sucked me in.

I opened my eyes and recognized the room, we were back at the packhouse. It was dark and I could see Raven was sitting in the armchair next to the bed. She had a few candles burning and her head buried in a book, it was an ancient book from my library about werewolf healing. I moved my hand and her head shot up.

"You're awake." I heard her say with my right ear. The left was still ringing, and I couldn't hear anything with that ear.

"How did we get here?" I croaked.

"You can hear me?" She asked.

"Just with the right ear. The left is still ringing." The sound of her beautiful voice sent warm sensations through me.

"We took you to see Kosta's physician, Dr. Homer. He removed the metal and performed emergency surgery to fix your intestines. After your surgery, we brought you back here. You've been asleep since yesterday and it's almost midnight."

"Are you okay? How's Rae doing?" I asked.

"We're fine." She gave me a warm smile.

"Where's Niko? Have we heard from your parents yet?"

"Everything is fine, Niko is with Clair, she knocked her head on something and had a concussion. She should be recovered by now. Your healing will take a few days, Dr. Vovos has been checking on you every few hours. She said that your hearing should return as you heal."

"Is Knox here? Have we heard from your parents? My sister?" I asked.

"Please try to take it easy. Knox and Rocky are here, he received a phone call from my mother today, my parents are with Georgios and Odessa. My mother hasn't had the opportunity to speak with Odessa alone yet. She's still unmarked but Georgios is keeping her close. Don't worry, if anyone can handle this, it's my mother." Raven assured me.

There was a knock on the door. "Come in." Raven called out and Knox stepped in.

"Glad to see you're awake."

"Thank you."

"I just received a call from Dad, Odessa went for a run this evening and was taken. Georgios believes Hades took her, or at least that's what Georgios is saying. Apparently, some of Hades' warriors were seen near the border of Georgios' pack territory. My dad thinks something is fishy, that Georgios has hidden Odessa somewhere and is blaming Hades."

"But if we believe Hades has her, then he knows we would attack Hades. Is this his way of using us to overthrow Hades? I thought he and Hades would be working together?" Raven said.

"Stefanos would naturally be working with Hades because Hades was Eros' heir. Maybe Georgios is counting on us taking out Stefanos and then he could use this as an excuse to take Eros' pack for himself." I said.

"Georgios' pack doesn't have a lot of financial resources, that would make sense." Knox said.

"So, what's the plan?" I asked.

"Our mom is going to challenge Georgios for his pack." Knox smiled like the Cheshire Cat.

CHAPTER 35 – PATIENT

"If he's done something to my sister, I can't just lie around and do nothing. I need to find her. I'm going to kill him myself." Dimitri growled trying to stand up.

"She's our sister now too. You won't be helpful to anyone if you don't allow that to heal." Knox replied.

"Dimitri please." I tried to calm my mate down. "She's his mate, he won't hurt her."

"Unless one of them rejects the other, then he will." Dimitri said.

"He wouldn't be that stupid, he knows she's your sister and doesn't want to make an enemy of you." I told him.

"Maybe, but Odessa might reject him first, she's not happy about this." He said.

"My parents are with Georgios; they know something isn't right. We'll find her, we just need you to heal. Dr. Vovos should be here to check your wound and change the bandage one more time for the night. You can speak to her about your progress." I said.

"I need to get to Georgios, if Odessa is still in his territory, I can find her." Dimitri said.

"We'll go together as soon as you're healed a little bit more." I told Dimitri and stroked his arm praying his healing would be quick. Rae whimpered in my mind, she was also concerned.

There was a gentle knock at the door and Knox pulled the door open. Dr. Vovos stepped in and walked over to Dimitri. "Good evening Alpha." She said.

"Dr. Vovos, how long until I'm fully healed?"

"That all depends on the patient. I'll have a better assessment once I've examined you and after you eat something." She told Dimitri.

"Should I get him something from the kitchen?" I asked.

"I'm going to mind link the kitchen staff for some scrambled eggs and toast. You need to start on something easy first." She said.

"So, no rib-eye steak?" Dimitri smirked.

"Not for the next day or so Alpha." She removed the bandages and looked pleased with the progress. She sprayed something on it and dabbed it with gauze. It looked much better already; wolf healing was fast but those born with Alpha blood seemed to heal faster.

"How's the hearing?" She asked while looking into his ears.

"Still ringing in the left, but I can hear out of the right ear."

"That may take a few days to heal." Dr. Vovos said.

"Will I live to have pups?" Dimitri asked and winked at me.

PAULINA VASQUEZ

"Of course you will Alpha, just don't try making any for the next day or two. You're healing faster than I expected. Also, no shifting for twenty-four hours. Eat what I've ordered from the kitchen, it should be here soon. I'll be back in the morning."

"Thanks, Doc." He said.

"Good night Luna, call if you need anything." She smiled warmly at me and left the room.

"I'm going to leave you two alone now, we'll talk about our plan in the morning. If anything changes tonight, I'll let you know." Knox said and closed the door behind him. A second later, Knox opened the door back up for the young lady delivering the food tray.

"Thank you." I told her and took the tray of food from her.

"Are you going to be my nurse?" Dimitri gave me a sexy grin.

"Mmm, mmh! Isn't he just delicious?" Rae purred at me.

"You have to behave yourself Alpha, you heard the doctor." I teased him and felt my heart skip a beat.

"I also heard Rae." His smile widened and I blushed.

"Here open your mouth." I forked some scrambled eggs and fed him.

"Do I get the toast too?"

"Yes, would you like butter on it?"

"Yes please."

I spread the butter on the toast and noticed I had some on my finger. He took my hand, lifted my finger to his mouth, and licked it slowly. Then he took my finger and placed it in his mouth, sucking on it. Dear Goddess, this man was going to torture me. I could feel my insides pulsing with heat for him as I gazed at his bare chest. He was completely naked under the blanket. I wanted to be naked too, pressed up against him, petting, rubbing, kissing, licking, and tasting.

"Well, what are you waiting for? An official invitation?" He laughed, clearly reading my thoughts. "Take your clothes off and come lie with me little bird. Rubbing and kissing is a prescribed part of my physical therapy."

"You don't have to tell me twice." Rae told me. I watched Dimitri finish eating and moved the tray to the table on the other side of the room. Then I turned off the lights and undressed. I slowly scooted over next to Dimitri and laid against his side.

"Nothing wrong with my chest." He smiled and rubbed his chest, inviting me to lay my head on it.

"I better not, I'm worried I might wake up laying on top of you."

"And why would that be a bad idea?"

"I don't want to hurt your wound." I whispered.

"I'm practically healed, the stitches are starting to fall

out. I should be near perfect by morning. Now kiss me!"

I leaned in and kissed him. I should have stopped while I could, after he kissed me, he moved to my neck. As soon as his mouth landed on his mark, a moan escaped me, and I felt myself getting aroused. I need to stop, I need to stop, I need to stop, I kept telling myself. His arm wrapped around my lower back and lifted me to bring my chest at eye level for him.

"What are you doing, you heard Dr. Vovos." I said, practically panting as he kissed down my neck to my chest.

"She said, I shouldn't make any pups for a day or two. Don't worry, I can wait until next week to put one in you." He teased and took my nipple in his mouth. At least, I think he was teasing.

I was completely lost, my head tilted back as I pushed my chest further into his face. The sparks shooting through my body and my need for him was growing stronger. No Raven, I mentally scolded myself, he's recovering. I tried to pull away, but he had a stronghold on me and growled when I tried to move. I looked down to make sure I was nowhere near his wound and noticed his erection under the blanket. Without thinking, I reached down and started petting it. Dimitri moaned and licked my other nipple before sucking on it.

I moved my hand under the blanket and wrapped it around his girth. It felt so hard and smooth, I wanted to please him, to taste it. Instinctively, I moved down his chest, kissing and licking. I placed a soft kiss over his wound and continued lower until I found my target. My lips parted and I looked up at this sexy man who was my mate before taking him into my mouth.

His eyes filled with intense desire and I heard a growl in his chest, obviously telling me he liked it. My hand wandered up to his thigh, caressing him, while my head moved slowly up and down, teasing him. I couldn't believe I had this effect on him and so much control. I began to suck a little harder and he threw his head back.

"Fuck!" He moaned in response. I moved a little faster and tried to take as much into my mouth as I could. His sweet scent engulfed me, and the taste made me hungry for more.

"Naughty little wolf. You heard the doctor's orders." He groaned.

"Should I stop?" I looked up at him.

He wrapped his fist into my hair and guided me back down to his throbbing cock. "How shall I punish you, I'm practically on my death bed and you're over here teasing me. You know I can't have my way with you right now." He groaned. I continued to stroke him while I sucked harder, I was on a mission.

"We could always get on top." Rae suggested to me, though I wasn't sure I could handle being on top and taking all of him at once.

"That's a great idea, Rae." Dimitri smiled.

"You want me to... get on top?" I asked.

"Do you need a spanking first?" He raised a sexy eyebrow.

I was soaking wet with excitement by now and the last thing I needed was a spanking that would tease me. I moved up to him and straddled my knees on each side of his hip, the only light in the room was the moonlight through the windows. "I don't want to hurt you." I whispered.

"Don't worry, you won't. Take my hands and move at your own pace." He said.

I slipped my fingers through his and he held them up to help steady me. I moaned out when I felt his bulge rubbing right where I wanted it most. I began rubbing his length between my wet folds and he moaned. "You're so hot and wet."

I lifted my hips up and felt his cock spring upwards, the tip was just outside my opening and I slowly started lowering myself onto it, moaning with pleasure. It felt so good to feel him filling me up. I paused a moment and started rocking up and down trying to adjust to him. "Yes." I breathed out greedily wanting this.

"Don't force it, baby, your body will get used to me. Just enjoy yourself and the rest will happen naturally." He cooed at me.

I took a deep breath and continued to focus on the pleasure and my mate. Dimitri threw his head back and moaned, "you feel amazing." I tried to take the last few inches but didn't seem to have enough room. I was fully stretched, and it felt so good. I continued to grind my hips when the first waves of orgasm hit me, and I cried out in ecstasy. "Give it to me," he breathlessly whispered. Colors floated in my vision and my body quivered as I released on him.

Like a madwoman, I couldn't stop. I needed him, to feel him, all of him in me. I began to rub my clit and ride him even harder. I heard his breathing getting faster and another growl rippled in his throat. I knew he was getting closer to release and I was building up for another.

I felt my insides gripping him tighter; his cock was so hard, and he was ready to explode. My body trembled as my orgasm rocked through me. Dimitri growled out, my spasming pussy sent him over the edge and I could feel his release inside of me.

After catching my breath, I rolled off Dimitri and looked up at his hooded eyes. He leaned down and kissed the top of my head. "That was the best physical therapy ever. I believe you have just saved me from the brink of death." He grinned.

Sunlight was pouring through the windows and I was tucked up into Dimitri's side. His arm was wrapped around me and when I tried to wiggle free, he held me down tighter.

"I have to get dressed before Dr. Vovos returns to check on you." I told him. There was a knock at the door.

"It's Spiro." Dimitri said. I pulled the covers up over my neck and wasn't sure what else to do.

"Come in" Dimitri called out and the door opened.

"Good morning Alpha, Good morning Luna. I wasn't sure if you were awake yet, please forgive the intrusion." Spiro said.

"What is it?" Dimitri asked.

"Alpha, we've just discovered a beaten body at the edge of the pack territory."

"Do we know who it is?" Dimitri asked.

"It's our former Beta, Kosta Stamos."

CHAPTER 36 – CLAIMING

Dimitri's POV

"He's going to be okay, won't he Dr. Vovos?" Niko asked.

"I've known Kosta since he was a pup, your Uncle is one of the strongest wolves I've ever met." Dr. Vovos assured us.

The pack clinic was a mile down the road from the packhouse. It was morning, we had to wait until Dr. Vovos had stabilized Kosta before we could see him. He was connected to machines and tubes, he looked pretty bad.

"How long until he wakes up?" I asked, I needed to talk to him. Find out who did this. He was savagely beaten and shot with a silver bullet. The silver should have killed him, it's a miracle that he even survived.

"He's stable for now, but he's not out of the woods yet. It could be a few days or a few weeks. We don't even know the status of his wolf yet." She said.

Shit! We don't have that kind of time to sit around and wait. I needed to get going, Georgios' pack was five hours northeast of here. I mind linked Alec and Spiro to meet me in my office in twenty minutes and bring Knox and Rocky with them.

"Dr. Vovos, my mate has some business to attend at another pack, is he okay to leave?" Raven asked.

"Aww how sweet is that? Luna is worried about the big bad Alpha." Niko mind linked me with a goofy smile on his face.

"All the stitches have fallen off already." I lifted my shirt to show Dr. Vovos.

"And how's the hearing?" She asked.

"Barely a low ringing in the left ear, but I can hear out of both now."

"That should correct itself once you've shifted, but I don't want you to shift today to make sure your internal wound is completely healed first Alpha."

"Thank you Dr. Vovos. I'm going to be away for a day or two, please keep Niko fully updated on Kosta's progress."

We entered the packhouse and made our way to my office. Alec, Spiro, Knox, and Rocky were already there waiting for us. Niko and Clair followed us back. I didn't exactly have a plan, so I was just going to wing it. I couldn't sit and wait any longer.

"I need to get to Georgios' pack, my sister has turned up missing. There's a good chance that she may have rejected Georgios and ran away. If she turns up here, let me know immediately."

"What if Hades has her to lure you in?" Rocky asked.

"I'm going to kill Hades as soon as Georgios is taken

care of." I said.

"Who are we bringing with us?" Niko asked.

"We're not bringing anyone Niko. You're the Beta and should remain here, in case Hades tries to attack the pack before I could return."

"Then the Alpha should be here to prepare for an attack, I can go look for Odessa." Niko said.

"An Alpha will be here. Knox is taking over the largest pack in the world in a few months, he can help prepare and secure Olympus Blood Moon for an attack. His aura is just as strong as mine, those who have never seen me before won't know the difference."

"I'm happy to fill in." Knox said.

"Alec, send some scouts out to Moon Warriors pack, I want to know what Hades is up to. Make sure they mask their scents. Kosta was going to send a few men out to survey things and report back but obviously, we won't know anything until Kosta is awake." I said.

"Alpha, my father is still Georgios' Beta, he's a good person." Rocky said nervously.

"I know Rocky, we won't let anything happen to him." I told her.

"When are we leaving?" Raven asked.

"Now."

Raven and I sat in the black Jeep just outside the territory boundary for Zeus' Howlers, waiting for their warrior to clear us to enter. He looked stunned when he heard my name. This was an unexpected visit and perhaps he didn't expect me to honor the formalities and request permission to enter. His eyes had glazed over as he received a mind link from Georgios. "You may enter, follow the road to the packhouse, Alpha will meet you there."

I nodded my head and put the Jeep in gear. The Macedonia side in eastern Greece is beautiful, the vegetation here was fuller with more varieties of tall trees. This also attracted lots of wildlife for hunting. My sister could easily hide and thrive in these dense forest lands, I thought to myself.

"She'll be fine." Raven said and squeezed my leg.

We pulled up in front of the packhouse and Alpha Georgios was standing there with his Beta and some warriors ready for us. Raven's parents were also standing behind him. "Remember, your parents hate me." I linked Raven before we stepped out.

"Mom? Dad? What are you doing here?" Raven faked shock.

"Council business." Diesel replied coldly.

"Where's my sister Georgios?" I growled.

"My mate was taken last night while on a run." Georgios said.

"Are you sure she didn't run away from you?" I replied.

"I'm her mate." Georgios growled.

"I don't see her mark on you." I replied.

"Have you come here to challenge me?" Georgios roared back, his eyes dark and his wolf on the surface.

"Is that what you think? Guess that would explain the warriors you have surrounding us!"

"Alpha Georgios we just need to see Odessa for a few moments, it's important." Raven said.

"As you can see, Luna, she's not here!" Georgios growled at my mate and I growled back.

"Stay out of this Raven!" Lucy barked. "Alpha Georgios, please call the rest of your pack and warriors to witness the DOWNFALL OF THE BEAST OF GREECE!" She snarled at us.

"What's she going to do?" I linked Raven.

"Oh, you'll see." Raven giggled back through the mind link.

"We should take this to the training grounds." Georgios said looking a little too excited for what might happen next. Perhaps he believed I was about to be taken down by my mate's father.

It almost felt like a preplanned ambush. I was certain Odessa was probably being held in a cell as bait to lure me here. The sooner Georgios was dead, the sooner I could look for my sister. I was sure I could kill Georgios with my bare hands while in human form, but I wasn't sure I could take on all of his warriors without shifting if they charged at me.

"No shifting." Raven reminded me.

"Fuck, I should have brought warriors with us." I told her as we walked towards their training field.

"That would have put our pack at risk having our best fighters come with us." She reminded me.

She was right. Leaving with half my warriors would have left the pack weaker if Hades and my father decided to attack. Hell, they were all most likely working together on this. We stopped at the field and were surrounded by warriors, pack members, and pups. Georgios stood close to Raven's parents believing they were his allies.

"We are Zeus' Howlers, and we stand together. Today our pack is being threatened by my mate's brother. He has come to challenge me. As many of you have heard, Alpha Dimitri Theodorus is not a natural werewolf like us. He possesses unnatural gifts from the devil and intends to use those to conquer our pack as well as the other packs across Greece." Georgios announced and the crowd growled back.

"Excuse me, Alpha Georgios, did I just hear you refer to the gifts of the Moon Goddess as gifts from the devil?" Lucy asked and the crowd went completely silent. I could see her eyes come to life and feel her aura all the way from where I was standing.

"The beast is evil after all." Georgios managed to utter.

"Tell me Georgios, do you believe everyone who possesses a gift from the Gods is evil?" She asked. "Do you know what I think is evil? I think slavery and sex trafficking is evil. You do have slaves here, don't you Georgios?" Her voice sounded lethal.

"Alpha LaRue, please control your mate. We are here to deal with the bastard who stole your daughter and wants to take our Luna away." Georgios snapped.

"I'm sorry Georgios, my mate can't be controlled, she is a descendant of not one, but two Gods. You know how temperamental Gods could be." Diesel smiled proudly and gasps could be heard around the field.

"Alpha Georgios, you have neglected this pack and your duties to it. You have been consumed by greed and power, putting this pack in financial peril. You have also failed to provide an heir and have managed to lose your mate, the Luna of this pack." She said. With every word she spoke, she walked around the center of the field so that everyone could feel her power.

"I didn't lose my mate." He growled.

I was ready to leap at him and rip his fucking throat out when Raven grabbed my arm. "Wait, he won't be able to lie to her, Lia is on the surface and she can compel the truth from him with her aura."

"Where is Odessa?" She demanded and stared him down from the middle of the field.

"W-with her father." He managed to utter and looked confused by his sudden truthfulness.

A growl ripped from me and Dom was at the surface. Lucy held her hand up at me for a moment telling me to stand down. I wanted this fucker dead. Raven pressed herself to my chest in a hug, not because she was crying, but because she wanted to calm both Dom and me.

"Wait, please. She's almost there." Raven whispered to me.

"You gave your mate away to a known murdering mafia boss! Why?" She asked.

"He would have taken the pack if I didn't. You don't know what Stefanos is capable of." Georgios said.

"Alpha Georgios of pack Zeus' Howlers, I, Lucy Michaels LaRue, challenge you for this pack to the death."

"You? You're not even an Alpha!" He growled.

"Then it shouldn't be a problem for you."

"You have to be an Alpha to lead a pack!" He growled and shifted into his wolf.

"You hardly qualify as an Alpha Georgios, besides I'M BETTER THAN AN ALPHA!" Lucy burst out of her clothes and shifted into her beautiful golden wolf. Her roar shook the ground and her amber eyes burned with fire. She truly was a sight to behold. Shocked gasps and screams rang out. Some were pointing and others dropped to their knees when they recognized what Lucy was.

Three foolish warriors tried to charge forward at Lucy to attack her. She turned her head and fire came shooting out of her eyes at them. Screams erupted as they fell to the ground in flames. I was stunned, Lucy could do more than manipulate fire, she could create her own.

Lucy stomped her front paw and growled at Georgios. He stood frozen with fear for a moment and bared his teeth at her, taking a few steps back. He was no dummy, he was not about to charge at a golden wolf.

She walked across the field towards Georgios, never breaking eye contact with him. No one moved. There was an eerie stillness in the air. His eyes shifted to his dead warriors and he knew he was no match for her. He turned to run, and Lucy lunged at him in one swift movement and ripped out his throat. Georgios' lifeless body lay at her feet and she howled out.

Those in wolf form howled back and the others still standing knelt before her. Lucy had just claimed Zeus' Howlers as her own.

CHAPTER 37 – PROGRESS

"I'm Lucy Michaels LaRue, Luna of Crescent Moon Pack. As a golden wolf of the Gods, I now claim Zeus' Howlers as my own. We are not enemies with Alpha Dimitri Theodorus. Our daughter Raven LaRue, is his mate and the new Luna of Olympus Blood Moon. We believe this will be a strong alliance for both packs and Zeus' Howlers will grow stronger and flourish." My mother said.

Applause and joyous howls erupted from the crowd. My mother stood in the middle of the field wearing nothing but my father's shirt after she shifted back. Dimitri and I stood with my father as my mother addressed her new pack.

"Beta Onassis, please step forward." She called out. The crowd became silent and some exchanged nervous looks. "Some of you may have already heard, our oldest son and heir of Crescent Moon, Knox LaRue, is the mate of the Beta's daughter. This will now connect the packs in more ways than one. We are honored to have Raquel Onassis, from Zeus' Howlers as the future Luna of the largest pack in the world, Crescent Moon, and our daughter-in-law." More applause and proud howls rang out.

"I have five Alpha sons. As mentioned, my oldest, Knox LaRue, will be taking over Crescent Moon and his twin Peter LaRue will be taking Dark Moon from his uncle. This means that we will have plenty of time to oversee things at this pack. I intend to eventually turn the pack over to my heir, my third son, Roman LaRue. He will receive training and oversight from my mate and I to ensure the success of this pack. If there's anyone who wishes to challenge me for the pack, please step forward."

Silence.

"Very well, let's move along, we have a few orders of business to take care of. First, we will not tolerate any disloyalty or treachery. If you do not believe you are capable of being a contributing member of this pack, or you simply do not wish to be here, I will give you until sunrise tomorrow to peacefully leave the territory. Second, everyone will contribute to the pack, we will not keep slaves. We will have some paid staff members as well as duties that everyone contributes to. If any slave is interested in becoming a pack member, we will take them in and provide appropriate accommodations for them. If they wish to leave or return to their original pack, I will be happy to help them. Finally, does anyone here have any knowledge of the whereabouts of Odessa Theodorus?"

There were some low murmurs and nervous looks exchanged. Rocky's father spoke first. "Alpha Lucy, Georgios met with a few men at the edge of the territory last night and gave her to them. She was shackled in silver so she couldn't shift or escape. Georgios owed Eros or the mafia money and because Stefanos wanted her, he gave her to him, to clear his debts."

"Thank you, Beta." My mother said. "You are all dismissed. We will have another pack meeting tomorrow evening to discuss pack changes and pledge our oaths."

"YES ALPHA!" They said and began to disburse.

"Alpha, I'll have someone take care of the bodies. I trust you know your way around here, if you need anything, please feel free to let me know." Rocky's father said.

"Thank you, I will. Let's meet in an hour to start discussing the changes we should implement Beta." She told him.

"You still want me as a Beta?" He asked.

"Of course, we're family now Phillip. My son Roman will likely want one of his cousins to come with him as his second. You have a great deal of knowledge and training to share with the future Beta in training." She smiled.

"It will be a pleasure." He returned the smile and bowed.

Dimitri and I followed my parents to the Alpha's office. When the door was closed the four of us all breathed a sigh of relief. My mom was now the Alpha of this pack.

"That was incredible mom." I said.

"Thank you. He was expecting you to come and had planned an ambush." She said.

"So if Roman gets this pack, what do we do with Eros' pack after we take it from Hades?" My father asked.

"Let's worry about that after I find my sister." Dimitri said.

"Do we have any idea where Stefanos may have taken her?" I asked.

"I would guess that he's in the city, hiding somewhere with her. Eros owns a lot of buildings and businesses that have been linked to mafia activities. There's also a possibility they're with Hades. Kosta was looking into it for me but we can't ask him until he wakes up." Dimitri told my parents.

"Wakes up?" My father asked.

"He was found at our border, hardly breathing, beaten and shot with a silver bullet. Dr. Vovos was able to stabilize him, but he's not awake yet." Dimitri said.

"Any guesses who it was?" My dad asked.

"Stefanos or his henchmen." Dimitri said.

"Do you think he will hurt your sister?" My mom sounded worried asking that question.

"After my mother died, my father became a heartless monster. I was only twelve when he started beating me and Odessa was four. He didn't lay a hand on her until she turned eight when he started beating her too, she ran away. She had crawled through a window and hid in the basement of the Beta's house. Kosta was the Beta and had no idea Odessa was in his basement. When my father found her there, three days later, he thought that Kosta's mate had helped her hide from him. He punished her by raping her in front of Odessa and me, then he killed her. Kosta was devastated."

"I'm so sorry." My mother whispered in shock.

"My father turned into a monster when he lost his mate. Kosta fell apart after losing his mate. Kosta was our best fighter, he was as strong and tough as any Alpha. Seeing what happened to him, how it destroyed him from the inside out; it showed me how vulnerable a mate really makes you. My father continued to beat me, and I did my best to protect Odessa too. He made me hate the idea of having a mate, he made me unwilling to love. After I took the pack from him, I was full of rage. I had a short fuse for abusive Alpha's and went on a killing spree that earned me the beast title. I took out my years of frustration and anger on bad Alpha's. I was broken. My father broke me. I never had any intention of accepting my mate, but then Raven swooped right into my life." Dimitri pulled me into a hug.

"I do believe he is capable of hurting Odessa, maybe even sending me her head. But I also believe he will keep her alive to lure me in." Dimitri finished.

"How do we find Stefanos now?" My mom asked.

"I think he'll find me. He's got an army of rogues, Eros' pack at his disposal and he may be planning an attack soon."

"Should we get back to your pack?" My mom asked.

"There's a good chance he may show up here, at this pack. Once word travels that Georgios is dead, he will want to know who you are. He may have even been counting on using warriors from this pack in the battle to take my pack." Dimitri told my parents.

"He's right." My dad said. "You'll have to stay here and prepare this pack in case he comes knocking."

"Raven and I should probably head back; I don't want to be gone long in case he shows up at my pack with Hades." Dimitri told them.

"We have scouts watching Hades' pack right now, if they make a move, we will know." I told my parents.

"Well don't worry about us, I can hold off an entire army." My mother said. "Raven, make sure you've got two lighters on you at all times."

"Dimitri, when you find out where Stefanos is, let us know, we can be there quickly to help. Lia can run much faster than the fastest Alpha." My father told him.

"Thank you. We'll be in touch." Dimitri said. I hugged my parents and we left.

We left the pack in the jeep and drove back. I kept thinking about what Dimitri had said, how his father had broken him. It explained why he struggled so much in the beginning to accept me. I need to train more and become stronger; I don't want him feeling vulnerable at the thought of having a weak mate. My phone rang pulling out of my thoughts, I noticed it was a call from Clair. I answered it on speaker. "Hi, Clair."

"Hi, Niko, Knox, and Rocky are here with me, you're on speakerphone." She said.

"We just heard from Rocky's father that mom took the pack." Knox asked.

"She sure did! Looks like Roman is moving to Greece." I

said.

"How's Kosta doing?" Dimitri asked.

"Still sleeping Alpha." Niko answered.

"Any territory breaches?"

"Nothing, it's been very quiet, but we've doubled the patrols." Knox said.

"Alec went to Moon Warriors to check on the scouts." Niko said.

"There's a good chance Odessa might be at Moon Warriors. Raven and I are heading there now, we should be there in about two hours." Dimitri said.

"Do you need backup?" Niko asked.

"No, not yet. If our territory is being watched I don't want them to notice that we're on the move. I need Spiro to work with his team and get me all the known locations in Athens that Eros owned or was affiliated with. Georgios turned Odessa over to Stefanos and he could be holding her in one of the buildings." Dimitri explained.

"That fucker!" Niko said outraged.

"Kosta was tracking Stefanos, we need to know what he knows the minute he wakes up."

"Will do Alpha." Niko replied.

I hung up the phone and Dimitri reached for my hand. He was on edge over his sister, and I couldn't seem to understand how he kept it all together. We needed to find her and soon. If Stefanos wanted to weaken Dimitri, killing Odessa would be the next step.

"Do you want to stop and get something to eat?" Dimitri asked me.

"I'm not hungry, my stomach has been kind of queasy today." I told him.

We arrived just outside of Moon Warriors territory in the Epirus region of Greece. Dimitri parked the Jeep in a wooded area and picked up his cell phone.

"We'll have to leave the Jeep here and get closer in wolf form."

"Is Alec here already?" I asked.

Dimitri's eyes glazed over, and he was mind linking with someone. A low growl rumbled in his throat and I could feel him get tense with anger.

"What's wrong?" I asked.

"FUCK! There's no sign of Hades or Odessa." He said.

"And Stefanos?"

"He's here, with lots of rogues. Looks like the warriors are preparing to move out for an attack. They won't be able to move in such large groups without being noticed until after sunset."

"That's about three more hours, we'll need to get back to the pack. Where's Alec at?" I asked.

Dimitri grinned. "Seducing information from the

Delta's daughter down by the river."

I rolled my eyes and scoffed. "Alec and his trusty penis."

CHAPTER 38 – SAVED

"Come on Alec! What the hell is taking him so long?" I huffed and paced back and forth. Dimitri and I have been waiting in the woods for nearly an hour.

"These things can be delicate. We don't want her to alert the pack that we're here, alone."

"Should we go down to the river and check to make sure he hasn't been caught?"

"He hasn't." Dimitri said.

"How can you be sure?"

"Because he's right behind you." Dimitri pointed and I turned around to see Alec, walking with his arm around a beautiful curvy woman.

"Alpha. Luna." He greeted us. "This is Helena. Her father is the Delta of this pack and was thrown in the cells a few days ago by the *new Alpha*." He informed us with an emphasis on the new Alpha.

"New Alpha?" I asked.

"Stefanos." Alec responded.

"What happened to Hades?" Dimitri asked.

"No one has seen him since Alpha Eros died. We believe that Stefanos killed Hades because he's claimed our pack. Our Beta challenged Stefanos for the pack and was also killed. My father tried to step down from his position and Stefanos threw him in the prison." Helena said.

"Is Stefanos planning to attack Olympus Blood Moon tonight?" Dimitri asked.

"Yes. Our pack has been overrun with rogues who are very loyal to him. They're planning on attacking and forcing three hundred of our fighters to join the rogues." She said.

"How many rogues would you guess there are?" I asked.

"Maybe four hundred." She said.

That would make about seven hundred fighters combined for Stefanos. Olympus Blood moon has about seventeen hundred pack members total, but only twelve hundred live in the main pack territory, the rest live on the three islands that belonged to us. We have about eight hundred fighters, which would make the numbers almost even. Stefanos was the previous Alpha of Olympus Blood Moon, he would know just how many fighters he would need.

"Do you know if a young she-wolf, Odessa Theodorus, is being held here?" I asked.

"There was a female they brought in recently. One of the guards is a friend, he's been helping me sneak into the cells to check on my father. I scented a female who's not from our pack down there." She told us.

"What did she smell like?" Dimitri asked.

"Strawberry sorbet." She said.

"That's her!" Dimitri's fists clenched.

"Is there any way we could sneak in? Is the prison heavily guarded?" Alec asked.

"There are normally two guards on duty, the bars are made of silver, so it makes escaping difficult. Everyone is busy preparing for the attack, with so many unfamiliar scents around, you should be able to get around unnoticed." She said. "Well, except maybe you Alpha. Your aura is very strong." She added and bowed her head.

"We need a plan." I said.

"The cells are in their own building, near the forest tree line." She told us.

"Maybe we can create a diversion." Alec suggested.

We crept down low behind trees and boulders near the tree line. The building that contained the prison cells was just ahead and Dimitri moved a little closer to scout the area out. Alec had linked the three scouts we had sent earlier to our location to help keep a lookout. A few moments later, Dimitri returned.

"Do you have your lighter with you?" He asked me.

"Yes!"

"There's a building near the training field on the other side. Do you think your flames could reach it?" He asked.

I wasn't sure about the distance from this far, but I would certainly try. "I think so."

I pulled out the lighter from my pocket and flicked it on. The flame seemed to send energy pulsing through me. I willed a ball of fire into my hand and it did as I wanted. I focused on the target building and took a few nervous deep breaths.

"Remember, your emotions control the level of energy. Focus your emotions on the energy." Dimitri mind linked me.

"We can do this!" Rae assured me.

I closed my eyes. I thought about Odessa and the pain she must have been suffering because of her worthless mate. I thought about what happened to Kosta and about Leo's death. I thought about Stefanos beating a young Dimitri. The ball of fire was practically glowing blue, it was so strong and hot.

I opened my eyes, walked closer to the edge of the tree line, and took aim at the building. The fire landed on the roof and I willed it to spread across the entire rooftop. Total chaos broke loose, and everyone seemed to be running in the direction of the fire.

"Bullseye!" Rae yipped.

"Quickly now!" Dimitri said and we ran towards the back of the prison cells. Alec, Helena, Dimitri, and I, stood with our backs pressed up against the building listening for footsteps. Helena looked around the corner and told us the prison guard at the front door ran in the direction of the fire. We made a move to the front door; Alec pulled the door open, and we stepped inside. A set of stone steps led down to an iron door. Judging by the foul smell coming from below, the cells were definitely down there.

Helena opened the iron door at the bottom first, we heard a low voice growl, "I told you, if you want to see your father, you'll have to suck me off first!"

"Someone else wants to speak with you David." Helena said and swung the door wide open to reveal Dimitri and Alec.

"What the fuck!" He managed to say before Dimitri shoved his elbow into David's nose. The guard fell back with blood sputtering out of his nose and mouth.

"If you try and mind link anyone, I'll rip your throat out!" Dimitri growled at him and he nodded his head.

"Where the fuck is Odessa?"

David's eyes moved down the hall and Dimitri grabbed the back of his neck, leading him in that direction. We looked into the cell all the way at the end and found Odessa. She was chained with a silver collar around her neck to keep her from shifting. Her eyes were closed, and she was sitting on the floor, near the corner of the cell.

"Odessa!" I called out and she lifted her head.

"Unlock the cell." Dimitri growled at David who didn't move. "I SAID, UNLOCK THE FUCKING CELL!" Dimitri pressed David's face against the silver cell bars and he howled in pain.

"Give me the keys!" Helena reached at his belt and removed the keys from the clip. She unlocked the cell door and we rushed inside.

"Quick we need to hurry." Alec said.

Helena unlocked the collar from around Odessa's neck and Dimitri quickly engulfed her in a hug. "Thank the Goddess. Are you okay?" He asked. Her neck was burned red from the silver collar.

A growl ripped from the wolf in the cell next to Odessa. She smiled at him. "It's okay, this is my brother."

"Who's this?" Dimitri asked, feeling a strong aura coming from the wolf.

"I'll explain later, we need to bring him with us." She insisted.

"We don't have time for this." Dimitri said.

"I'm not leaving without him!" Odessa protested.

"FUCK, HURRY!" Dimitri eyed Alec, who moved quickly to unlock the cell next to Odessa and remove the silver collar from him. His neck had also been burned by the silver and would take time to heal.

"He looks familiar." Rae said to me, but I couldn't place him.

Helena grabbed the keys and ran to her father's cell. She unlocked him and helped him out. He had been beaten pretty badly and the silver collar prevented him from healing.

"Are we ready?" Alec asked.

"Let's get out of here. We need to get back to the pack before Stefanos does." Dimitri said.

Alec grabbed David's head and snapped his neck; we couldn't afford to have him alert anyone. We made our way back up the stairs and Helena thanked us for our help. She and her father decided to hide until Stefanos left for the attack. They planned to get her mother and run north into Albania, to seek refuge with her mother's old pack. Alec hugged her goodbye and we headed in different directions into the woods. The fire was still at a full blaze and the smell of smoke would hide our scents.

We continued running deep into the woods before Dimitri stopped. "We're going to have to shift, the car is about ten kilometers away, just outside the territory. It will be much faster." He said.

We all stepped behind a tree and removed our clothing to shift. I picked up my clothes in my mouth and stepped out. I heard a low growl and saw that Dom was ready to attack. He was looking at the other big black Alpha wolf with brown eyes and circling him. Another low growl was heard, and I looked to see Odessa. Odessa was Alpha born and her wolf, Olympia, was an average sized black wolf with a white bib. She jumped between the Alpha males and bared her teeth at her brother to protect the unknown wolf. What the hell was going on here?

Dom stopped for a moment and was also shocked at his

sister's behavior. "Can we get moving please, we're still in someone's territory." I reminded him through the mind link.

Dom picked up his clothes and ran east towards the direction of the Jeep. We were almost to the pack border when a group of rogues jumped out to attack us. There were five of them and five of us.

The unknown black Alpha immediately lunged at them and started snapping and biting. Dom also jumped in and immediately tore out a rogue's windpipe. One of the rogues jumped at me and Dimitri sent a big boulder sailing through the air that crashed right into the rogue. He fell at my paws and Rae sliced her claw right through his neck. Dimitri used his element to open up a hole in the ground and Alec pushed the rogue bodies in. A few seconds later, Dimitri had filled the rest of the hole up with dirt.

We made it to the Jeep and shifted back on different sides of the car to get dressed. Odessa and the unknown Alpha stood hugging. It looked like he was resting his head in her neck, scenting her.

"Who are you?" Dimitri growled.

"Can we talk about this in the car? We need to get the hell out of here!" Odessa said.

"He's an Alpha! Who are you?" Dimitri demanded.

"I'm Hades Kappas." His gruff voice said.

"YOU'RE EROS' SON!" Dimitri's eyes flared and the ground shook beneath us. He was struggling to control his emotion.

"It's not what you think!" Odessa said.

"I'm no threat to you. My father hardly ever had contact with me. My mother was a chosen mate, he never loved her or treated us well. I could care less about him or the pack. I just want my mate!" Hades said.

"Oh Fuck!" Alec whispered.

"Your mate?" I asked.

"Yes, Hades is my mate!" Odessa happily grinned at us.

CHAPTER 39 – RACE

The sun was setting as we raced back in the Jeep to our territory. Dimitri was at the wheel and his eyes kept glancing in the mirror at the occupants in the back seat. Odessa was seated in the back, between Alec and Hades. The tension in the car was thick.

"What the hell happened Odessa? I thought Georgios was your mate?" Dimitri asked and a low growl came from Hades at the mention of Georgios.

"It's kind of a long story." She replied.

"We've got time. No one is leaving this car for a few hours." Dimitri said.

Hades spoke first, "My mother was originally from Georgios' pack, Zeus' Howlers. When my father claimed her as a chosen mate, she switched packs and joined Moon Warriors. He wasn't very good to us and took little interest in me. Growing up, I spent a great deal of time visiting with my grandparents at their pack. Georgios' father had the pack then, he was good to me, let me come and stay whenever I wanted to. My grandparents were wonderful people and I enjoyed visiting them every chance I had. They lived next door to the Delta couple, and I became good friends with their son, Leonidas."

"Leo!" I whispered as realization set in.

"Yes, Leo. He was one of my best friends. When I heard

what had happened, I wanted to kill Eros myself. I went to Zeus' Howlers to attend his funeral and pay my respects to his parents. I caught the scent of my mate and followed it, that's when I found Odessa. Georgios wasn't too happy that Odessa found her mate. He asked me to join him in his office and when I did, I discovered Stefanos and his men waiting for me. I don't remember much else, they drugged me and left me chained in the dungeon until after the funeral. At some point, I was moved to Moon Warriors in a cell next to my mate where you found us." Hades told us.

Odessa continued, "Georgios told me to play along and pretend I was his mate so that Stefanos wouldn't hurt me. He told me he had an alliance with my father. I knew he was lying and overheard him speaking about the plan to lure Dimitri in by using me. I don't think he had expected me to find my true mate. When Raven's parents showed up, he told me he would kill Hades if I didn't convince them he was my mate. I wasn't sure what to do, I thought I could get a message to Raven's parents somehow, but he never left me alone with them."

"It's a good thing Georgios wasn't your mate! Raven's mother killed him and claimed the pack!" Alec told her.

"That's fantastic! Stefanos had agreed to wipe out Georgios' debit if he sent his warriors to help with the attack." Odessa informed us.

"So, does this mean that Hades is the next Alpha of Moon Warriors?" Alec asked.

"Yes, once we take out Stefanos, Hades is the rightful heir." Dimitri growled back.

"I don't want my father's pack." Hades said.

"It's not your father's pack or my father's pack, it's our pack. Those wolves deserve to finally have a good Alpha. We can turn things around." Odessa said.

"Spoken like a true Luna." Hades whispered to Odessa and kissed her on the side of her head. A low growl rippled in Dimitri's throat and I placed my hand on his leg to help calm him.

The look in Hades' eyes when he looked at Odessa was enough to convince me that she was the center of his universe. He had the same thick dark brown hair as his father and soft brown eyes. He also had the same sharp facial features and jaw which gave him a unique but handsome appearance. I tried to read Dimitri's thoughts and he was struggling in his mind. This was Eros' son and Eros was a bad person, he wanted to dislike Hades. But, if anyone can relate to the situation, it would be Dimitri. The same had been said about Dimitri because of his terrible father, Stefanos. He knew he couldn't judge Hades based on who his father was.

"You're right." I mind linked Dimitri reading his thoughts and he smiled at me.

"I guess I should be happy Georgios isn't her mate after all." He linked back.

"Hades seems better matched for her and she looks so happy." I told him through the link.

"She's barely eighteen, still a pup." Dimitri protested.

"Did you forget I'm only a few months older than her?"

I linked back and Dimitri didn't say anything else.

"The sun is almost down, Stefanos and his warriors will be moving at dark." Alec reminded us.

"The run should take them at least three to four hours. We'll reach the pack in about two hours. Alec, call Niko and let him know to be ready." Dimitri said.

We had been traveling in silence for over an hour. We were almost to our pack border when Dimitri suddenly slammed on the brakes. I looked out the window and dozens of red eyes circled us and blocked the small bridge we needed to cross.

"Rogues." Dimitri growled.

The front of the Jeep was being lifted by six rogues. They were trying to flip the Jeep over. The ground started shaking and the rogues dropped the front end of the Jeep back down, stunned by the earth quaking Dimitri had created. I looked at the bridge and willed the water beneath it to rise up and knock into some of the rogues with so much force they fell over into the river.

"Our back tire is going flat; we'll have to get out." Alec said.

"Raven, can you put a ring of fire around the Jeep so we can shift before we are attacked?" Dimitri asked.

I took my lighter out and flicked it on. "Open the sun roof." I had witnessed my mother create rings of fire in so many sizes before. I focused on the fire and it grew larger. I closed my eyes and pictured it completely surrounding the car with enough room for us to get out. I pictured it at least ten feet high. My arm lifted up and the lighter was sticking out of the sunroof.

"You can do it." Dimitri said to me.

He had so much faith in me and believed in me. It gave me the confidence I needed. The fire ripped up with a roar of its own and then circled the Jeep. The rogues jumped back, and someone screamed "witchcraft."

"Is she a witch?" I heard Hades whisper to Odessa.

"No, she's elemental, like my brother." She told him proudly.

"We'll have to leave the car here. We're going to shift, kick some rogue ass and run the rest of the way to the pack." Dimitri said.

We stepped out of the car and shifted as fast as we could, our clothes shredded everywhere. A rogue jumped over the fire and Hades was the first to jump on him and sent his claws right into the rogue's heart.

"Lower the flames." Dimitri told me.

When the flames came down, Dimitri sent dirt and sand flying towards the rogues to blind them. Many of them howled as they were blinded. I almost laughed out loud thinking about the first time Dimitri did that to me. This trick never gets old, I suppressed my giggle. Dimitri turned and opened up a sinkhole that took about ten rogues down. Rae was so impressed by her mate she let out a happy bark.

I used the flames from the circle to send fireballs at the rogues. Two of them were engulfed in flames and dropped to the ground screeching and whimpering in pain. Another one whose tail caught fire jumped into the river. Alec pounced on the rogue near him and ripped his throat out. Dom stomped his paw and the ground shook again, he floated swinging boulders in the air, and I continued to shoot balls of flames.

The remaining rogues stopped the attack and ran off, there was no way they would be able to take out four black Alpha wolves and a Gamma. Dom unnaturally towered over all of us and they believed we had a witch. Dom tipped his head back and let out a howl. Hades returned his howl and the rest of us also joined in.

Rae rubbed herself up against Dom and he nuzzled into her neck breathing her in. When all this was over, she was going to need some quality time with Dom. Alec barked and motioned his head in the direction of our pack. Time was ticking. We continued to race back the rest of the way through the forest.

Howls started ringing through the air as we approached. Our warriors and fighters were in fight formation ready for the coming attack. Spiro met us behind the pack house with an arm full of clothes. We shifted back and headed inside to the office. Niko, Clair, Knox, and Rocky were all standing in the office.

"Hades!" Rocky said and engulfed him in a hug.

"You know each other?" Niko asked.

"We've been friends since we were pups. His mother was from our pack." Rocky said confirming what he had told us. "I thought we would see you at Leo's funeral, what happened?" She asked.

"Long story." Odessa replied smiling.

"Odessa is my mate." Hades told her.

"Oh, my Goddess! That's wonderful!" Rocky screeched.

"We're not celebrating just yet. We've got a fight coming." Dimitri said.

"We did as you requested, we've set up and started fire pits burning around the entire pack territory for the Luna. The swimming pool is full, and the big water fountain is at maximum water capacity. Luna, we have fire hydrants throughout the pack territory as well." Niko told us.

"That's perfect, thank you." I said.

"If you look closely, all the rocks and decorative boulders around the pack territory aren't there by chance or just for decorations." Niko grinned at me. That was a smart idea, to have elemental weapons strategically placed around the territory for Dimitri's use. Maybe I could get him to build me a big pond.

"Stefanos will have some unshifted rogues, they will be the biggest threat. They've got guns with silver bullets." Hades said.

"I think we need to put Raven in the bird's nest and reinforce the steel around it for silver bullets." Dimitri said.

"What's the bird's nest?" I asked.

"It's a metal look-out box on top of the roof, we call it the bird's nest." Spiro answered.

316

"I'm not hiding, I'm the Luna. I'll fight with my pack!" I said.

"You won't be hiding. You're our greatest resource and surprise Raven. If they figure out what you are, you will be the main target. If you're up in the bird's nest, you'll be in a bulletproof box able to control the fire and water attacks below. You'll still be fighting." Dimitri told me.

"Better listen to him sis, you'll be able to do far more damage with your elements from up above than on the ground." Knox said and I knew he was right.

"Alpha, I've got more steel reinforcement heading up to the bird's nest, it should be ready in twenty minutes." Spiro said.

"Move fast Spiro, I don't think we've got twenty minutes." Niko said. "Alpha, the scouts report the rogues are almost to the edge of our territory."

Dimitri let out a growl. "Everyone in place now!"

CHAPTER 40 – ATTACK

"Be a good little bird and stay in the nest. Don't come out for any reason, understand?" Dimitri told me.

"Okay."

"Keep the door locked from the inside. Don't open it for anyone. If you set one foot out this door, before I come back for you, I'm going to spank your bottom red!" He crashed his lips into mine. His kiss was hungry, demanding, and filled with emotion. The promise of another spanking sent an exciting quiver down my back. I couldn't wait until this was over to spend time tangled up with him.

"Please be careful." I whispered as we broke away.

"I'll be back as soon as this is over." He said and closed the door to the nest.

I was standing inside of a closet sized metal box, that was perched on top of the roof of the packhouse and looked out over the pack lands. The fire pits were burning bright, if someone didn't know any better, they would just assume the fire pits were there to light up the grounds for battle.

"Let's test the reach of our element." Rae suggested.

"Good idea." I wasn't sure how well my reach would be from this far.

I focused on one of the fires and its dancing flames. I closed my eyes and tapped into my energy, feeling my own emotions flow through me. I could feel my heart pounding in my chest, as I took a deep breath. I opened my eyes and willed the fire to rise, it moved a few feet higher into the air. I concentrated harder and it flared up ten feet more towards the sky.

"Are you doing that?" Dimitri mind linked me.

"Yes, just getting a feel for my reach." I linked back.

"Try the water too." He told me.

I willed the swimming pool water to rise and fall. "I can reach. I don't want to blast open a fire hydrant yet, it'll cause a muddy mess before they get here."

"Some of our fighters got spooked, I guess I forgot to tell them their Luna has two elements. Niko just told them about your elements and that you're in the bird's nest helping to protect them. They're excited and very proud to have you as our Luna." Dimitri told me.

"Where are the pups and vulnerable pack members?" I asked.

"Our safe room is under the packhouse, everyone who needs to be in there is safe."

Dimitri stood in the middle of the field in human form surrounded by our warriors. Niko and Alec stood in wolf form next to him as his second and third. Spiro is a sharpshooter and was positioned in the window of the attic. He had two other shooters with him and silver bullets of their own to neutralize shooters from

Stefanos' side.

I stared down at the open field and saw Hades, Odessa, Clair, Knox, and Rocky standing behind Dimitri in wolf form. Knox had insisted on fighting to help protect his sister's pack and Rocky wanted revenge for Leo. I felt an uneasy tension in the air, and I knew Stefanos was close.

A row of red eyes emerged from the tree line and growls filled the air from both sides. Niko let out a loud howl and the rogues charged forward. Dimitri stomped the ground and a huge trench opened up beneath a dozen rogues. I looked to the fire and willed it to fill the trench. "YES!" I called out as painful howls filled the air and burning wolves tried jumping out.

"Nice!" Rae said to me.

Dimitri sent a cloud of sand towards the other rogues running in our direction as our fighters clashed with them. More red eyed rogues came charging out from the far end of the tree line and I sent balls of fire at them. I hit four of them and their mangy fur caught fire. Another group of rogues charged from the opposite end and Dimitri brought a tree crashing down on a few of them.

Our warriors and the rogues continued fighting. The rogues were vicious but didn't stand a chance against our trained fighters. I realized the first attack of rogues was a distraction when I heard the popping sound of bullets coming in our direction.

"They have shooters in the trees." I linked Dimitri.

"Spiro can't see them, can you send some flames to the trees, so they move or try to climb down?" He asked.

"Coming right up!"

I looked closely and spotted a tree with a shooter, I sent a ring of fire around the tree and willed it to start climbing up the bark. I heard a popping sound and the shooter in the tree fell. Spiro had hit the shooter. I did the same to a second and third tree and Spiro picked them off. Another shooter jumped down and tried to run, I aimed a ball of fire at him and hit him.

I looked down and saw half a dozen wolves struggling with water bubbles around their heads. Knox had pulled water out of the swimming pool and was drowning six rogues at once. How did he learn to do that? I had only learned to hold one water bubble at a time. I was going to have to give my dad a piece of my mind when this was over.

"Focus on trying multiple water bubbles at once. I have faith in us." Rae told me.

I was so frustrated the water burst out of the fire hydrant with little effort and I could feel the power of the water pulsing through the air. I looked at several rogues and imagined the water bubbles engulfing their heads. The water did as I wanted. All four of them thrashed around trying to knock the water bubble away. I focused my energy on holding the bubbles in place and two of the rogues shifted back and dropped to the ground. The other two struggled for a moment longer before they fell lifeless on the ground. I dropped the water and felt a little weaker myself.

"Using this much elemental power is draining." I told Rae.

There were still over three hundred rogues fighting with our wolves. I heard another popping sound and spotted a shooter hiding behind a big boulder. Before I could send a ball of flames at him, Dimitri rolled the boulder over on top of the shooter crushing him. Dimitri was still in human form and was waiting to shift, Dom was so big, he would have been an easy target for the shooters with silver bullets.

Dimitri was insanely strong and able to kill rogue wolves without fully shifting. His claws and teeth had shifted so that he could rip out throats. I looked to see Hades tearing through any rogue that dared get close to his mate. Clair sent a rogue flying into the swimming pool and I willed the water to hold him underneath the surface. The more he struggled the harder I had to focus on holding him down with the water. My head was light, and I felt a wave of dizziness before the rogue finally floated up dead.

"We need to rest." Rae told me.

"We can rest later, in case you missed it, there's an attack happening."

"We're getting weaker and weaker the more you use your elements." She said.

"It's because we haven't trained the way we should. Did you see Knox holding six water bubbles?"

"Knox is also two and a half years older. He's had more training and practice." Rae reminded me.

"I'll be fine." I continued to send flying balls of flames at rogues.

Dimitri sent more sand clouds towards the rogues still rushing in. He stomped the ground and tree roots came out tripping up rogues. Warriors around the field were dropping dead rogues everywhere, it was a bloody mess.

I heard a yelp from Rocky, Knox growled and jumped onto the rogue who tried to bite into her neck. I tried to water bubble two more rogues, but the water moved slower, and I dropped to my knees. I sat for a moment listening to the fighting taking place. I was out of breath and felt drained. Like someone who hasn't exercised in a long time and overdid it the first time out.

A loud powerful growl rang across the field and the fighting seemed to stop. I managed to stand up and peaked out at the field. A couple of hundred warriors, from Eros' pack, were at the edge of the tree line ready to attack us. They had sent the rogues in first before they sent in their trained warriors. In the middle stood a familiar looking black wolf who was unnaturally bigger than the typical Alpha. He looked just like Dom, except he was missing an eye.

"Stefanos!" Rae whispered to me.

"Look who decided to join the party." Dimitri called out.

Stefanos shifted back to his human form and a gasp escaped my lips. He looked so much like Dimitri. "I've taken Eros' pack and now I'm back for my pack. When

I'm done with you, I will take Georgios' pack from your mate's parents."

"In case you forgot, when you take a pack, you have to challenge the Alpha. The rightful heir to Eros' pack is Hades and he's standing behind me. I hear you and Georgios, drugged him up and chained him in silver with your daughter. I'm pretty sure those warriors you have are technically still bound to their rightful Alpha. Since you never actually challenged him, HADES IS STILL ALPHA." Dimitri said for everyone to hear.

"I will deal with Hades when I've dealt with you." Stefanos growled.

"And are you going to cheat with silver bullets *father*?" Dimitri said and several low disgusted growls were heard.

"You're the one cheating, are you not? Both you and your mate seem to have unnatural talents. **RAVEN MY DEAR, WHERE ARE YOU?** Where did you hide her son? The fire is her handy work isn't it?" Stefanos called out.

"You'll never get your hands on her!" Dimitri growled back.

"Relax, I just want to meet your little Raven." He smiled with an evil grin that looked nothing like Dimitri. Then he turned his head to the bird's nest and his smile widened. He looked right at me with his one eye and I felt the urge to vomit. "What a suitable place for a raven, in the bird's nest! Tell me son, is the bird's nest bulletproof? I can't seem to remember if we made it bulletproof when we built it." He was trying to provoke Dimitri and I could feel his anger raging.

"You have ten seconds to surrender the pack to its rightful Alpha before we turn the bird's nest into Swiss cheese!" Stefanos demanded with a sick grin on his face.

A familiar, thunderous, God like, growl ripped across the land and shook the ground. Everyone turned their heads and stood frozen at the sight before them. Even Stefanos looked like he had just seen a ghost. A beautiful golden wolf stepped out of the tree line, her teeth bared, her eyes glowing with fire. She looked like something that stepped out of Greek mythology and my father stood proudly in human form next to the wolf that emanated so much power.

"IF YOU WANT A PACK STEFANOS, YOU WILL NEED TO CHALLENGE THE ALPHA AND FIGHT FAIRLY. ANYONE WHO FIRES OFF A SINGLE SILVER BULLET WILL BE INCINERATED ALIVE!" My father called out and my mother shot flames from her eyes that immediately turned dead rogues into ash.

"AND WHO THE HELL ARE YOU?" Stefanos demanded.

"YOUR WORST NIGHTMARE, STEFANOS. WE'RE THE IN-LAWS!"

CHAPTER 41 – FINALLY

Dimitri's POV

"Relax, I just want to meet your little Raven." He said with a sick smile.

"He knows about mate." Dom growled at me.

"We need to make sure and end him this time." I told Dom.

He turned his head to the bird's nest. "What a suitable place for a raven, in the bird's nest! Tell me son, is the bird's nest bulletproof? I can't seem to remember if we made it bulletproof when we built it."

I mind linked Spiro, "tell me you had the chance to line the bird's nest with another layer of steel?"

"I did Alpha, but they won't be shooting regular bullets. We've never tested it against silver bullets!" Spiro linked back.

"You have ten seconds to surrender the pack to its rightful Alpha before we turn the bird's nest into Swiss cheese!" My father demanded.

I was about to unleash Dom and lunge at him when an earth shaking growl, with intense power, ripped across the land and shocked everyone. Greeks were taught from a young age to fear and respect the power of the Gods. I could smell the fear sweep the land as everyone realized what Lucy was. Even my father seemed to have realized what he was looking at.

"IF YOU WANT A PACK STEFANOS, YOU WILL NEED TO CHALLENGE THE ALPHA AND FIGHT FAIRLY. ANYONE WHO FIRES OFF A SINGLE SILVER BULLET WILL BE INCINERATED ALIVE!" Alpha Diesel called out and Lucy sent flames from her eyes displaying a fraction of her strength by incinerating corpses.

"AND WHO THE HELL ARE YOU?" My father demanded.

"YOUR WORST NIGHTMARE, STEFANOS. WE'RE THE IN-LAWS!" Diesel grinned back and walked closer to us. I sure am happy to have them on my side.

"CHARGE!" Stefanos yelled, ordering the warriors to attack.

Hades shifted back and his Alpha voice boomed out, " **MOON WARRIORS, YOU WILL STAND DOWN. THIS IS NOT YOUR FIGHT AND HE IS NOT YOUR ALPHA!"**

"I AM YOUR ALPHA!" Stefanos called back with his Alpha voice, but the warriors didn't move.

"Yeah, I don't think it works that way Stefanos. Now that they know their true Alpha is alive, they are compelled to follow his orders." Diesel told him.

"Your fight is with me. You brought rogues onto my land, you've used silver bullets against my pack, you tried to steal a dead Alpha's pack by drugging his heir, you've threatened my mate and now you're trying to claim my pack! I ACCEPT YOUR CHALLENGE

STEFANOS!" I growled.

"When I beat you, I expect your *in-laws* will leave." Stefanos growled.

Hades stepped forward and roared, **"I ALSO ACCEPT YOUR CHALLENGE STEFANOS. IT SEEMS YOU HAVE TRIED TO STAKE A CLAIM ON MY PACK TOO!"** I was starting to like Hades more and more.

"I believe you also threatened to take Zeus' Howlers from my mate's parents. You don't have a problem facing off with a female Alpha do you father?" I asked.

"I should also warn you; the golden wolf is not only the strongest of our kind, but also the fastest. You won't be able to outrun her, though you're welcome to try." Diesel smiled proudly.

"YOU CAN KEEP YOUR PACKS! I ONLY WANT WHAT WAS MINE. OLYMPUS BLOOD MOON IS MINE!" He growled.

"BECAUSE YOU WERE SUCH A GOOD ALPHA?" A deep voice echoed from the door of the packhouse. I turned my head to the voice and saw Kosta stalking forward with his fists clenched ready to jump at my father.

"Kosta? You're alive!" My father sneered.

"It took a dozen of your thugs and a silver bullet to bring me down because you were too much of a coward to face me! Look at the disgusting foul creature you've become, your father would turn over in his grave Stefanos." Kosta said with a lethal tone.

"I will deal with you after I deal with my ungrateful

son!" Stefanos said.

Lucy's golden wolf walked over to Kosta and sniffed him as if making sure he was okay. She greeted Kosta by rubbing her head against him and he smiled. It was clear that she was fond of her friend and angry that he had been attacked. She turned her gaze to my father and released an angry growl that emanated a power that was out of this world.

"You won't make it past Dimitri. It will be a pleasure to watch him rip your shriveled little black heart out of your chest!" Kosta growled and gave me a nod of approval. I knew what needed to be done.

"ANYONE WHO TRIES TO INTERFERE OR CHEAT WILL BE MET WITH THE WRATH OF THE GODS! MAY THE BEST ALPHA WIN!" Diesel called out.

"You're going to use your gift and cheat!" Stefanos growled.

"Relax old man, I don't need to use my gift, I'm going to kill you with my own hands." I said and we both shifted.

A growl came out of Stefanos' wolf Silus, who was just as mad and crazy as my father. He lunged at me with teeth bared and Dom got low to claw the exposed underbelly of Silus. I rolled to his left side which was his blind side and jumped on his back. Silus spun in circles and bucked me off sending me flying into a tree. Dom quickly jumped up and locked up with Silus, snarling and nipping at each other. He bit down on my back leg and Dom let out a yelp.

"Dimitri." Raven whispered my name faintly through the mind link.

"Something is wrong with mate." Dom looked up to the bird's nest to make sure no one had breached it.

"Alec, go check on Raven." I quickly linked him.

Silus took advantage of my distracted moment and jumped on my back trying to sink his teeth deep into my neck and dug his claws deep into my sides. I stepped back into a tree and reared up on my hind legs to smash Silus against the tree, over and over again. He drops to the ground and I turned around to dig my claws into his chest. His hind legs came up and kicked me off sending me stumbling backward.

Silus lunged at me and Dom ducked to the side and bit down on Silus' neck. Silus rolled onto the ground in circles, and we separated. We continued to trade blows and bites. Silus was snarling and determined to kill me. Dom was faster and stronger. Silus charged with his head low, and Dom rolled out of the way. Dom quickly stood up and dug his right claw into Silus' right eye blinding him completely.

Silus howled in pain and Dom knew we had won. Silus started snarling and snapping trying to feel for Dom and fight without vision. Dom charged into Silus and dropped him to the ground. I shifted back to human form but kept my wolf claws shifted. I kicked Silus in the head several times.

"SHIFT!" I yelled at him. My sides were dripping blood, but it didn't stop me. **"SHIFT!"** I growled and continued to kick him.

Silus shifted back and Stefanos laid before me panting on the ground, blinded and groaning. "IT'S TIME TO MEET YOUR MAKER IN HELL." I said and plunged my claw into his chest.

"This is for everyone you ever hurt, you heartless bastard!" I ripped out his heart and held it up. The nightmare was finally over, and his lifeless body lay on the ground. Howls and cheers erupted. I'd like to say that I wished he would find peace in the afterlife, and finally be reunited with my mother. But I'm not even sure he deserved that. He was so cruel and monstrous, he deserved to rot in hell. I tossed his heart into a burning fire pit and moved to go check on Raven.

The remaining rogues started running back through the woods trying to escape. Lucy let out a roar and chased after them, Diesel shifted into his wolf and I gave my pack the approval to join the hunt for the rogues.

"MOON WARRIORS JOIN THE HUNT, NO ROGUE LIVES!" Hades called out.

"YES ALPHA!" They responded and joined the hunt.

"Alec, how's Raven?" I linked him and ran up the southern stairs of the packhouse to the roof.

"She's not responding." He replied.

I arrived on the rooftop and ran to the bird's nest. "RAVEN, open the door." I called out. "RAVEN?" I pulled the door open, and the nest was empty.

I tried to mind link her and got nothing. I linked Alec "are you with Raven?"

"Yes Alpha, I found her on the northern stairs, she's not responding."

I raced to the other end of the roof and pulled the door open to the northern stairs. Raven was lying on the floor and Alec was trying to wake her up. "There doesn't seem to be a physical injury to her, I think she passed out." Alec said.

I picked her up and ran to the clinic. Dr. Vovos directed us into a room and started examining her.

"Alpha you're bleeding on my floor, please let my nurse wrap those wounds for you." Dr. Vovos said.

"Attend to my mate first." I told her.

"Your mate will be fine. I just need to run a few tests on her. I understand she has two elemental gifts that she used tonight?" She asked.

"Yes, we kept her safe in the bird's nest and she was able to use her gifts from the roof." I explained.

"Alec, make yourself useful. Wrap these around the Alpha so he stops bleeding on the floors." She tossed some large bandages at Alec and pulled the curtain back between Raven and us, so she could continue examining her.

The nurse entered the room and stepped behind the curtain to help Dr. Vovos. Alec helped me roll the bandages around my waist to help stop the bleeding from

Silus' claws that dug into me. I could hear them removing Raven's clothes and Dr. Vovos speaking to the nurse who was taking notes. "Heart rate is steady, temperature is good, pressure is normal, keep her on the monitor until she wakes up, here's the order for the blood work. If she's not awake in a few hours we'll start her on an I.V."

"Alpha, she's just resting. The usage of too much elemental power, too soon, could have exhausted her. There's never been a wolf with two gifts so her energy and strength may have just been depleted. I'll start Luna's blood work now; it should take about an hour." Dr. Vovos told me.

"I'll leave you two alone and go check on things. Let me know if you need anything." Alec said.

"Fresh clothes would be great." I said.

"I'll have Spiro run some over in a few minutes." Alec told me and stepped out.

I sat with Raven watching her sleep. She looked pale and exhausted. Maybe it was too much, too soon. I should have sent her to the safety shelter with the others. I took her hand in mine and laid my head on the edge of her bed. I heard Dom let out a whimper, he was worried about our mate too.

A while later, I felt Raven's hand running through my hair and looked up to find her beautiful blue eyes staring back at me. "Raven, do you remember what happened?"

"I started feeling weak after using my element so

much. I could hardly stand and managed to make my way to the stairs, I sat down for a moment and that was it." She told me.

"You nearly gave me a heart attack. Didn't I tell you not to set foot out of the bird's nest?" I said.

"Does this mean you owe me a spanking?" She grinned back at me and my heart fluttered.

"Luna you're awake! How are you feeling?" Dr. Vovos entered the room and asked.

"I'm feeling much better thank you. I guess I just need some rest and maybe endurance training with my elements. I've only had the gifts for a few months and probably need to spend more time developing them." Raven told us.

"Well, you're going to have to put off training for a few months, because it will drain your energy while you're pregnant."

"Pregnant?" Raven asked. My heart swelled with pride a Dom was yipping with excitement.

"Yes. It takes a lot of energy to grow an Alpha pup, so nothing strenuous with your gifts until our future Alpha is safely delivered." She smiled.

CHAPTER 42 – NEWS

"Wake up little bird, the plane just landed." Dimitri stroked my back to wake me up. I had fallen asleep in his lap on our flight from Greece to Canada.

My father had sent the LaRue Enterprises jet for us. We have two mating ceremonies to attend this week. Knox and Rocky's ceremony is tomorrow. Then we will travel to Dark Moon for Peter and Mandi's ceremony. I was excited to show Dimitri where I had grown up, have some Chinese food in the village, show him Crescent Point. I've also missed my younger brothers and couldn't wait to see them.

It's been two weeks since Dimitri and I found out about the pup. We haven't told anyone and wanted to do it when we were all together. My parents had returned to Crescent Moon with Knox and Rocky last week to get ready for the mating ceremony. They would officially become Alpha and Luna of Crescent Moon after the ceremony.

My parents plan to travel back and forth between packs but will spend the majority of their time in Greece getting Zeus' Howlers ready for my brother Roman and training him. Kosta has also agreed to help my parents manage affairs while they go back and forth. My father even started looking for buildings to purchase in Athens for the new LaRue Enterprises branch. My two youngest brothers, Seth and Levi couldn't wait to come spend some time in Greece. Seth just turned sixteen and Levi is thirteen.

Uncle Ranger will be turning over the Dark Moon pack to my brother Peter and his mate Mandi after their mating ceremony. This will leave my Uncle more time to travel between packs and help my brothers. Last week, my brother Peter announced they were expecting a pup. My parents seemed excited about grand pups so I'm hoping my father doesn't freak out when he hears our news.

We stepped off the plane, which landed on a private airfield about twenty minutes away from Crescent Castle. A caravan of black Escalades lined up to transport us and our luggage to Crescent Moon. Rocky's parents and younger sister, Kiki, got in the first car. Clair, Niko, and Kosta took the second car. Odessa, Hades, and Alec filled the third car, while Dimitri and I sat in the last car.

Dimitri was looking out the window admiring the scenery. "The mountains are so beautiful here! Raven, is that a real castle?"

"It is, it was built over two centuries ago by my LaRue ancestors. That's Crescent Castle."

"You grew up in a castle?" He asked astonished.

"It's also the packhouse. The east and west wing are primarily pack rooms, the south wing is the biggest with all the common areas, there's a dining hall, ballroom, theater, game room, lounge, parlor, infirmary, offices, and more. But there's also a north tower, which is the private family quarters."

"Wow! You're like modern day royalty." Dimitri said still shocked.

Our vehicles pulled up to the castle and we stepped out. Niko was looking up at the castle with his mouth open. "A real freaking castle!" He was just as shocked as Dimitri.

"A massive castle!" Hades said in awe.

"THEY'RE HERE!" My Aunt Payton squealed as she ran down the stairs to hug Clair. Uncle Max followed and gave me a warm hug. After everyone was introduced, we made our way into the castle and my parents greeted us. Uncle Ranger and Athena stood with all my brothers and cousins. Gamma Zeke and Vannica stood with Delta Elliot and Aunt Megan. My parents took us all through another round of introductions, hand-shakes, and hugs.

"I'm so happy to have everyone here. Let's get you to your rooms and situated, lunch will be served in the private family quarters in an hour." My mother said.

I took Dimitri up to my room and everything was just as I left it. Seems strange, how so much has changed so quickly. I went from being daddy's little princess to an expecting Luna and I was anxious about breaking the news. Maybe I should wait until after the ceremonies? In case my father doesn't take it well.

"We'll tell them whenever you feel the time is right." Dimitri was reading my thoughts. He stood behind me and wrapped his arms around my waist. "So, are you going to give me the tour? Lock me in a dungeon or take me to a secret passage to make out with me." He joked.

"All of the above!" I smiled back. "After lunch, I want to take you to Crescent Point, it's my favorite spot in the territory. Dom will enjoy the run too."

"Sounds wonderful."
Rae yipped with joy, she was excited to show Dom around.

Lunch was a chaotic mess of energy with nearly two dozen of us around a big table talking and getting to know each other. Niko was seated between Aunt Payton and Clair, Uncle Max, Alec, and Kosta sat with my father discussing the training grounds and arena, they were planning on joining my father this afternoon to observe Crescent Moon training. Uncle Ranger, Hades, and Peter were engrossed in conversations with Dimitri. I was catching up with my younger brothers Seth and Levi. Roman was discussing his future pack with Rocky's parents, he seemed to have an instant connection with Rocky's little sister Kiki. My mother was gushing about her future Grand pup with Mandi. Odessa, Vannica, and Aunt Megan discussed mating ceremony details; Odessa was listening intently because we would need to plan ours for next month as well.

After lunch, Dimitri and I took the wolves out for a run to Crescent point alone. "This is a beautiful location. I can see why it's your favorite spot." Dimitri mind linked me.

"This is also my family's favorite picnic spot." I linked back.

Rae was enjoying her run with Dom, she kept nipping at his tail and jumping up to nip at his ears. Dom was a gentle giant with her and protective of her condition, though it didn't stop Rae from trying to seduce her mate. She had Dom wrapped around her paw always trying to please her.

Later that evening we all gathered at the village for Dinner. Knox and Rocky had selected Chinese Chopsticks for dinner, which was excellent because I was craving Chinese food. The entire restaurant was reserved to accommodate all of us.

"The first time I took your mother out on a date, this is where we came for dinner." My father told us.

"WE KNOW DAD!" My siblings and I chimed in unison. He told us every time we came to eat here about their first dinner date. Their love was timeless, my parents would still come here for sleigh rides and dinner dates.

"When your mother was pregnant with Raven, we practically ate here every night." My father joked. At least, I think he was joking. "I sure hope you have good Chinese food in Greece."

"Where's the food, I'm starving!" I practically growled.

"I caution you now Dimitri, my little Raven has always been demanding. Gets it from her Aunt Payton." My father laughed.

"Payton was the worst when she was pregnant." Uncle Max chuckled and got a playful elbow to his side from Aunt Payton. Dimitri and I just exchanged nervous looks and a giggle escaped me.

Platters of food were placed on the table and it looked like everything on the menu was being served. The platters were being shuffled back and forth across the table as everyone tried a little bit of everything. Niko looked like he was in heaven forking mouthfuls of food into his mouth and I realized, I looked just as bad as him wolfing down my food.

Dinner was almost over when my mother asked the million-dollar question. "So, are you going to tell us or make us wait until after our grandpup is born?"

Dimitri coughed, practically choking on a piece of garlic chicken and I stared back at my father like a deer caught in headlights.

"How do you know?" I whispered.

"I'm your mother, how could I not know. And, I could also hear a faint heartbeat when I'm close to you." She said.

"We umm, well, we wanted to wait. Didn't want to steal any thunder from the excitement of this week." I managed to say.

The table erupted with congratulations and hugs. Odessa practically jumped onto Dimitri crying tears of joy for her brother. I looked at my father who was still seated as if trying to process what he had just heard. "Dad, are you okay?" I managed to ask.

He looked up at me with glistening eyes. "My baby girl is having a baby." He said and hugged me tightly.

"I should kill him." My father growled.

"Dad!" I said and my father laughed.

"Are you for real? First Peter and now you!" Knox sounded a little envious and everyone laughed at him. He was the oldest and always a little late to the party.

"Oh no! Now he's got pup envy." Clair teased and everyone roared with laughter again.

The mating ceremony at Crescent Moon was beautiful and we traveled to Dark Moon two days later for Peter and Mandi's mating ceremony. Mandi was the daughter of Dark Moon's Gamma, Blake. She was a twin with her sister Paige. As soon as Alec set eyes on Paige, we knew he had found his second chance mate.

We later found out that Paige was rejected by Alpha Liam's son, from the neighboring pack, because she was gamma born. Blake was happy that she found Alec and was given a second chance. Alec was practically floating on air and couldn't wait to introduce Paige to his mother back home in Greece.

After the mating ceremony at Dark Moon, my older brothers both left for their honeymoons. Peter and Mandi went to Hawaii, while Knox and Rocky went to Barbados. We discussed our plans for next month's mating ceremonies in Greece. Both of my older brothers would be back from their honeymoons and join the family in Greece for my mating ceremony which would be followed by Hades and Odessa's mating ceremony as well.

We were currently sitting in the living room of the LaRue house that my Grandfather, Alpha Knox LaRue, built almost fifty years ago when he claimed Dark Moon Pack. Uncle Max was telling us stories about their childhood and we were all practically in tears laughing. My mother entered the room with fresh flowers in her arms.

"Dimitri. Raven. Will you come with me please?" She asked.

"Of course, let me carry those for you." Dimitri said and went to unload my mother's arms.

We made our way to cemetery hill and stopped at my grandparent's graves. My mother placed flowers on her parent's graves first and told us about Peter and Alice Michaels. She explained how Peter was a descendant from the Apollo bloodline and how a golden wolf is born from that bloodline once every hundred years. She also told us about my grandmother Alice, who was a descendant from the Moon Goddess with the fire element.

We moved a few yards over to my other grandparents, Alpha Knox and Luna Clair LaRue. We placed flowers on their graves as well. She explained how Luna Clair and my grandmother Alice, were from the same pack in Alaska. Even though Luna Clair didn't have the water element, she passed it down to Diesel. Luna Clair was also a descendant from the Moon Goddess. She went on to tell us about how great my grandfather Alpha Knox was. How he helped train her gifts and loved everyone unconditionally.

"When I received my prophecy, there was a pack war that followed, and we lost Alpha Knox. The prophecy said, there is a war coming and a lost wolf. The war happened and the lost wolf was the head of our family." She told us. "The grief of losing him showed me my own strength."

My mother took a moment to wipe a tear from her cheek. "It also said, only the one born from Gods can set the course. I was born from two Gods and set the course by having pups and passing the gifts."

"But, I'm the only one with both." I said.

"Yes, and your mate also has one. Now you're expecting a pup. Dimitri's destiny is with you and your offspring. He will play an important role in training your pups and grandpups, just as his prophecy said."

"But what's the importance?" I asked.

"War. A great war is coming someday." Dimitri said connecting the dots.

"In a hundred years, a descendant will possess the power of all four and save us in the Great War to come. The key here is a hundred years. There is a golden wolf every hundred years." My mother said. "Raven, there was no way your father was going to let you go all the way to Greece. We had to force him to let you follow your destiny. You can't stop fate or try to interfere. There's a reason behind every joy and every sorrow. It makes us who we are for better or worse."

"Thank you, Luna, I can't tell you enough how much I love your daughter and our pup." Dimitri beamed.

"Oh, I can see it. It's just the same way Diesel looks at me." She smiled and hugged him.

"Now, have you decided on any names for my grand-pup?" She asked.

"Since your twins are named after their grandfathers, and Clair is named after Luna Clair, I was thinking that Alice would be a perfect name if we have a girl. If that's okay with you Luna?" Dimitri smiled.

EPILOGUE

Seven years later

"**MOM!** Uncle Niko ate the rest of my moussaka!" Kyros pouted.

"Uncle Niko has a habit of doing that. He doesn't like perfectly good moussaka to go to waste." I laughed.

"Are you going to finish yours or should I take care of that for you too?" Niko asked me.

"Touch my plate and you might lose a few fingers." I growled and shoveled the rest of the food in my mouth.

Dimitri chuckled and kissed me on the side of my head. "Don't mess with a pregnant woman's food Niko, you should know better by now after three pups of your own."

Kyros was our oldest, Damien followed two years later, they both looked just like Dimitri. Our twin daughters Alice and Anabeth looked just like me with the strong LaRue family genes. I was currently expecting pup number five in about two more weeks.

"How's baby Lukas doing?" Clair asked me.

"He's kicking a lot, hopefully, he won't try to break out before Levi's mating ceremony this weekend." I told her. We had found out the gender of the baby last month and decided to name him Lukas.

After my brother Roman took over Zeus' Howlers, he found his mate, Kiki, who is Rocky's little sister. They currently have two pups of their own. My brother Seth took over the Silver Moon pack, which is next to Dark Moon when Alpha Liam's son was killed by rogues three years ago. Seth is twenty-three now and has yet to find his mate.

Four days from now, we will all be traveling to western Greece to the Spartan Shadow pack where my youngest brother Levi will be taking over as Alpha. Alpha Atlas only had one daughter, Imara, before his Luna died. Levi discovered that Imara was his mate a few months ago at a shifter's ball. Alpha Atlas has been thrilled to turn the pack over to another LaRue and his daughter.

"Daddy, when is Aunty Odessa coming for a visit? She promised me loukoumi the next time I see her." Damien's little voice squeaked. He loved his sweets.

"You'll see Aunt Odessa, Uncle Hades, and your cousins this weekend, but you'd better be good if you want loukoumi." Dimitri told him.

"Let's go, it's bath time and then bed. The sooner you go to bed, the sooner grandma and papa will be here to take you to the beach tomorrow." I told them.

"Ohhh I hope papa floats us on top of the water with his magic!" Kyros jumped up and down with excitement.

We had spent a few weeks at Crescent Moon this summer and my dad had fun floating the pups on the water like he used to do to us growing up. The twins are now three and they enjoyed taking rides on Lia's back. The girls always squealed about how her golden fur was so "pwetty." Lia enjoyed having the girls climb all over her.

"Come on, you two. Let's go, it's bath time!" I called out to the twins who were playing with Uncle Max on the floor.

"Ewww mommy peed her pants!" Alice said pointing to the gush of water coming down my leg.

"My water just broke!"

"I'll link Dr. Vovos." Dimitri said scooping me up.

"Don't worry about the kids, I'll get them bathed and put to bed." Aunt Payton called out.

"I'll call your parents." Uncle Max added.

We entered the infirmary and Dimitri placed me on the bed. "Owwww." I cried out as the contractions hit me. Dr. Vovos busied herself setting everything up and connecting me to monitors.

"Okay Luna, you know the routine. We're going to wait until you're fully dilated before we deliver. Alpha, you know what to do." She told us.

Dimitri kissed the top of my head and rubbed circles on my back to ease the anxiety and pain. "The girls are going to be so excited to have a baby." He grinned.

"Yeah, until they get a whiff of a full diaper." I laughed and then cried when another contraction hit me.

Four hours later, Dimitri was holding baby Lukas. He had raven black hair and blue eyes. "He looks like his mama." Dimitri smiled at me.

Moments later, Lukas let out a really loud cry. "wahh-hhh wahhh." He fussed with his little hands locked in tight fists.

"Looks like he has his mother's temperament too!" Dimitri laughed.

"He wants his mama." I smiled extending my arms out.

Dimitri handed him to me, but Lukas continued to wail. I tried to bounce him a little to soothe him. I gasped when his blue eyes opened and flashed to an amber color, then back to blue.

"What's wrong?" Dimitri asked.

He was like me, my eyes did that when I had strong emotions. "His eyes! They flashed colors like mine!"

BROKEN TRILOGY

Released 2020

Broken Luna

Broken Alpha

Broken Omega

GOLDEN SERIES

Coming – 2021

Golden Prophecy

Golden Wolf

Golden Wars

COMING - The Alpha Chronicles
Alpha Hades - April 2022

Follow Author on Facebook at

"Author Paulina Vasquez"

A storm is coming!

Lukas Theodorus is unlike any other Alpha. A descendant from the Gods, Lukas possesses elemental gifts never before seen and couldn't care less. This powerful Alpha isn't used to being challenged. Feeling cursed by the Moon Goddess a fire burns deep inside that has turned into a slow burn. After years of suffering and slavery, Syble Martin has a secret that needs to remain hidden. She tries to hate him but craves his touch.

Bound by the Moon Goddess and tied by a prophecy, his pride is no match for her will as he fights his destiny. These star-crossed lovers risk everything for future hope. From New York to New Orleans the storm will rage!

This book is the end of the Broken Trilogy and the end of this book is the start of the Golden Series!

Warning: This werewolf trilogy is not intended for anyone under the age of 18 or anyone who doesn't enjoy a good spanking. It will take you on adventures around the world, make you laugh, fall in love, crush your heart, and possibly leave you drooling. Side effects can only be cured by reading the next book in the Golden Series Spin Off – GOLDEN PROPHECY!

Printed in Great Britain
by Amazon

19360943R00200